Gingerbread Dead

A Hilarious Holiday Mystery

Kirsten Weiss

misterio press

About Gingerbread Dead

A TEAROOM OWNER. A *Tarot reader. A murder. Solving this quirky case may take a Christmas miracle.*

Tea and Tarot room owner Abigail is having a hard time getting into holiday mode. She's working her assets off to make the tearoom a premier holiday destination, searching for an appropriate Christmas gift for her new boyfriend, and trying to forget her aggravating but oh, so tempting neighbor, Brik. But when one of the Tarot readers finds a nearby business owner dead, Abigail and her Tarot-reading partner Hyperion are on the case.

Now, with a cranky cop on their tails, the duo must find a way to solve the crime and stay out of the slammer before a killer cancels their Christmas.

Gingerbread Dead is a fast-paced and funny cozy mystery, packed with oddball characters, pets, and murder. Buy the book and start this hilarious caper today!

Tearoom recipes in the back of the book!

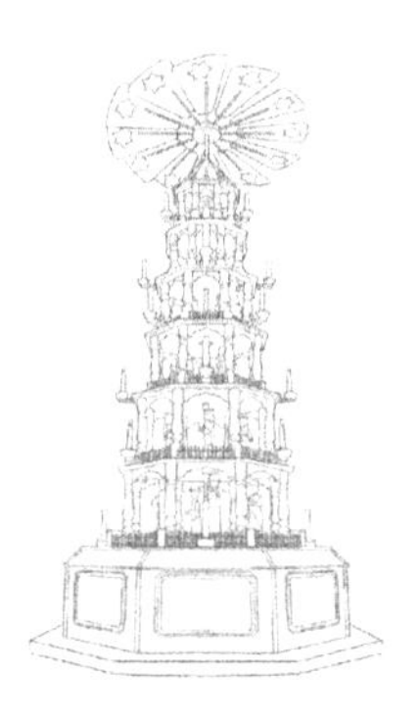

Copyright

THIS BOOK IS A work of fiction. Names, characters and incidents are either the product of the author's imagination or are used fictitiously. Any resemblance to actual persons, living or dead, is entirely coincidental.

The publisher does not have any control over and does not assume any responsibility for author or third-party websites and their content.

Visit the author website to sign up for updates on upcoming books and fun, free stuff: KirstenWeiss.com

Cover art by Dar Albert.

misterio press / print edition September, 2022

ISBN-13: 978-1-944767-86-0

Chapter One

"Face it, Abigail. I love Christmas more," Hyperion caroled in front of the white quartz counter. He brought a cup of sugar plum tea to his lips. A Santa hat perched rakishly on his sleek, dark head.

"Ya think so?" From behind the counter, I motioned at the full tearoom.

Waitstaff passed beneath snowflakes dusted with glitter and dangling from the chandeliers. Guests sat around white-clothed tables with Christmas tree centerpieces. Pine boughs dotted with twinkle lights swagged the front windows and the walls.

My partner's Santa hat, fisherman's sweater, and fashion-model good looks might have said, "I'm a quirky holiday aficionado." But my tearoom roared *holiday spirit? Bring it on!*

A massive gingerbread house, lit from within, stood on one end of the counter. Smaller houses found places between the brushed-nickel tea cannisters on the shelves behind me. Originally, each table had boasted a gingerbread house centerpiece. But guests had assumed they were part of the tea and nibbled on the peppermint windows and iced roofs.

We were hip for the holidays, right down to my frilly red and white checked apron. The problem was, I wasn't feeling the spirit. And I wasn't one of those people who loathed the commercial excesses of the season. Especially when it was *my* commercial excess.

Hyperion arched a brow. "Being an elf doesn't count."

I laughed. "Oh, come on. Now you're just being mean." It wasn't my fault I was height challenged.

Absently, he reached for the gingerbread house with one long arm.

"Uh-uh." I smacked his hand. "That's not for eating."

He rubbed the back of his hand. "Then what's the point?" His brows lowered over his expressive brown eyes. "It's all faux ho-ho-ho. Eating a gingerbread house is way more in the holiday spirit than simply displaying one."

"It's also more expensive." The gingerbread house had taken me ages to make. And though the tearoom was doing well now, I expected a post-holiday slump. We'd started Beanblossom's less than a year ago, and I still couldn't quite believe it seemed to be succeeding.

The thought sent a quiver through my insides. I checked my bun, making sure my longish caramel-colored hair was still tucked away.

"Whatevs." He checked his watch and frowned. "Why isn't Sierra back yet?"

Since Hyperion managed the Tarot readers at Beanblossom's Tea and Tarot, the question was rhetorical. The Tarot readers weren't on a clock. They were contractors and gave my business partner Hyperion a cut of their earnings. Their services had grown even more popular as the year was drawing to an end. And Sierra was never late.

I glanced at the oversized clock on the far wall. "She may have gotten hung up in traffic," I said. "I heard a tomato truck overturned on 101."

"She wasn't on 101. She was just going down the block to buy a last-minute gift. And that's another thing. I'll bet you've already done your Christmas shopping."

"I had it done by December first." *Mostly*. I was trying to get more organized. You had to be organized when you ran a tearoom, or the tearoom would run you. Besides, I wanted time to enjoy the season. I'd spent too much time this year racing around like a madwoman.

He shook his head. "Talk about a snooze fest. You can't plan Christmas spirit."

A police car raced silently down the drizzly street outside. Its blue and red lights flashed, a mockery of holiday lights.

I smoothed my checked apron. "Says who? And how is last-minute shopping spirited? By getting so much shopping done in advance, I had time to put thought into my gifts." I shifted my weight.

I'd recently begun dating a local attorney, Gino Redmond. I'd only gotten him a bottle of wine. Since we hadn't been seeing each other long and he liked wine, I'd thought it sensible at the time. Now the gift seemed a little impersonal.

"But you're missing the holiday shopping experience," he said. "The bustle. The hustle. The holiday lights. The kids screaming on Santa's lap. I'll bet you haven't even been to the Christmas market on the pier yet."

My face heated as fast as our industrial dishwasher. My grandfather and his best friend, Tomas, were sharing a booth at the pier. The Christmas market was competitive, and they'd worked hard to get that booth. I really did need to get down there and show some support.

Hyperion braced his elbows on the counter. "So what'd you get me?"

"I'm not telling."

His eyes narrowed. "I bet you got me a Tarot deck."

Two more police cars, lights flashing, sped past outside. Uneasily, I pulled my gaze from the window. We didn't usually see that much police action on Main Street.

"Please," I said. "Do you think I'd be that obvious? You've got so many Tarot decks, odds are I'd just get you something you already had." Rumor had it he had a storage locker for all his Tarot paraphernalia.

But I knew what I was getting Hyperion, and it was the best ever. He'd never see it coming. Once I figured out where I could buy it.

"Everyone's making decks now," he agreed. "It's making me long for the classics just to be contrarian. Rider-Waite-Smith. Marseilles. The Thoth deck. OMG, have you heard? An academic has come up with some pretty good evidence that the 14th century Sola-Busca Tarot was based off Renaissance black magic. It's totes creepy."

"Beg all you want, I'm not getting that deck for you." Black magic didn't worry me. Maybe it should have, but it didn't. But I could do better than a Tarot deck for a professional Tarot reader.

He shuddered. "I wouldn't want it anyway. Bad mojo."

A waitress in black and white zoomed to the counter. "Table six wants a tin of the spiced chai."

"Sure thing." I turned and reached for the brushed-nickel tin, jostling a lit pine bough in the process. It shivered, golden ornaments tinkling. Wary, I eyed the greenery.

I handed the tin across the counter. The waitress whirled and sped away, her elbow coming within a whisker of the gingerbread house. I nudged the house an inch closer to the center of the counter.

"What *did* you get me?" Hyperion asked.

"I'm not telling."

"Is it bigger than a breadbox?"

"It cannot be compared to breadboxes." Especially since his was the one present I hadn't actually bought yet. At this point, it was only a vague idea.

"It's non-corporeal?" He propped his chin on his fist. "Did you buy me a ghost?"

"Yes," I said. "You nailed it. I bought you a ghost."

"A service of some kind then." He drummed his fingers on the white counter. "What sort of service could the man who does everything need?" He snapped his fingers. "New ideas for my Tarot blog." He sighed. "It wouldn't be a bad gift. I'm almost through writing about every card in the deck. What else am I supposed to write about?"

Since he was getting uncomfortably close to the truth, I changed the subject. To myself. "What did you get me?"

"I told you, I haven't gotten anyone anything yet. I do all my shopping Christmas Eve."

I gaped. "Are you nuts?" Who does that intentionally?

"I like the adrenaline rush. And speaking of which, what's going on?"

"Hm?" I tracked his gaze to our front windows. A cluster of elderly guests had risen from their tables and peered through the drizzle outside. It was probably a fender bender. Nothing else ever happened on this street. "No idea."

I walked around the counter and joined everyone at the window. "What's happening?" In the early afternoon gloom, holiday lights glistened off the damp cars.

"The police are at your neighbor's shop." Mrs. Ingram touched her white hair, done up in a smooth chignon. "Do you think that old miser was robbed? It would serve him right."

Her wrinkled companion shook her head. "Is it my imagination, or is the criminal element growing bolder?"

I angled myself to see better. Beneath cement skies, three police cars were parked pell-mell in front of the shop. It sold beach souvenirs to tourists and had the highest prices in San Borromeo. That many police cars could not be good.

I'd gone in there once, to introduce myself. The owner had been abrupt and disinterested. I'd left him a plate of scones and never heard from him again.

A spatter of rain drops pebbled on the windows. We gasped and took an involuntary step back, then glanced at each other with embarrassed smiles.

Hyperion nudged my side. "That's a plainclothes detective's car." He pointed at a brown sedan, parked between the black-and-whites.

But it wasn't our friend Tony's car, and my heart gave a quick, spikey pinch. Tony Chase had recently quit the San Borromeo PD. He was closer to Hyperion than to me, but I liked him. And I'd gotten the sense that the ex-detective was floundering.

The phone rang on the hostess stand. Hyperion stepped smartly behind the podium and picked up the receiver. "Beanblossom's Tea and Tarot, where the dress code is flashy and unapologetic."

I rolled my eyes and snatched the phone from him. "How can I help you?" I asked.

"Er, I'd like to make a reservation?" a woman asked, hesitant.

I took the reservation for an afternoon tea, then turned to scowl at my partner. "You can't answer the phone like that. People will take you seriously."

"But wouldn't you *like* the dress code to be flashy and unapologetic?" he asked, arch.

"That's not—" A movement outside the window distracted me.

Sierra hurried down the sidewalk, her red sweater-coat billowing about her knees. The Tarot reader opened the front door. She stumbled inside, her face pale, her dirty-blond hair plastered to her head.

She shut the door and turned. Her lake-colored eyes were bleak and wide, and dread coiled coldly in my stomach.

Rivulets of water trickled down her slender neck, vanishing into the collar of her matted sweater and down the v of her red t-shirt. Her hands clenched and unclenched spasmodically, the knuckles white. “He’s dead,” she gasped. “He’s dead.”

Chapter Two

The Tarot reader swayed beside the tearoom's blue door, her teeth chattering. I hurried to her. Hyperion grasped Sierra's slender shoulders and steered her into a recently vacated chair. Teacups and half-eaten scones and mini sandwiches littered the plates in front of her.

"What's happened?" I asked in a low voice. On the sidewalk outside the window, pedestrians stopped and pointed down the street.

"I went to... I can't believe it," she stammered. "He's dead."

Hyperion met my gaze. I nodded. "I'll get some tea," I said.

Worried, I strode behind the counter and prepared a cup of her favorite English Breakfast. We had several drama queens working in the tearoom, but Sierra wasn't one of them. If she was this rattled, someone was dead in the literal sense.

I returned to the table. Its prior occupants clustered around the Tarot reader. A white-haired lady patted her hand and murmured quietly. I handed Sierra the tea.

"Tell us *everything* that happened," Mrs. Ingram said.

Sierra took a gulp, then winced. "Hot."

"If you want iced tea..." I began, smothering my impatience. Sierra'd been through something, and I could give her a minute to gather her thoughts.

"No," she said. "This is fine."

"What happened?" Hyperion said briskly. "Who's dead?"

The Tarot reader drew a shaky breath. "I went to the Beach Shop to look for gifts for my nieces in Connecticut. No one was there, but I... I had this weird feeling, like the store *wasn't* empty. That someone was there, waiting. You know?"

Hyperion nodded, expression grim. "I know. So you looked around?"

"There's a door toward the back of the shop," she said, "to a storage area. It was open. I knocked and pushed it wider, and I saw..." She blinked rapidly.

"What did you see?" An elderly woman in pearls asked breathlessly.

"Mr. Callum, on the floor. He looked so peaceful, like he was sleeping. But there was blood..." Sierra's face spasmed, and she touched her red *Drink Up Grinches, It's Christmas* t-shirt. "There was so much blood—and his eyes..." She shook her head, droplets of rainwater splattering the white tablecloth.

"Then what happened?" Hyperion asked.

"I knew he was dead. I called 9-1-1. And then the police came—it took them forever—and then they told me to wait, and I couldn't stand it anymore, and I came here."

"Wait," I said. "You left without giving a statement?" Could you do that?

"Of course I gave a statement. I told the first policeman who arrived what had happened, and then more police came, and everyone got busy, and I was just freezing in the rain. No one would talk to me or tell me what was going on and—"

"You came here," I finished for her, and my stomach did a sickening barrel roll. This was bad. "Sierra, we need to go back." Preferably before the cops noticed she'd gone.

The lady in pearls slid a small umbrella from a crimson purse hanging on the back of a chair. "Take this. There's no sense in you getting any wetter."

Sierra took it with a grateful smile. "Thanks Mrs. Peters."

"I'll get mine," I said.

Sierra looked up. "You're coming with me?"

"Of course we are," Hyperion said stoutly. "The police were idiots to leave you standing outside like that. Tony—" His lips flattened into a straight line. But it didn't take a psychic to complete the thought for him. *Tony wouldn't have done it.*

Maricel, the tearoom manager, appeared at my elbow. Her round face creased with concern. "I'll take over," she murmured and smoothed her near-black hair, done up in a bun and held in place by a discreet net.

"Thanks." Striding to the industrial kitchen, I ditched the apron and retrieved my raincoat and umbrella, hanging from a hook on the wall. I met Sierra and Hyperion at the front door, and we stepped outside.

A gust of oceanic wind bulleted me with rain, tossing the hem of my coat. I staggered back a little at the force of the gust.

Hyperion tugged his Santa hat lower on his head. Cars crawled down the street. A parking enforcement officer waved cars around the cluster of police vehicles blocking one side of the wet road. Blue and red lights flashed, reflecting off the slick pavement and the shop windows.

We walked to a policeman, his hat covered in protective plastic against the rain. The uniformed officer raised his hands in warning. "Sorry," he said, "you'll have to go around."

"I'm Sierra Franklin," the Tarot reader stammered. "A witness. They told me to wait."

"And you left anyway," a man behind us said roughly.

We turned to face him, and I felt myself shrinking. Six foot two. A paunch. Ruddy face. Brown hair. Comb over. Bad attitude. *Detective Baranko.*

He hated dirty cops, which should have meant he was a good one. But he'd also hounded Tony Chase from the San Borromeo PD, and Tony had been innocent. We weren't fans.

"What are you doing here?" I blurted.

The detective's broad face darkened. "What are *you* doing here?" he snapped.

"But you work in Santa Cruz," I continued. I knew I should shut up. But one of my least useful traits was a distrust of authority figures. It's why I'd started my own business. Mostly.

"Uh, Abigail..." Hyperion tugged on my coat sleeve.

"Not anymore," the detective said. "Now for the last time, what are you doing here?"

"It's my fault," Sierra said. "You told me to wait, and I was waiting, but it got cold, and—"

"You decided to pop over for a cup of tea?" The detective's lip curled.

"To get warm," I said tartly. "Look how wet she is. It's freezing out here, and you just left her." I didn't know how Hyperion could stand it without a coat, even if fisherman's sweaters were notoriously warm.

The detective stared blankly at Sierra, then shook his head. "You can wait in a car." Taking her elbow, Baranko walked her to a black-and-white. He opened a rear door, and she slid inside.

"I don't know if waiting in a squad car is an improvement," Hyperion muttered, rolling up the collar of his sweater.

No, the back of a police car was never a good look. "Yeah," I said, drawing out the word.

I craned my neck at the Beach Shop. The usual shell wind chimes that hung outside the door hadn't been hung today. T-shirts covered the inside of the windows in a colorful display. They also blocked my view of what was happening inside. So that was annoying.

"What's going on?" a man asked from behind us, and we turned again.

Jonasz Albrekt, Callum's sole employee, stood on the brick sidewalk. His narrow shoulders hunched in a damp overcoat glistening with water droplets. He had bone structure Hyperion could envy—high cheekbones and wide, soulful brown eyes. A red knit cap covered his brown hair.

"What?" he asked in a faint Eastern-European accent. "What has happened?"

"Uh..." Hyperion shifted his weight. The cops wouldn't like us telling a potential witness—or was he a suspect?—what had happened. They'd want to talk to Jonasz first and see his reaction for themselves.

"They wouldn't let me in the back door," Jonasz said. "I had to walk around the block to get here. Was there a robbery?"

"I don't know," I said. There could have been a robbery too, for all I knew. If I could just see past those t-shirts in the windows... I still wouldn't know if the store had been robbed. "Maybe."

Jonas's angular face darkened. "The phone call. That explains it."

"What phone call?" I asked.

"I got a call around nine-thirty this morning, after I'd arrived for work. The woman said she was a nurse, and my daughter had been admitted to hospital again. But when I got to the hospital, she wasn't there. I called my wife, and she said they were both home and well."

"Which hospital?" I asked. The question was automatic. Under the circumstances it was likely also inappropriate. But to my surprise, Jonasz answered.

"St. Borromeo's," he said.

"But that's only fifteen minutes away by car," Hyperion said. "It's after one o'clock now." And this was why Hyperion and I made such a good team. He was also naturally and unabashedly suspicious.

"I made the mistake of taking the freeway," Jonasz said. "A tomato truck overturned in front of me. Then the person behind me slammed on their brakes, and the person behind *him* didn't stop quickly enough. I was surrounded by accidents. A crash in front, a crash to the left, a crash behind. I was the only one who didn't get hit. No one was badly hurt, fortunately. But I was stuck there with everyone else until they could clear the truck aside. Now what has happened?"

"What are you two doing outdoors on a day like this?" Tony drawled from behind us, and we swiveled again like a pair of nervous groundhogs. Tony adjusted his cowboy hat, its mocha-colored edges darkened by the rain. "You two just can't resist a crime scene, can you?"

"We're here to give Sierra moral support," Hyperion said.

The tall Texan cocked a brow. "And she is...?"

Hyperion winced. "In Baranko's car."

Detective Baranko strode toward us, his brows lowered, his chin down. "Chase," he growled. "You've got no business here."

"Nope," Tony said. "I'm just an innocent civilian ambling down the sidewalk, until I happened to see my friends here. We'll get out of your hair." He grasped Hyperion's shoulder.

"Right," Hyperion said, unmoving.

"But you may want to chat with this gentleman." Tony angled his head toward Jonasz. "I couldn't help overhearing he works at the Beach Shop."

Baranko bridled, his nostrils flaring. "Now listen here, Chase—"

"What is happening?" Jonasz asked. "Was there a robbery? Is Mr. Callum all right?"

"This way." Baranko led Jonasz into the Beach shop. I glanced anxiously at the police car. Sierra sat rigid in the back.

"Sierra will be fine," Tony said. "Unless she had a reason to want Mr. Callum dead. I hear he wasn't very popular."

"Where did you hear that?" Hyperion asked.

"Your tea and Tarot room. Everyone's talking about the murder. That's how I knew to find you two here. It looks like I arrived in time to interrupt you interrogating a witness," he said pointedly.

Since Tony was no longer a cop, I felt a lot less guilty about the interrogation than I might have. Still, a change of subject seemed in order.

I tried to cross my arms and nearly took out an innocent pedestrian's eye with my umbrella. "I'm sure Sierra had nothing against Mr. Callum," I said. "If she had, she wouldn't have gone shopping there. Sierra's not even from San Borromeo. She's a Santa Cruz native."

"Right," Hyperion said. "The police have no reason to suspect her. Aside from the whole discovery of the body thing. And the bit about leaving the crime scene—"

"But she was freezing," I protested. A cold droplet that had evaded my umbrella slithered down the back of my neck. "And why didn't one of the cops behind the shop bring Jonasz to talk to Baranko? They just drove him off, and he's a potential witness."

"There's a new recruit on the rear door," Tony said. "He made a mistake, and he'll hear about it later."

A car started nearby. *Okay.* A newbie had made a mistake, and Baranko, who I didn't like but who was probably a good cop, was in charge.

It was no big deal. They had no reason to suspect Sierra. She'd been in the tearoom until noon. Depending on when Emery Callum had been killed, she likely had an alibi. Baranko would take her statement and let her go. She'd be fine.

A police car cruised down the street. Sierra looked out the rear window, a panicked expression on her face.

My heart went cold. *Just fine.*

Chapter Three

THE POLICE CAR DISAPPEARED around a bend in the crooked road. Clusters of gawkers—of which I was one—stared after the cruiser. Rain pattered off my umbrella and onto the brick sidewalk.

"Okay," I said to Hyperion. "That's not g—"

"I don't understand," Jonasz said, exiting the souvenir shop. "I've told you. You recorded it on your recorder thing. Why do I need to sign a statement at the police station?"

"Because this is murder." Glowering, Baranko paced close on his heels, herding him forward. "And you're going to the station."

"You can relax," Tony told us in a low voice. "Sierra's not being arrested. They just want a signed statement from her too."

I glanced at Hyperion. Rain dripped down his face. No, taken to the station for a statement wasn't the same as being arrested. But it wasn't great either.

"We're in the way here," Tony said. "Let's get out of their hair."

We walked back toward the tearoom. "Should we get her a lawyer?" I asked Hyperion.

My partner shook his head. A droplet caught in his thick eyelashes, and he dashed it away. "She's already got one."

"Really?" I asked, surprised. "How do you know?" I didn't keep a lawyer on speed dial. Given the number of run-ins I'd had with the local authorities, maybe I should.

"Sierra's loaded. Flush. Rolling in dough. Drowning in Ducats."

"I had no idea." I didn't stray into the Tarot side of the business. But I knew Tarot wasn't the sort of thing you normally got rich off, unless you were running a con. And I knew Sierra wasn't doing that.

"Family money," my partner explained.

"Oh." I hadn't expected that either. Now I was a little embarrassed I knew so little about Sierra. She was one of my favorite readers, and a tearoom favorite as well.

Ahead, white lights glistened through the tearoom's windows, and I sped up. Not that it made much difference. The two men had longer legs than me, and I was already struggling to keep up. But the tearoom had become a second home, a refuge, and I wanted to get back.

Naturally, Maricel had everything well in hand when I stepped through its blue door. The guests had returned to their tables and conversation to its usual genteel murmur.

Unspeaking, the men walked through the tearoom and into the hallway to Hyperion's office. I hurried to the counter, where Maricel filled a pot of tea.

"Where's Sierra?" she asked quietly.

Another Tarot reader strode through the tables and into the hallway after Hyperion. I guessed she wanted the answer to the same question.

"She had to go to the police station to make a statement." I tapped my forefinger on the cool counter. The gingerbread house was askew again, and I moved it back into a safer position.

Maricel bit her plump bottom lip. "They don't think Sierra was involved, do they?"

"No, no, of course not. She was just unlucky enough to find the body, and the police..." *The police what*? I hated to say it—I'd been raised to think of the police as our friends—but cops were people too. And people made mistakes, got things wrong, had agendas. "They just want to make sure they get everything locked down," I finished.

"And old Callum is really dead?" Maricel asked.

"*Old* Callum?" I said, looking up from the gingerbread house. "Did you know him?" Gentle laughter rose at a nearby table.

My assistant manager grimaced. "I applied for a job with him once. It was years ago. As part of my interview, he had me work behind the counter for a day. He offered me the job. But the pay was minimum wage, and it was clear there'd be a lot of hours I wouldn't get paid for... And then he never paid me for my try-out. I felt like such an idiot. But..." She shrugged. "Lesson learned."

"What he did was illegal and wrong," I said hotly. And he was dead, murdered, so there was no point in getting mad about it now.

"Yeah," she said, "probably. But what was I going to do? I don't know how he found anybody to work for him." She handed the teapot to a waitress. "I'd better get back to the kitchen."

"Thanks." I braced one elbow on the counter and frowned at the rows of brushed-nickel tea cannisters behind it. Baranko hadn't exactly done an outstanding job when Tony had been accused of murder. There was no reason for him to suspect Sierra, but I still didn't trust him.

A pair of well-clad arms slipped around my waist. "Hey," a masculine voice rumbled in my ear.

Smiling, I turned. Gino brushed against me, close enough to scent his exotic cologne. One corner of his mouth lifted, then his dark eyes sobered. Droplets darkened the shoulders of his charcoal business suit and glittered in his curling, near-black hair.

"What are you doing here?" I asked, pleased. My heart beat a little faster.

"I heard what happened up the street and wanted to make sure you were okay."

My insides warmed. It had been a long time since I'd been in a relationship. It was nice having a man around who cared. "I'm fine. What did you hear?"

"That Emery Callum was killed in a robbery," Gino said. "Did you see anything?"

"Just the police cars after the fact. And I'm sorry to say I didn't know Mr. Callum well." I really should make more of an effort to get to know the people on the street. "Can I get you something?"

He glanced at his watch. It was simple, basic, and I liked the seeming contrast to the man who wore it. "Sorry, I can't stay. Like I said, I just wanted to check in." He reached for the gingerbread house.

"Ah! Look, don't touch."

He grinned roguishly. "My grandmother had a gingerbread house she wouldn't let me get near. It was guerrilla warfare to sneak candy off it." His forehead crinkled. "Come to think of it, that candy must have been years old."

"And you still ate it? I don't know if I should be impressed or horrified." Honestly, I was a little of both.

"Ah, youth." Gino kissed my cheek. "I'll see you later." He exited down the back hallway, and I got to work.

I poured tea and checked in with the guests, making sure all was as well as it could be. The murder down the street hadn't seemed to have dampened any spirits. But that was life. Unless you knew the deceased personally, it was just a news story, gossip.

The blue front door swung open. An elegant sixty-something woman with a white streak in her gray hair stepped inside like a stranger in an old-west saloon. The tearoom quieted, the silence as pregnant as in any western movie.

I hurried to the hostess stand. "Happy holidays. How can I help you?"

"I don't have a reservation." She wobbled on her low heels and grasped the edge of the wooden stand. "I'm sorry. I was just... The souvenir shop. My ex-husband. I heard he was dead and..."

I drew up short. Emery Callum was her ex? No wonder the woman looked so pale. "You were married to Mr. Callum? I'm so sorry for your loss."

That was the thing about living in a small town. Everyone was connected somehow. It was both blessing and curse.

The older woman straightened and pulled her navy coat more tightly about her. Beneath the long coat she wore a simple navy pantsuit. "It's silly. You must be full up. I was just standing there in the rain, and I saw your window. I felt like I had to come in, that tea would be the thing..." She laughed unevenly. "I suppose I've been watching too many British costume dramas."

"There's space at the counter." I motioned toward the gingerbread house.

"The counter will do. I just left my office for some impromptu Christmas shopping when I saw..." She swallowed.

"Of course. Here." I took her coat and hung it on a nearby wall pegs beneath a garland of pine and twinkle lights.

Mrs. Ingram rose from her chair. Smoothing her sweater and plaid skirt, she tottered to the counter. "Ivette," she said to the woman. "What a thing to happen." They gave each other awkward hugs, their bodies not quite touching. "Come sit with us," Mrs. Ingram said.

"No, thank you," Ivette said. "I'd rather be alone. I just need to think."

"Are you certain?" Mrs. Ingram asked. "Thinking isn't always the answer. In fact in cases like these, it can be the last thing you want to do."

Ivette's smile was bitter. "You're probably right, but I need some time to get my head around this."

"Of course. If you change your mind, I'm sure we can add another chair to our table."

"Yes," I said quickly. "We can make it work."

Mrs. Ingram raised a crooked finger. "And Abigail, we'd like to each buy one of those little gingerbread houses."

I glanced at their table. Its dishes had been recently cleared; they'd need their checks. "I'll take care of it."

I added the gingerbread houses to the bill while Ivette looked over the menu. Motioning to Mrs. Ingram's server, I explained about the addition. We brought the houses, wrapped in red cellophane, to their table.

"So good of you to make room for Ivette," Mrs. Ingram said in an undertone. She glanced at the woman at the counter. "Emery did not make things easy on her during the divorce. Lawyers." Her lip curled. "Ivette left that marriage without a cent."

"I suppose it was difficult to divide up the souvenir shop." I set a gingerbread house in front of her.

"That place?" She tsked. "Do you know how much property Emery Callum owns around San Borromeo? He has buildings up and down Main street. They're worth millions. He learned early on that real money is made in business and property. Not that I imagine his little shop makes much." She sniffed. "I think he just kept it so he had a place to keep an eye on his other properties."

"Hm." I returned to the counter, and Ivette set down her menu.

"What sort of tea would you like?" I asked her.

"I think something calming like chamomile is best right now."

"Done." I prepared a tea strainer, warmed a white ceramic pot then filled it with boiling water.

I glanced at the older woman at the counter. Having the ex-wife of the murder victim was too good an opportunity to ignore, and I didn't like Baranko. And yes, I was being petty and unfair. Baranko would talk to Ivette eventually. But she was here now.

Besides, with Sierra involved, it only made sense to learn what I could. The Tarot reader might not be a suspect, but the police wouldn't know that yet.

"Where's your office?" I asked Ivette while the tea steeped.

"Three blocks from here on Gull Street, just outside the shopping district. I'm a speech-language pathologist."

"That sounds like interesting work." Largely because I had no idea what it was. "What's a typical day like?"

"I work with people who have trouble communicating—mainly children, but adults recovering from injuries as well."

"I see you didn't get a chance to find any gifts." I poured her a cup of tea and set the ceramic pot beside her.

She tilted her head. "Why do you say that?"

"No shopping bags."

"Ah." Ivette nodded. "No time. I'd just reached this street when I saw the police cars and..." She shuddered. "Emery and I had a difficult marriage, and there was no love lost in the divorce. But we were together a long time."

My lips pressed flat. If she was only three blocks away, she might have had opportunity to kill her ex. Had she really just left her office? "Is December a busy season for you?"

"Not especially. I had two clients this morning and then an unexpected—"

A chill breeze shivered my skin. Belatedly, I realized the tearoom had again fallen silent.

A woman stood inside the slowly closing front door, her black coat belted at the ample curve of her waist. She looked about my age—mid- to late thirties.

The woman caught my gaze, and her expression shifted to anger. "You." She strode toward me. "I can't believe this."

I took an involuntary step back. "Ah..." Who was this woman? "Pardon me?"

Ivette twisted on her high stool. "Didn't we say enough to each other this morning, Merry?" she asked wearily. "This isn't the time. Not with... You *do* know your husband is dead, don't you?"

Wait. Husband? Then this was...

"Allow me to introduce Merry Callum," Ivette said to me. "And I think she'll need something stronger than a cup of tea."

Chapter Four

MERRY'S FISTS CLENCHED. HER cloud of red hair trembled. "You did it. You finally did it. You killed Callum."

No one in the tearoom was even pretending not to listen now. Customers sat wide-eyed, heads turned, teacups raised. Even the Tarot readers had frozen, cards poised above the white-clothed tables.

"Don't be absurd," Ivette said. "How did you even find me here?"

Merry's face darkened. "I saw you in the window, sipping tea as if nothing..." She shook herself. "I was just at the shop with the police. They called me. I'm supposed to go to the station to give a statement."

Ivette studied her manicured nails. "And I guess they'll want to know where you've been all morning?"

"You know where..." Merry's chest heaved. "Oh. You!" She lunged toward Ivette.

And for some idiotic reason, I stepped between them. You'd think I'd have learned by now. But I was still clinging to the illusion that the tearoom was an elegant oasis of gentility, and I didn't want a brawl. "Ladies," I squeaked.

But Ivette was faster than me. She eeled sideways. Merry stamped on my foot. I tried to go in two directions at once, which just proves—should anyone be wondering—I'm really no good at the physical stuff.

Finally, my body opted for the *away* direction, and I stumbled over Ivette's empty barstool. I tumbled backward, arms windmilling, and realized with slow-motion horror what was behind me.

The gingerbread house.

I once saw Bastet miss a leap onto the back of one of Hyperion's office chairs. The tabby had twisted in mid-air and landed on all four paws like it was no big thing. It wasn't the sort of maneuver I could usually pull off.

But desperate times, desperate measures. I wrenched myself around, grabbed the counter and stopped my fall, nose centimeters from the frosting-covered chimney.

Ivette laughed lightly—and coldly—behind me. I did a push-up off the counter. Roughly, I smoothed my holiday apron.

Ivette's folded her arms. "You picked the wrong morning to pitch a fit in my office," she told her rival. Her hazel eyes narrowed. "Or maybe exactly the right morning, since now you have an alibi too."

Merry sucked in her flushed cheeks. "You—"

"May I be of assistance?" Hyperion asked. His Santa hat was mercifully gone. In the hallway entry, he stood with his hands clasped, solemn as a funeral director. Ivette snorted.

Hyperion glided toward us. Before I knew it, he'd laced Merry's arm through his. "Sometimes," he murmured, "one needs something more than tea."

Ivette opened her mouth. I cleared my throat, catching her eye. Her mouth snapped shut, her face pinking.

Hyperion led Merry away. Ivette returned to her seat at the counter. The older woman smoothed the lapels of her navy blouse.

"Sorry," Ivette said shortly. "She was the last person—" She shook her head. "I made a scene, and I apologize."

Conversation resumed in the tearoom. Teaspoons clinked against the sides of cups.

"It's fine." I adjusted the gingerbread house, mainly to make sure it was undamaged. "No one's at their personal best in circumstances like these."

"Where's he taking her?" she asked.

"To his reading room, I imagine," I said. "That, the restroom, and the kitchen are the only things back there." A Tarot deck shuffled loudly behind us.

"Ah, yes." Ivette glanced over her shoulder at a reader laying out cards at a two-top. "You do Tarot here as well."

"Not me. The readers and Hyperion." But I could see she was embarrassed and changing the subject, and I let her. Her ex-husband dead. A fight with the new wife... My pulse had only just begun to slow after the minor conflict.

"Merry came to my office this morning to rant," she said. "It was a good thing my nine AM client had canceled, or she would have interrupted our session."

I made a sympathetic noise and topped up her teacup at the counter. I didn't know why she was telling me all this. Maybe it was her way of making excuses for the drama. But I was happy for her to bend my ear. Like I said, Hyperion wasn't the only nosy partner in this relationship.

"Emery," she continued, "may he rot, had hidden several important assets during our divorce. He lied to the court. It was years ago, but my attorney thought something could be done, and we were doing it. Merry wasn't happy about it." She laughed shortly. "Emery wasn't either."

"Not a fun way to start your day."

"It took me nearly an hour to get her to leave. At one point, I considered calling the police. I wished now I had."

And Emery hadn't been discovered until after noon. I'd have to ask Sierra exactly when she'd found him. Emery could have been killed any time between nine-thirty and the body's discovery.

Unless Jonasz had lied about everything and killed him. I cleared my throat. "An hour's a long time."

"Huh. Merry's one of those people who can rant for hours about the same topic, going round and round and getting nowhere. But if she did kill him..." Her mouth pinched. "I can't say I blame her. He was a difficult man."

"The police will likely be interested in all this," I said neutrally.

"Yes." She sighed. "Though I hate to volunteer information. I should wait until they contact me, don't you think?"

"After Merry chats with them, I'm sure they will."

An expression of distaste crossed her features. "Oh. Yes. No doubt." She rose. "I should go. My office..." Ivette hurried from the tearoom.

I set her teacup and pot in a bin beneath the counter for washing. It was getting full. When I straightened, Mrs. Ingram stood beside the gingerbread house.

The older woman slid a hundred dollar bill across the counter with her receipt. "For my share. I'm afraid I have to leave, and keep the change."

"Thanks. That's generous of you. I'll make sure your waitress gets the tip."

"You handled those two well, my dear. They've been battling for years through various San Borromeo social clubs and restaurants. This scene today was the least damage they've done. Perhaps Emery's death has cooled them off." She nodded and walked out the door.

Thoughtful, I took the bin from beneath the counter to the kitchen. I loaded dishes into the industrial washer. Was that why

Ivette had been so free with information? Their contentious relationship was public, so why not tell a tearoom owner about it too? I checked my watch, then glanced around the tearoom. The tables were emptying for our next seating.

I walked down the hall toward the blinking red and gold twinkle lights that surrounded Hyperion's office door. It stood ajar. This was the signal that nothing private was happening inside—private being a Tarot reading.

I knocked and pushed the door wider. Hyperion sat slumped in his high-backed velvet chair.

On the scarlet-clothed table before him sat his massive tabby, Bastet. The cat's striped orange and white tail flicked. Bastet swiveled his head in an eerie, liquid motion to regard me.

Hyperion frowned at the table. "Well?"

"Ivette's gone." I eased inside the room. "She told me Merry came to her office this morning. They had a blow-out over some legal action Ivette was taking against her ex-husband."

"Merry admitted as much to me. She was pretty embarrassed and..."

"Worried?" I shut the door behind me.

Hyperion looked up. "*I'm* worried."

I sat in the matching velvet chair across from him. "What's wrong?"

"You know Tarot readings with my clients are private," he said, and I nodded. "Merry didn't pay me," he continued. "This was a freebie, just to get her out of the tearoom's hair. But the same privacy rule applies."

"But?"

"The cards were... She was surrounded by danger and deceit. I know you don't believe—"

"I trust you." It wasn't that I didn't believe in Tarot. I did believe we were all connected by... a web of something bigger than ourselves. I also believed certain people could touch that web and see more than the rest of us.

I thought Hyperion was one of those people. Though Tarot wasn't something I wanted to count on, it could be useful.

"And Tony's..." His dark brow furrowed.

"Not a cop anymore."

"He's floundering. I thought it was bad when he was accused of murder, but he had a purpose then. Now..."

"Maybe we should tell him about your latest reading."

Hyperion's mouth crooked. "That's the last thing he'd listen to. He's a strict rationalist."

"I'm not so sure about that." Sure, Tony was a skeptic. But like me, he believed in Hyperion's instincts.

Hyperion straightened in the thronelike chair and smiled. "I don't think dragging him into one of our madcap capers is the best idea right now."

I folded my arms over my checked apron. "If you don't mind my asking, why not?"

"Because he needs to find his own madcap caper. Or at least rescue us from ours. If I ask, it will look like I'm trying to help him. He needs to help *us*."

One corner of my mouth quirked. "So we do what we always do? We stick our nose into a problem that's not our own?"

He studied the deck on the table for a lot longer than its blue and white back warranted. Finally, he said, "It *was* a strange Tarot reading." Hyperion motioned toward the deck.

"And we can't ignore that."

"But more importantly," he said, "Sierra is my best Tarot reader."

I nodded, sobering. "Who knows how this will affect her?" There'd never been any question—of course we were going to nose around this murder. But we needed some rationale. Otherwise we just looked like two busybodies.

Being a busybody was one thing. *Looking* like one was a whole other kettle of fish.

"Exactly," he said.

"And I like Sierra too," I said. "She's a good person. She deserves our support."

"The poor woman's down at the police station right now making a statement. She found the body. She could be a suspect. It's our duty to step in."

Bastet meowed an agreement.

"Then it's settled," I said. "We investigate to help a Tarot reader out."

His office door burst open. Sierra strode inside, smiling. "You don't need to worry about me. Everything's fine."

Chapter Five

My relief at Sierra's return was immediately followed by — I'm not proud to admit this — chagrin. I mean, *damn*. What was our excuse going to be for nosing around now?

Hyperion looked equally taken aback for approximately half a second. Then he slouched, a picture of unconcern, in his high-backed chair. "Oh? How'd it go at the station?"

Bastet hopped from the round table. The tabby sauntered to Sierra, standing in the office doorway framed by twinkle lights.

The Tarot reader bent to pet him, and the cat twined around her ankles. "My lawyer came down, and I signed a statement," she said. "Easy peasy."

"I told you she'd have a lawyer," Hyperion said to me then grinned at the Tarot reader. "You know Abigail. Worry, worry, worry." He rolled his eyes.

My neck tightened. I was worried? "Did Baranko take your statement?" I rose from my chair.

"No," she said. "Someone else did."

"He's not taking this seriously," Hyperion said.

Her pale eyebrows lifted. "Because the detective in charge didn't take my statement? I think he was busy with something else."

"Exactly." Hyperion nodded, a satisfied look on his face. I knew what he was doing. Excuses. Rationalization. I'd been doing it too—neither of us were going to ignore a murder practically next door.

"There's something I need to show you." She pulled her phone from the pocket of her long sweater coat. "I don't know why I did this, but while I was waiting for the police, I took a picture."

Hyperion's brown eyes widened. "You took a crime scene photo?"

She nodded sheepishly and handed him the phone. I crowded behind him to look. On the oversized screen, Emery Callum lay on the ground beside a simple metal desk. A pencil holder and pencils lay scattered on the desktop. Boxes were stacked nearby. On the concrete floor lay a pillbox—one that held a week's worth of pills. Blood seeped from the older man's head. I swallowed, sickened.

"Good composition, awful subject matter." Hyperion handed the phone back to her. "I'm sorry you had to see it."

"Someone had to," she said heavily.

"I wasn't worried, but I'm glad you're okay." Oh, *that* didn't sound defensive. Not at all. Edging past her, I returned to the kitchen. Hyperion could figure out an excuse to investigate on his own.

Dishes had piled up on the metal counter. We were between seatings, tidying up time. I grabbed a sugar-plum scone, still hot from the oven, took a quick bite, and rolled up my sleeves.

I was particularly proud of this new recipe. The scones used dried Angelino plums instead of prunes, and the Angelinos had a lovely, garnet color and tart flavor. Dusted with sugar crystals, the scones almost looked magical. I wasn't sure if I preferred them with berry jam or lemon curd or just dripping in butter. Clearly, I'd have to keep testing.

We filled the dishwasher and switched out the tablecloths and place settings. The next round of guests, chatting and laughing, entered the tearoom. I took up position behind its quartz counter.

But as I got into the groove of prepping teapots, my mind wandered to murder. Hyperion would say the appearance of two suspects in the tearoom today was the work of Fate. I wasn't sure I believed in her. Beanblossom's was only a few stores down from the murder scene. And upset or in shock, it did make sense for Ivette and/or Merry to stumble inside. Sort of.

Sierra emerged from the hallway into the tearoom. She roved, Tarot deck in hand, stopping to chat with guests at their tables.

My forehead wrinkled. *Had* Ivette really just wandered downtown for shopping? Sure, her office was only a few blocks away. And yes, this was prime shopping time, even if it was rainy. As for Merry, she'd been called to the scene by the police. I poured boiling water into a teapot.

But why hadn't Merry gone straight to the station afterward? Why stop in the tearoom? Surely the police would want to talk to her more about her husband. Or maybe that would happen later?

Or maybe this murder investigation was already in trouble. Boiling hot water overflowed the teapot, and I skipped backward. Water splashed across the counter and onto the floor.

"Oh, Abigail," Mrs. Ingram sat at the counter. The older woman smoothed her green and red plaid skirt over her knees. "Is it all right if I sit here?"

"Of course. It's nice to see you again." Bemused, I grabbed a towel and blotted the counter. Mrs. Ingram was a regular customer. But not even she returned twice in one day. Had she come back for murder gossip? Not that I could blame her. I was angling for gossip too. "What brings you back so soon?" I set the teapot in the sink beneath the counter.

"A spur of the moment inspiration and a pot of Earl Grey. Please."

"A pot of Earl Grey coming right up." I wiped the floor with the damp rag then pulled out a fresh pot to fill. "And the inspiration?"

"I was thinking of gift certificates for Tarot readings from Hyperion as Christmas gifts. Have you ever had one?"

"Yes, and he's great. You should do it."

She fiddled with the beaded chain on her reading glasses, hanging against her chest. "I should have thought of it before. It will be such a unique gift."

Helena, my newest waitress, appeared at the counter. "Have you—?"

"I'll bring the tea to table five," I told her hastily.

"Thanks." She whizzed into the hall and presumably to the kitchen.

I made tea for Mrs. Ingram and for Helena's table. Setting the pots on a tray, I stepped from behind the counter. "I'll get the gift certificates from Hyperion," I told Mrs. Ingram.

Something whispered above my head, and a dark mass swooped downward. Mrs. Ingram squeaked, and a bell jangled faintly.

"Look out," a man's voice rumbled behind me.

I hunched, instinctively protecting the teapots. Granted, this was not the brightest instinct, but I had my priorities.

And then... nothing happened. I straightened and turned.

My neighbor, Brik, held a strand of pine garland that had slipped from its spot high on the wall. He turned and hooked it onto its nail. I'd have needed a step stool to get it up there, and my heart did an irritating, fluttery thing.

Brik was tall and brawny, and his blond hair was pulled back into its usual ponytail. I'll be honest. Normally, I'm not a fan of long hair on men. My hair's longish, and it feels like too much competition. But Brik could make a mohawk look good.

"You need a real hook on that," he said, "or it'll fall again. I can install one later if you want." In spite of the fact it was cold and wet outside, all he wore was a white t-shirt and jeans. They showed off his muscles admirably. Not that I noticed that sort of thing.

And I didn't want him doing favors for me. I jerked down the hem of my apron. "What are you...?" Also, he was distracting me from work. "I'll be right back." I deposited the teapots at the table, made sure the ladies were taken care of, and returned to the counter.

Brik jerked his thumb toward the hallway. "Hyperion finally wants me to start on that ceiling in his office. He said he needed to wait to make sure he had the budget for it."

My eyes popped. *Hyperion? Budget?* Those two words rarely went together, unless I was the one griping that my partner needed to watch the budget.

Mrs. Ingram raised her teacup to her mouth. I noticed she didn't drink though.

"Yeah." Brik laughed lightly. "Don't worry. I won't be drilling or hammering while the tearoom's operating."

Brik was a contractor, and a good one. Installing a fake ceiling to hide the pipes in Hyperion's office was a small job for him. But I was selfishly glad he was doing it. Brik was a perfectionist when it came to contracting.

I was also glad we'd gotten past that whole will-they-or-won't-they awkwardness and settled comfortably into "won't." I was seeing someone else, and Brik... With his god-of-thunder good looks, he never had trouble getting a date.

He scanned the other swags of pine with a professional eye. "Yeah, those nails aren't very stable. I'll take care of the rest of them tomorrow if you want."

If he was going to be doing work for Hyperion anyway... I climbed off my high horse and relented. "That'd be great. Thanks."

He shifted his weight. "So, uh, I'm planning a holiday party next weekend. You're invited, of course, but it'll be a big crowd."

The shoe dropped. He wasn't here to save me from falling holiday décor. He was offering favors so I wouldn't complain about the street parking.

I forced a smile. "No problem." And at least he was giving me advance warning. There'd been a time when he'd held parties near nightly—noise had been the rule. I frowned. Come to think of it, he hadn't thrown a loud party in weeks.

Hyperion appeared at Brik's elbow. "Everything okay?"

"The new ceiling's a go," the contractor said. "See you around, Abigail." He ambled from the tearoom, female (and some male) heads turning as he passed.

Hyperion folded his arms. "You two still on the outs?"

"No, we're not *still*, because we were never on the outs. Or in for that matter." I strode behind the counter and dumped the water from the overflowed teapot.

"It's the twenty-first century," he said. "You should just ask him out. I've heard women can do that now."

Mrs. Ingram shook her head, her mouth pulling downward. "Oh, dear. No."

"Um," I said, "I'm seeing someone, remember?"

Hyperion smirked. "Ah, yes, the analytical estate attorney."

"What's wrong with being analytical?" I asked.

Hyperion yawned, making a show of covering his mouth. "Snoozeville."

"Gino's plenty fun," I said grumpily.

He slid onto a bar stool beside Mrs. Ingram. "Mm, if you say so." He shot the old lady a shrewd look, and she raised her wintry eyebrows.

Heat flushed my cheeks. "And Brik and I are friends." And we were going to stay that way, since Brik had issues with my independent, high-risk lifestyle. "That's all."

"Sure you are," he said. "So... What are you doing?"

"What does it look like I'm doing?" I brandished the empty pot.

"I honestly have no idea." He propped his elbows on the counter. "Your tearoom shenanigans baffle me. But I think we should strike with our investigation while the iron is hot."

"You want to break into the victim's souvenir shop?" I asked, sarcastic, and immediately regretted it. Hyperion might think it was a good idea.

"Ooh!" Mrs. Ingram's brown eyes widened. "Could you?"

"Not while the cops are crawling all over the place," he told her.

"I suppose that's fair," she said. "Disappointing, but fair."

"I thought we should hit up your grandfather and Tomas for gossip," Hyperion said. "If anyone knows what's up with our victim, it'll be those two. I'm actually surprised they're not here."

"They're working the Christmas market on the pier," I said.

"They managed to get booths?" Mrs. Ingram asked.

Hyperion whistled. "I heard those were almost impossible to snag."

"They got *a* booth, which they're sharing." Normally, my grandfather and Tomas worked the weekly farmer's market. Their horseradish and salsa were in high demand. But the farmer's market was closed for the winter season, to be replaced by the Christmas market.

"Then we should leave now," my partner said, "before the market closes."

"But the tearoom—"

"Is under control and can survive another thirty minutes without you."

"It really can." Mrs. Ingram sipped her tea.

I scanned the room. It seemed like Beanblossom's *was* under control. And maybe I could find a more personal gift at the market for Gino. "Talk to Mrs. Ingram about Tarot gift certificates. And I need to talk to Maricel."

I hurried into the kitchen. My assistant manager assured me she could manage without me. And while this was convenient, it was also a minor blow to my ego. We like to think we're indispensable and irreplaceable, but none of us are.

Hyperion and I strolled to the pier. The rain had stopped, but masses of low clouds had turned the December afternoon to twilight.

White twinkle lights glittered above wooden stands, sheltering beneath forest-green marquees. A Dickensian choir belting out holiday tunes muffled the sound of lapping water.

Hyperion jammed his hands in the pockets of his charcoal slacks. "Maybe I can get some holiday inspiration for my blog." He'd been writing about a different card each week. If he kept to it, he'd finish the deck by the end of the year.

"You still on track?"

"Yes," he said gloomily. "I'll be out of cards soon. Then I'll have to come up with another genius idea for a year's worth of blogs. There's only so much I can say about Tarot cards."

We walked past stands selling wooden toys and pine wreaths and found my grandfather and Tomas near the end of the pier. A long line extended from their stall, and we moved to its back.

As the line edged forward, I studied the twenty-foot Christmas tree at the end of the pier. Tourists and locals snapped selfies in front of it its gleaming lights. It was so charming I almost wanted a photo.

Hyperion nudged me. We stepped up to the stall, a pine garland swagging its wooden counter.

"Hey, Abigail." Tomas waved from the back of the stall, where he was wrapping salsa in red tissue paper. Nearby, a mallard duck sat on top of an empty horseradish crate. It quacked and waggled its tail when it saw Hyperion.

Gramps leaned over the wooden counter and adjusted his cabbie-style hat. "No Bastet?"

"He hates the rain," Hyperion said. "In that respect and that only, he's a typical cat."

My grandfather jerked his thumb toward the duck. "Peking will be disappointed. What brings you two here?"

"Did you hear about Mr. Callum's death today?" I asked. My grandfather was one of those innocent-looking old men who knows too much. Waitresses flirt with him. People come to him to unload their dark secrets. It made him a font of local intel.

My grandfather nodded. "It's all over the pier. What happened?"

We explained, and he shook his head. "I'm surprised no one bumped him off sooner," he said. "To be honest, he wasn't a likable man."

The carolers assembled around the tree and launched into a new song.

"Why not?" I asked him.

"He was a skinflint. Never treated his employees well. Told the community to pound sand whenever something needed doing. And he was mean about it too. You won't be lacking for suspects. No one liked him."

"He was married," I said. "Someone liked him." He'd been a handsome man as well, if you liked cold and aloof and elegant.

"Yes," he said dryly, "well, for some women, money cancels a multitude of sins."

"Not just women," Hyperion said, and my grandfather laughed.

"How's Gino doing?" Gramps asked me.

"Gino?" What *was* I going to get him? "He's great. I was just shopping for his present."

"I mean with the murder," he said.

"The murder?" I said blankly. What did Gino have to do with the murder?

Gramps scratched the back of his neck. "Didn't you know? Gino's Callum's nephew."

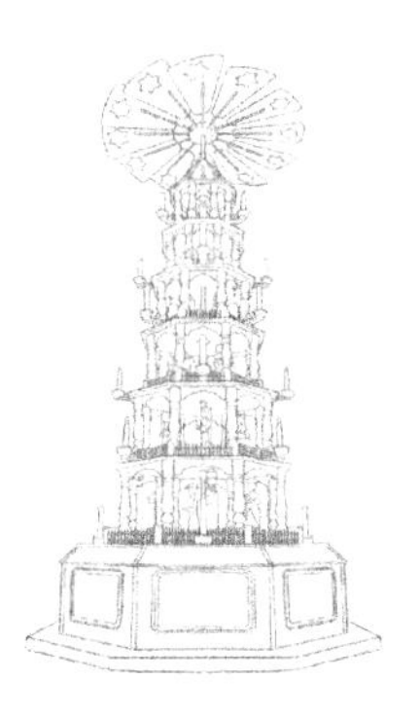

Chapter Six

"Easiest investigation ever," Hyperion said, and we strolled back down the pier. "You've got an in with Gino. All you need to do is work your feminine wiles—you've got those, right? Whatever. He'll tell you what I want to know."

"Mm," I said, noncommittal. But my stomach curdled. It wasn't as if Gino were a suspect. So why was I dreading talking to him about this? And why hadn't he mentioned they were related earlier? He'd had the perfect opportunity in the tearoom earlier.

Twilight darkened the pier, the crowds thinning. Clouds and ocean converged in gradations of steely blue, and the lights on the pier brightened. On the shore, a thirty-foot Germanic Christmas carousel, a Weihnactspyramide, made a stately rotation. Its giant plastic candles gleamed.

"So out of all your done holiday shopping, why don't you have a gift for your boyfriend yet?" he asked. "You're not hitting a romantic slump, are you? Because that could put a serious kink in our investigation. And not the good kind."

I hunched my shoulders in my thick coat. "I have a gift for Gino. I just don't really like it."

Hyperion stopped beside a wooden stand selling Christmas ornaments. "Don't like the gift or the guy? Trouble in paradise?"

"No. I'm just..." I shook myself. What *was* wrong with me? "Murder kind of puts a damper on the holiday spirit."

"No kidding. I know what you need." He dragged me to a photo stand with wooden cutouts and stuck his head through a dancing Christmas tree. "Ta dah!"

"I need to take your picture?" I asked.

He withdrew his head and walked around the wooden tree. "No, you need to stick your head through this ridiculous cutout so I can take *your* picture. We can put holiday photos of all the employees on the wall at Beanblossom's."

That wasn't a bad idea. "Why not?" It would only take a minute, and then we could get back to the tearoom.

I walked to the back of the cutout and stuck my head through. "I could never figure out if you're supposed to stick your head through or just *look* through the hole."

He aimed his phone at me. "Smile and say *die*."

"Do not even—"

"Hey," a familiar masculine voice said from behind me.

I jerked, the top of my head banging against the curve of the wooden cutout. "Ow." Wincing, I extracted myself from the dancing tree and turned.

Gino, in his sleek gray suit, grinned. "A little jumpy?" Moisture glittered in his curling dark hair.

I reached back to smooth my own and realized I was still wearing a snood to keep my hair out of the scones and sandwiches. I whipped it off, and my braid tumbled down my back. "Heh, heh. Hey yourself."

"I cannot *stand* the sexual tension." Hyperion's gaze flicked skyward. "I'm going back to the tearoom." He strode down the pier toward town, mist dimming its pastel buildings.

Gino's grin widened. "You're playing hookie too?"

"Something like that. Gino, I…I didn't realize. Your uncle…"

He sobered. "Why would you? It's the real reason I was on Main Street earlier. Merry called me."

"I'm so sorry."

He shook his head. "Don't be. We weren't close. I tried, but my uncle wasn't interested in family." He grimaced. "But I couldn't bring myself to go back to work after I left you. I've been wandering ever since."

"I wish you would have told me earlier." I slipped my hand into his. "I could have wandered with you."

"I didn't want to interrupt your work." He paused. "I saw Merry after I left you. She mentioned she stopped in your tearoom and got into it with Ivette."

"Yeah." I glanced away. On a floating pier, a dozen sea lions lolled. "It was a little awkward."

"Those two have always hated each other. The mystery is why they felt my uncle was worth fighting over. I told Merry she picked the right tearoom though," he said jokingly.

"Oh?"

"Because of your love of crime."

"I'm not sure I'd call it a love…" Though it certainly was more than idle, morbid curiosity. Mostly. I couldn't exactly explain *what* it was. Someone had been killed on my street, only a hundred yards away from me. It didn't seem right to just go on, business as usual. "Have the police spoken with you?"

The carolers strolled past singing a cheerful tune. It now seemed awkward and inappropriate.

"I don't know why they would," Gino said. "Like I said, my uncle and I weren't close." His chocolatey eyes narrowed. "Hold on. You don't think you're going to... You're not really playing amateur detective? This is my uncle you're talking about."

I hesitated. "I thought you said you weren't close."

"We weren't. But still. I know these people."

"Who do you think would have wanted your uncle dead?" I hedged. If Gino really didn't want me asking about it... But he said they hadn't been close.

Gino folded his arms. "It was a robbery gone wrong. Nothing more. There's no reason for you to be concerned about it."

Had the police told him it was a robbery? I leaned against the pier's railing. Nearby, a mass of seaweed bobbed in the darkening ocean. "One of our Tarot readers found the body."

Gino drew in a breath. "Damn. I'm sorry." He pulled me into a hug. I rested my cheek against the soft fabric of his coat and inhaled the faint scent of his spicy cologne. "Of course you're worried about her. I didn't think—" He ran his hand down my back, and I shivered. "I don't think you need to worry about your staff's safety. Your tearoom is a totally different situation. You have people in there all the time. My uncle's shop... He was alone when it happened."

"But he shouldn't have been," I said. "The man who works for him would normally have been there."

"Jonasz?" He stepped back, his expression clouded. "And that's the second reason you shouldn't be worried. Odds are, it was an inside job."

"You think Jonasz did it?" I didn't know the man well, but he didn't seem like a criminal.

That said, I'd been fooled before.

He ran his hands down my arms. "I'm saying odds are it was an inside job. And Emery only had one employee."

"Is that what the police are saying?"

"That's what they told Merry. You have nothing to worry about."

I wasn't worried, but I was disturbed. "It's more than that," I fumbled.

His olive brow creased. “The police don’t think your Tarot reader is a suspect, do they?”

“No. No, I don’t think so. Why would they?”

“They shouldn’t. Your tearoom is safe, and so are your employees. San Borromeo is still a low-crime town.” His arms encircled my waist, and his cheek brushed mine.

In spite of everything, a lovely cocoon of warmth enveloped me. Yes, we’re all whole and complete on our own. But having a boyfriend is *really* nice. “Dinner tonight?” I asked.

He stepped backward, releasing me. “I can’t. Merry’s panicking about all the thing she has to do now that Emery’s gone. I told her I’d help her with… You know.”

“I know,” I said, my insides squeezing with sympathy. I kissed him lightly. “You’re a good man for helping her out.”

“It’s sort of my job.”

“Are you your uncle’s estate attorney?”

He snorted. “Emery didn’t believe in them.” His brows slashed downward. “And I’m afraid he may have left a mess for Merry. Not having a will or trust is practically spousal abuse these days.”

“He doesn’t have a will?” I asked, shocked. Though I didn’t have any kids, even I had a simple trust. My grandfather, a retired CPA, had drilled record keeping and financial probity into me from an early age. For that, I was grateful.

“If I know my uncle,” Gino said, “he found some do-it-yourself website to save money. And then he screwed the whole thing up. But he’s dead now, so what does he care if he left a mess?”

“Did he have any children?”

“No, thank God. He told me kids were parasites. I was eleven at the time. I can’t imagine him as a father.” The first threads of bitterness wound through his voice. He smiled. “I’m meeting a client at the Fish Restaurant for a drink and then headed over to Merry’s. Raincheck on dinner?”

“Call me.”

We kissed again, and I hurried down the pier toward Beanblossom's. I hadn't been concerned about robberies before talking to Gino. The idea of someone attacking Beanblossom's still seemed unlikely. But the thought had jammed in my brain now, and I couldn't quite shake it.

The rest of the day whizzed past in a flurry of holiday teas. Since I'd spent so much of the day out of the tearoom, I offered to let the waitstaff leave early. They all did, mumbling about Christmas shopping and holiday parties.

Cleaning up on my own was a welcome end to the day, even if I did make double sure the front and back doors were locked once I was alone. There was a certain satisfaction to getting everything back in order. But that didn't keep me from thinking about Emery Callum as I stooped over the cold-holding unit and attacked it with a sponge. It didn't keep me from thinking about Gino's fraught relationship with his uncle. Or about Gino's reaction when I'd asked him about the murder.

When we'd first met, Gino had accused me of having some psychological disorder that compelled me to investigate crimes. He'd later apologized, and I'd thought that was that. After all, I got where he'd been coming from.

On the face of it, amateur detecting didn't make a whole lot of sense. We had a perfectly fine police force. It was their job to solve murders, and they had the resources to do it.

But Hyperion and I were *good* at what we did. Okay, true, we'd almost solved our last case by accident. But we'd solved it, and we'd cleared Tony's name. And that had meant something, even if Tony had gone on to leave the police force anyway. At least he wasn't in jail.

That hadn't been a case we could exactly ignore. Hyperion hadn't been about to let Tony go down for a murder he hadn't committed. And I couldn't have left Hyperion to do it all on his own.

Of course, that wasn't the situation now. Now...

CRASH.

I started at the unmistakable sound of breaking glass. The sponge dropped from my nerveless fingers and splatted wetly inside the cold-holding unit. A chill breeze stirred the tendrils of hair around my ears.

I jumped to standing and raced into the dining area. The curtains billowed around a jagged hole in a front window.

Stunned, I stared for a moment, not quite processing what I was seeing. Someone had thrown a rock through our window. The rock had knocked over a mini-Christmas tree centerpiece and now squatted malignantly on the tablecloth. Pebbles of safety glass littered the tables and floor and glittered beneath the twinkle lights.

"Abigail?" Hyperion asked from behind me, and I sucked in a quick breath. I thought I'd been alone.

"The window," I sputtered. Hot rage flooded my brain. I dashed to the blue, front door and tried to open it, discovered it was locked. Unbolting it, I ran onto the sidewalk.

A couple emerged from a nearby restaurant across the street. But no one else walked the brick sidewalks. My neck corded. I'd been too slow.

Hyperion came to stand beside me and loosed a good fifteen-seconds worth of Lovecraftian curses. He had a Lovecraft word-of-the-day calendar. It was obnoxious, though my vocabulary was definitely growing, if in a mildly disgusting way.

But his anger leached off some of my own, even if an unpleasant knotting in my stomach replaced it. A murder on the street. A robbery. And now vandalism, here at the tearoom.

My flesh pebbled. I touched the sleeve of his sports jacket. Together, we backed inside the tearoom, and I relocked the door.

Chapter Seven

WE CALLED THE POLICE and waited. I took photos for our insurance company. But I wasn't sure it would be worth it to file a claim. The insurance company would likely just raise the rates. Again.

"On the bright side," Hyperion said, lifting a table by the window. "No one died."

Droplets sleeted into the tearoom, and I glared at him. "Bright side? Do you have any idea how much windows cost?"

"No." Hyperion shifted the table out of the rain. "I can honestly say I don't."

"You soon will." I strode into the kitchen and retrieved my sweater and a mop. Too late, I realized mopping was pointless until the window was boarded up. In the dining area, I tossed the mop down with a clatter. Hyperion raised a brow.

"It's just not right," I burst out.

Two youngish police officers arrived and took a report. One snapped pictures of the destruction with his phone. The other filled out a form on his computer tablet.

"Do you think it has anything to do with the murder at the souvenir shop?" I retrieved the mop and jerked my head in the direction of the souvenir shop.

The cop with the tablet looked up. "A broken window connected to a murder/robbery? I doubt it. Kids probably did this."

My hand tightened on the mop's wooden handle. "It's just—"

Hyperion laid his hand on my shoulder. "He's right. Two crimes in one day on a low-crime street like this? That's *definitely* a coincidence."

The policeman shot him a confused look, then nodded. Ten minutes later, they left. A gust of wind blew splatters of rain into the tearoom and flapped the hem of my long sweater.

I clawed a hand through my hair and surveyed the wreckage. This was a disaster. Sure, tomorrow was Monday, and the tearoom would be closed. But how long would it take to get the window replaced? It was the holidays. I could cover the gap with plywood, but that wasn't exactly the elegant and genteel holiday atmosphere I'd been aiming for.

And yes, I *knew* there were bigger and more important things going on—like murder. It was hard to believe it was only this afternoon that a man had been killed. So much had happened today, and I should be focusing on Gino and the widows.

But this was Beanblossom's. Someone had thrown a rock through *Beanblossom's*. I frowned at the rock on the table. The police had declined to take it as evidence. That just seemed lazy to me.

Hyperion slung an arm over my shoulders. "It'll work out. It always does."

"Maybe the cops are right." I rubbed the back of my neck. "Maybe it was just a coincidence."

"They do happen." He shook his head. "It's just a Ten of Swords day."

The Ten of Swords depicted a man lying on the ground, ten swords in his back. Tens were about endings, and the ten of swords was a very final one. But the sun was also rising on the scene, making way for something new.

"I hope so," I said, and shook myself. "I think I've got some duct tape. I can put plastic wrap over the hole for tonight. But—"

"Plastic wrap?" Brik asked, and I turned. He strode from the rear hallway into the dining area. "Only a baker would think that was a good idea." His blond hair was windblown, strands escaping from his ponytail. Rain dripped down his black windbreaker and stained the front of his jeans.

I jammed my hands on my hips and turned to face Hyperion. He'd obviously been the one to call my neighbor, since I hadn't. "Plastic wrap's all I've..." I trailed off, noticing the toolkit in Brik's hand. "I don't suppose you have any plywood?" I asked meekly.

"I always have plywood." He shrugged out of his windbreaker and dropped it over the back of a wooden chair. "But we may not need it. I might have a window I can cut to fit."

I blinked. "You... really?" I asked, torn. I needed that window fixed. And I had a good idea it wasn't going to get done quickly if I found another repair shop. Of course I'd pay Brik, but it felt awkward taking another favor from my neighbor.

He set his toolkit on the laminate floor and unlatched it. "The glass is for another job, but they don't need it right away. I can re-order in time."

"If you're sure it won't cause you any problems down the road." I rubbed the back of my neck.

"What problems? And I got nothing else going on tonight."

"But it's a—" *Sunday*. I clamped my mouth shut. Once upon a time, Sundays had been prime party nights for Brik. But he'd seemed to have given them up—a step forward for us both. Not because the loud music and lack of parking wasn't crazy-making (it was). But because I'd finally figured out why he threw so many of them.

He didn't want to be alone.

In his hometown of Eureka, he'd been wrongly accused of murder. Brik didn't want to be alone because he feared not having an alibi, and a knot tightened my gut. He didn't deserve that hell.

"A Sunday?" Brik finished for me and cocked his brow. "I don't throw parties every night, you know."

"I was going to say a huge favor." I pulled my sweater tighter. "And I appreciate it."

Hyperion checked his watch. "And I've got to bounce. Brik will you...?"

"I'll make sure Abigail gets home."

I folded my arms. "You don't need to—"

"Or I can take you home now and come back to work on this," Brik said.

If he was going to be that way about it... "No. I'll stay and help with the window. We can go home together." Heat rose to my cheeks. That hadn't come out the way I'd intended. "I mean, since we live next door, we can drive back at the same time."

He crossed his arms over his chest. It was much more impressive when he did it, his muscles bulging. "What do you know about replacing windows?"

"I assume we'll have to take the broken one out first," I said.

Hyperion choked back a laugh. "I'll see you two later." He strolled into the back hallway. The heavy, metal door clanged at the rear of the building, and the lock clicked shut.

Replacing the window took time. I wasn't much help, aside from the cleanup. But I'd like to think I at least provided moral support in the form of hot drinks and scones.

When we finished, the rain had stopped. Brik followed me home, the headlights of his pickup blinding in my rearview. We pulled into our driveways and stepped from our vehicles at the same time.

My yellow bungalow was 1940s California-style, and my muscles unknotted at the sight. There's just something about home sweet home, humble and all.

Brik had expanded and modernized his bungalow into neat, blue cubes. Like mine, his windows were devoid of holiday lights. In my defense, all my decorating efforts had gone into the tearoom. I didn't know what his excuse was.

He walked across the narrow strip of lawn between our bungalows. "Hyperion told me about Callum's murder this morning. Why didn't you?"

It had been an intentional omission, and warmth flushed my chest. Brik didn't need more murder in his life. Not after Eureka. "I didn't really know the man," I said.

"He wouldn't want to know someone like you. His loss," he added quickly.

I cocked my head. "Did you know Emery Callum?"

"I did some repair work for him when I was first starting out in San Borromeo. He was too cheap to remodel, which his store desperately needed. He'd just gotten remarried."

"I met his wife. Merry came into Beanblossom's today."

His arctic eyes glinted. "Which you figured was a sign to investigate?"

I stiffened. This was the reason Brik and I had never got off the ground. What was really irritating was I understood where he was coming from too. The murder victim in Eureka had been his girlfriend, killed by a stalker.

The police had eventually dropped Brik as a suspect. But the real killer had never been caught. It had left Brik with a wariness around cops. He also wasn't a huge fan of people who put themselves at risk nosing around murder investigations. "No," I said dryly, "we took Sierra finding the body as a sign we should investigate."

"Sierra found him?" His blue eyes darkened. And why did *that* raise my hackles? Was I jealous? "Is she all right?" he continued.

"She was shaken when she first found him, but I think she's okay. They took her down to the police station to sign a statement. She had a lawyer with her, and she returned to work later today."

"It's too bad Tony's not in charge anymore. How's he doing?"

"Trying to figure out next steps. Steps for his career, not for an impromptu investigation of Emery Callum's murder."

He huffed a laugh. "I didn't think he was going to join your little mystery team. Not his style."

"Well, jinkies," I said, and his smile broadened. "Now you're just being mean."

He sobered. "And now someone's broken your window."

"It can't be connected to the murder. There's a bottomless chasm between a broken window and murder. And the police seem to think Emery Callum's death was a simple robbery gone wrong." And it all sounded false coming out of my mouth.

"But you don't."

I hesitated. No, I didn't. "When I opened Beanblossom's, I did some research into security."

He arched a skeptical brow. "Really," he said flatly.

"I did," I insisted. "Most robberies happen right when the business opens, in the morning. Don't ask me why; I can't remember. Callum's store *was* hit in the morning. His employee, Jonasz, had been called away. But the call was a hoax."

There was every reason to believe it *had* been a robbery gone wrong. So why didn't I want to believe it?

"A hoax?" he asked.

"Someone phoned and told him his daughter was in the hospital." Calling Jonasz away seemed a little elaborate. But if robbers had been surveilling his business, it wasn't outside the realm of possibility. Maybe I was making more of this than there was.

Brik's expression hardened. "Bastards. His daughter has some sort of heart disease."

My breath caught. "Oh, no." I pressed a hand to my stomach. "How old is she?"

"I'm not sure. Ten or twelve by now, I'd guess. I got to know Jonasz a little when I was on the job there. I'm surprised he's stuck it out this long. At the time, he told me he couldn't quit because of the great health insurance."

"But I thought Emery was a cheapskate?"

"Yeah, he probably figured it was cheaper to pay up on the insurance than to pay a better wage. Or maybe Ivette had pushed him into it. I don't know." The clouds parted, revealing a slip of moon, and the shadows on Brik's face lightened.

"Well." I edged backward toward my porch steps. "Thanks again. Send me the invoice for everything."

"Don't worry. I will."

We parted, and he walked to his front door. He waited until I was inside before closing his.

Chapter Eight

DESPITE MY LATE NIGHT fixing windows with Brik—or maybe because of it—I spent most of the night lying awake. No sooner would I shut down thoughts about the murder then I'd think about vandalism or Brik instead. Then I'd get angry with myself for doing it. That didn't help either.

Eventually, sunrise brightened my bedroom curtains. Unable to deny I was still awake, I dragged myself from my warm bed. I dressed and made my way to the kitchen.

Yawning, I ran my hand along its gray granite counter and fumbled to the butcherblock work island, stubbing my toe in the process. I hopped around, cursing, on the white tile floor. *That* got my blood pumping.

When swearing at inanimate objects got old, I wandered into the pantry. I studied the herbs and flowers drying from the ceiling rack.

I rubbed my burning eyes. Mondays were always a good day for testing out scone recipes. The tearoom was closed. And scones made for good breakfast eating.

But I was getting tired of all the holiday spices, delicious as they were. Moving more slowly than usual, I mixed up my usual basic scone recipe. I added lemon juice to the milk, then zested my lemon and tossed that into the mix as well. Since I had dried cherries in the cupboard I tossed those in. If it worked, I'd call them cherry-lemonade scones.

I slid the scones into the oven, and there was a knock at my front door. I shut the oven and rinsed my hands. Grabbing a tea towel from the refrigerator handle, I dried my hands as I walked to the door. I peered through the peephole.

A giant brown eye stared back at me, and I smiled. *Hyperion.*

I swung open the door. "Good morning."

He bounded into the living area and sniffed. "I don't smell scones." He was dressed like a male model on winter vacation. Skinny blue-gray slacks. A white tee beneath a denim shirt and wool navy coat.

"That's because I just put them in the oven."

He rubbed his long hands together. "Outstanding. If it's a new recipe, I'll help you test it. If it's not, I'll have one anyway. I'm starving." He looked around the living area, done up in soothing blues and whites. "Brik's not here?" he asked casually.

My eyes narrowed. "Is he supposed to be here? You didn't call and invite him over, did you?"

"No, no. I just thought... After last night."

"Oh, come *on*." I tossed my towel onto the ivory sofa beneath the front window. "Why are you so determined to get Brik and me together? I'm seeing Gino."

"Yeah, but Gino's a lawyer, and only an estate attorney at that. Think of how much more useful dating a contractor would be."

I considered. There was actually something to that. "How's Tony?"

He sat against the back of my blue, gaming couch. "In a mood. He's refusing to help with the Callum murder, even after someone threw a brick through our window."

"A rock."

"Whatever. You haven't decorated."

"I haven't had time," I snapped, and immediately felt guilty for snapping. It was the holidays, after all, and I loved the holidays. So why *hadn't* I decorated yet? "That's my project for today."

"No time for household projects. We've got to canvas the street and find out if anyone saw who threw that rock."

"Today?" Okay, yes, I *did* want to catch the jerk who'd broken our window. But it was my day off, and insomnia made me whiny.

"You know the more time that goes by," he continued, "the less people will remember."

I hung my head. I knew. I also knew this was about more than a broken window. The police might think there was no connection to the murder, but I didn't. And if I was wrong, talking to local business owners could still be useful.

The scones finished baking. We ate said scones, and they were light and lemony and delicious. Come January, they were going on the menu.

"They're good," he said slowly. "But they're not very holiday, are they?"

Ignoring that (since it was true), I rose from the table. "I'm going to change."

"Don't ever change, Abigail," he said seriously, then grinned.

I left him examining my collection of fortune telling teacups and hurried to my bedroom. Since 'twas the season, I slipped into a cranberry turtleneck, plaid skirt, and matching boots.

I faced myself in the mirror and smoothed the short skirt. I might not be feeling the spirit, but at least I looked the part.

We took Hyperion's Jeep to downtown San Borromeo. Letting him drive was a major Christmas concession on my part. Hyperion thinks he's a stock car racer. I've never taken anything stronger than a glass of wine, but his driving made me wish valium was available over the counter.

The street was blanketed in a thick ocean fog. A few holiday lights gleamed pallidly, red and gold globes in the mist. A car pulled from its spot on Main Street, and we squealed into it.

"Thank you, parking gods," Hyperion caroled.

I pried my fingers from the grab bar. "So what are we thinking? Ask about the broken window and Emery Callum?"

He stepped from the Jeep. "It only makes sense. I'm sure he'll come up in any case."

We walked down the street from Beanblossom's, passing Emery Callum's closed shop. We popped in and out of businesses asking if anyone had seen anything. But no one had. We crossed the street and walked back, doing the same.

In the shop across from the tearoom, Mr. Jamison braced one elbow on his dusty counter and listened to our spiel. T-shirts in neat formation marched across the back wall. None would make a good gift for an estate attorney.

The shop owner clawed a hand through his thick, longish blond hair and grimaced. His face was tanned and lined by the sun. "Sorry. My shop was closed by that time last night. I didn't see a thing."

"I'm more worried about Callum's murder than your window, to be honest," Mr. Jamison continued. "This town used to be peaceful. There's some talk of organizing a neighborhood watch."

"Can they do that in a business district?" I asked.

He shrugged. "Why not? It's just a bunch of people getting together to, you know, watch. Nothing illegal about it."

"I do like to watch," Hyperion said gravely.

I shot him a quelling look, then wondered why I'd bothered. As usual, it had no effect.

My partner grinned impishly, then sobered. "Emery Callum ever give you any trouble?" Hyperion asked him.

"Aside from the annual rent raises, no."

"He owns—owned this building?" I corrected, surprised.

"This and a bunch of others on the street." Mr. Jamison glanced longingly at the surfboard propped in the corner, behind the counter.

"Was he a good landlord?" I asked.

The shop owner barked a laugh. "Are you kidding? Look around." He motioned around the shop.

It looked like it hadn't been updated since the seventies. Graying ceiling tiles. Linoleum floors. Scratched windows facing the street. Shame on me, I'd chalked up the casual disarray to Mr. Jamison's easy-breezy surfer attitude.

"How was he to deal with?" I asked.

"Don't know," Mr. Jamison said. "I never had to. He had a management company."

"Really? Which one?" Hyperion asked.

"Acme. Like in the cartoons."

We chatted some more and moved on to the restaurant next door. It hadn't opened for business yet. But the owner, Mr. Salazar, recognized us through the glass door and waved.

He let us inside. "I can't believe you got your window repaired so quickly." He locked the door behind us. He was a balding, dark haired man, with a seventies-era mustache. "What's your secret?" He adjusted his thick, black-framed glasses.

My mouth tightened in remembered annoyance. "We got lucky," I said. "Aside from someone breaking it in the first place. Did you see anything last night?"

He shook his head. "I heard the crash and ran to the front of the restaurant." He motioned to the picture windows. "I did see someone running down the street. They were at the next block by the time I got here though, so I didn't get a good look."

"Man or woman?" Hyperion asked.

He scrunched his forehead. "Hard to tell. It was dark. I think it might have been a woman though."

I glanced at the paper sign taped to the hostess podium. It advertised a hundred and twenty dollars in gift card for only a hundred dollars.

Mr. Salazar noticed my gaze. "It makes a great Christmas gift."

It would for me. I ate here quite a bit. But a gift certificate seemed a little impersonal for Gino.

"I heard Callum owned this building," Hyperion said. "Any idea what will happen to it now he's, er—"

"Dead?" Mr. Salazar supplied cheerfully. "All I know is whoever gets it can't raise the rent any more than Callum's been raising it. We lost three restaurants on this street because he pushed the rent so high. I mean, I don't mind losing competitors. But the empty windows aren't good for anyone."

"They left because of the rent?" I asked.

The restauranteur laughed shortly. "Oh, yeah. Their leases ended this year, so he was able to ask for the moon. Fortunately, I've got four more years on my lease, so his rent raises are limited." He cocked his head toward the neighboring wall. "Jamison's lease was coming up this year though. He's worried, and I can't blame him."

Hyperion and I exchanged a look, and my pulse beat a little faster. Mr. Jamison hadn't mentioned that.

"Abigail's organizing a neighborhood watch for the street," Hyperion said. "I hope you can join us."

Hold on. We hadn't agreed on that. "Wha—?" Hyperion stepped on my foot. "—aah—aah." I jerked my foot away and bent to rub the top of my crimson boot.

"Really?" Mr. Salazar asked.

"We can't afford to ignore the rise in crime," my partner said. "Of course, we'll be providing refreshments."

I sucked in an outraged breath and straightened. *We*? Since when had Hyperion done a lick of baking? "I don't know if starting something up over the holidays makes sense." I looked meaningfully at my partner. "Everyone's so busy."

"We can do a Secret Santa," Hyperion said, oblivious. "First meeting's next Monday night at seven at Beanblossom's. Can you make it?"

I scowled, my foot throbbing. *Secret Santa? Refreshments?*

The restauranteur ran a hand over his balding pate. "Yeah, I can do Monday. Monday's are dead here."

"Excellent. We'll see you then." Hyperion grabbed my arm and steered me from the restaurant.

I jerked my arm free. "What the—? Why did you volunteer *me*?"

"Because no one would believe *I'd* organize it." He studied his manicured nails. "And it's ideal. We can get everyone together to spill what they know about Callum. No one will suspect we have an ulterior motive. Besides, crime really is going up. We need a neighborhood watch."

"Well, sure, but—" The back of my neck prickled. A bulky shadow chilled my shoulders. It swallowed my own slender shadow, stretched waveringly across the brick sidewalk.

"Who's organizing a neighborhood watch?" a man rumbled.

I turned. Six feet of well-padded muscle glowered down at me. *Baranko.*

Chapter Nine

"WELL?" BARANKO PROMPTED. "CAT got your tongue?"

I stiffened. I did not need this aggravation on a Monday morning. Not when my eyeballs felt like they'd been dragged across the Death Valley salt flats. The detective wasn't stupid, and my brain wasn't up for clever. Our so-called watch was an obvious ruse. Baranko wouldn't be happy about it.

I wasn't thrilled with the idea either. It was a lot to organize, and I already had my hands full with the holidays. But neighborhood watches were for residential neighborhoods. We were in a commercial district. If there was any justice in this world, we wouldn't be able to organize one.

A Santa on a motor scooter buzzed past on the crooked street. Baranko cut a glance in its direction.

"We're starting one," Hyperion said. "For the business district."

"A business watch then." the detective rubbed his chin. His hand made scratching sounds against his bristly jowls.

"You mean that's really a thing?" I asked. *Damn.* I scuffed my boot on the brick sidewalk.

"If you didn't know it was a thing, why did you offer to start one?" Baranko said.

"Duh." Hyperion rolled his eyes and motioned toward Callum's closed souvenir shop, across the street. "Murder. Vandalism."

The detective studied him for a long moment. "You'll need a representative from the police department. When's your first meeting?"

I winced. "Ooh, too bad. We haven't organized anything with the SBPD yet. We'll have to put the meeting off."

"Next Monday at seven at Beanblossom's," Hyperion said.

Baranko nodded. "I'll be there. The first topic will be observation skills." He pivoted and strode into the fog.

My shoulders sagged. *Check and mate.* We were stuck hosting the meeting.

"He—What?" Hyperion sputtered. "*He'll* be there? He'll ruin everything. How are we supposed to subtly interrogate other business owners with *him* there?"

"It is a mystery."

"Are you laughing?" he asked, accusing.

"I'm trying not to cry." I *could* organize the meeting. Expectations for the promised snacks wouldn't be all that high. But Baranko had known what we were up to, and I didn't like that at all.

My partner scowled. "With him watching, we're going to have to hold a *real* neighborhood watch. Or business watch. Whatever."

"Then no Secret Santa?" If we were stuck holding the meeting, at least I could enjoy watching my partner squirm. Sometimes it's nice to share the pain.

"I don't know how to organize a watch," he complained.

"I'm sure there's a website."

We visited other store owners to ask about last night and invite them to our watch meeting. No one had seen anything.

But everyone agreed to come to the watch, and that surprised me. Emery Callum had not been well-loved. Maybe people were more upset by his murder than I'd thought.

Mrs. Henderson at the costume shop certainly was. The older woman's eyes were pink behind her cat-eye glasses. Her chins trembled. "I can't believe it. I just can't believe it," she said in a quavering voice.

"Did you know Mr. Callum well?" Hyperion asked, oozing tea and sympathy.

I glanced around the cluttered shop. Christmas and Victorian-themed costumes crowded the walls.

She grabbed a tissue from a box on the glass counter and blew her nose. "We both started our businesses the same year. So yes, I'll come to your watch party. It's our duty to catch whoever did it," she said fiercely and burst into tears.

We couldn't get much out of her after that. Hyperion and I murmured condolences and departed.

"Could the murder have just been a robbery gone wrong?" I stepped off the sidewalk to make way for a gray-haired woman on a mobility scooter. The wicker basket on the front of her scooter was piled with shopping bags.

"Yes," Hyperion said quietly. "And if it is, we aren't going to be any help in catching the guy who did it. The cops might not be any better off than we are. No offense to the SBPD, but crimes like this go unsolved all the time."

"I know." I stopped and turned to him. "But I don't want to stop asking questions. Maybe the business watch *is* the best thing we can do."

"I hope not. You know I hate meetings. And this one sounds dreadfully dreary."

I refrained from pointing out he'd been the one to get us into this mess. There was no sense rubbing it in.

We stopped for lunch at a Mexican restaurant. The blue shuttered window by our table overlooked the Pacific, but we couldn't see much ocean. The December fog had thickened, blotting out the small pastel houses along the shore.

A blur of white flashed past, and I jerked backward. Hyperion didn't react to the window's near-miss with the seagull. He scrolled through his phone searching for information on how to run a watch.

"Is the management company open today?" I tilted back my pomegranate margarita, finishing off the icy dregs. It didn't boost my holiday mood, which was flagging again. Why *hadn't* I decorated my bungalow yet? It looked adorable strung with twinkle lights and pine boughs.

"Huh?" He looked up, a shock of ebony hair falling across his forehead.

"The one that Callum used—Acme."

"Oh. Right." He looked down again at his screen and typed frantically with his thumbs. "Yes, they are."

"Then we may as well pay them a visit," I said. "Unless you have an in with Merry or Ivette?"

"I actually sort of do, with Merry at least. She gave me her card."

"She did?" I propped my elbows on the colorful tile table. "Was she selling something?"

He shot me an annoyed look. "People do give me their cards for reasons other than wanting something."

"I just didn't think that was usual during a Tarot reading, that's all."

"It's not," he admitted. "I think... I think she wanted to tell me something. Or maybe she was just— She was upset about her husband's death and wanted someone to talk to. I'll call her."

"But we can't see her tonight," I said quickly. "I'm taking lasagna over to my grandfather's house and helping him decorate."

He lifted a dark brow. "That's going to be a chore. His house is monstrous. He should invite a crew over and have a decorating party." Lifting one hip, he pulled his wallet from the back pocket of his navy slacks.

"Gramps and I can handle it." We'd been doing it ourselves since my grandmother had passed, when I was ten. It was a tradition, and one I looked forward to repeating. We'd put on Bing Crosby and Doris Day carols, and drink eggnog, and... And maybe that's why I hadn't gotten into the spirit yet. For me, decorating his house had always been the true beginning of the season.

Hyperion fished a business card from his wallet, dialed, and pressed his phone to his ear. My partner shook his head and frowned. "Merry's not answering. I'll call her later." He bounded to his feet, and his chair wobbled alarmingly. "Away, to the management company." He pointed dramatically to the restaurant's arched door.

Our departure was delayed by having to collect our coats and pay the bill. But eventually, away to the management company we went. It was in a low building on the outskirts of town and tucked deep in a stand of gloomy, fogbound cypresses.

A slender young man looked up from his cluttered desk when we walked inside. "Can I help you?"

"We're interested in Emery Callum's San Borromeo properties," I said.

"Oh?" he cocked his head. "Are you looking to rent?"

"To buy," Hyperion said.

The man's dark-eyed gaze sharpened. "Which property?"

"All of them," my partner said. "We represent a consortium looking for investment opportunities."

My stomach spasmed. True, anything we said would have been a lie. But I wasn't sure we could fake representing an entire consortium.

"Ah..." The young man rose and ran his hands down the thighs of his khakis. "Unfortunately, Mr. Callum has recently passed on. I don't know what the status of his estate is, but we're not in a position to talk about sales right now."

"I noticed there are several buildings on Main Street which are empty," I said. "And they've been empty for some time. What sort of rent are you asking for?"

He named a figure, and I tried to keep my eyes from bugging out of my head. *Good Lord.* Was that what we had to look forward to when our lease was up? "That's, um..."

"It's the going rate these days." The realtor smiled. "Which is why it's such an excellent investment property."

"I'll bet that makes for a strong return on assets," Hyperion said smoothly. But beads of sweat had popped out on his brow. And I'd thought he hadn't been paying attention to my lectures on Beanblossom's finances.

"I'm Sam, by the way." The realtor extended his hand, and we exchanged grips.

"I'm surprised the rental price hasn't come down," I said. "They've been sitting vacant for months." A Harley roared past the realty's window.

Sam shook his head. "Mr. Callum was willing to wait for the right tenant. He knew that once he was locked into a lower rent, it would be difficult to raise it to its true value. He was an excellent businessman."

"Why did the last tenants leave?" I asked.

The realtor tilted his head. "Ah, they weren't willing to meet the price, I'm afraid."

And I hadn't seen their restaurants reopen anywhere else in town. Had they gone out of business permanently or moved to another zip code?

"They mustn't have been too happy." Hyperion said.

"No. But business is business, and they couldn't deny that the rental market had changed."

"I heard threats were made." Hyperion's voice dropped.

The realtor leaned against the wooden desk. "They did threaten a lawsuit, but that fell through. They knew they didn't have a case. Or maybe the lawyer they consulted talked them out of it."

"How big of a price jump was it?" I jammed my hands into my coat pockets.

"The rent on both buildings tripled," Sam said. "But several tech companies have shown interest in the properties. I'm confident we'll have tenants in them soon."

I swallowed. If that happened at Beanblossom's... We were barely breaking even. Sure, it was still our first year of business, and I expected we'd keep growing. But if our rent tripled when the lease was up, we couldn't afford to stay. "Are any renovations or upgrades planned on those buildings? They're kind of old."

Sam shrugged. "That'll be the responsibility of the tenants."

Tripled rent *and* they were responsible for upgrades? The burrito I'd had for lunch churned unpleasantly in my stomach. I was a die-hard capitalist, but the free market could be Darwinianly merciless to the slow and weak.

"That's progress for you," Hyperion said dryly. "Who can we talk to about the buildings?"

"Leave your card. If the owner decides to sell, I'll get in touch."

Hyperion patted the pockets of his thick wool jacket. "I don't think I brought mine. Did you, Abigail?"

I rummaged in my purse and frowned. "I gave my last card away yesterday and forgot to refill. Can we call you back?"

"Certainly," the realtor said.

We walked to the door with promises to be in touch and escaped to Hyperion's yellow Jeep.

He slumped behind the wheel and turned to me, his face sketched with horror. "*Tripled* the rent? It's ludicrous. How many more years do we have on our lease?"

I buckled my seatbelt. "Four."

"Am I a bad person for hoping the rental market collapses? I mean, I'm as much a cock-eyed optimist as the next Tarot reader. But you can only serve so many teas."

"Yeah," I said shortly.

"Our landlord might not raise the rent that much." Hyperion rubbed the back of his neck. "He seemed much more laissez-faire to me."

To all intents and purposes, our landlord was the lawyer managing the property. He'd do what his realtor recommended. And if rents were all up... Four years didn't seem that far away.

Chapter Ten

Singing along to carols on the radio, I drove toward my grandfather's house. The Christmas spirit might still be evading me, but come hell or high water, I was going to recapture it tonight.

I drove slowly up the winding road. The trees that lined it glowed with twinkle lights. It was the perfect street for my grandfather's fairytale home.

Some people said the 1920s houses were cheap imitations of the fairytale homes in Carmel. But who cared? My grandfather's had turrets, a wavy, shingled roof, and stone chimneys. It was awesome.

When I'd lived with my grandparents, my room had been in the turret. Childhood Christmases there had been magic. But the real magic I'd longed for was for my parents to turn up in time for the holiday.

They never did.

Every December, I'd ask Gramps if my parents would come. And every December, he'd had to give me the bad news. If I could go back in time, I would have told young me to drop it and give the poor man a break.

I was working on forgiving my parents, but I couldn't forget. I also couldn't forget how my grandparents had stepped up. An ache of hopeless gratitude squeezed my heart.

I turned the corner onto my grandfather's cul-de-sac and leaned forward in my seat.

My anticipation shifted to puzzlement. The eaves of my grandfather's house were strung with Christmas lights. A familiar ramshackle pickup sat in the driveway.

My hands tightened on the wheel. *Brik.*

I forced myself to loosen my grip. Gramps had hired him at Halloween to decorate the exterior. He must have drafted him again to do the exterior lights, and that was a good thing. Gramps didn't like climbing the ladder. I hadn't been looking forward to it either.

But I couldn't help thinking that maybe Brik should decorate his *own* house. I shook myself. At least Gramps and I could do the interior together.

I parked beside Brik's pickup and grabbed my plastic carrying case with the food. Striding to the arched front door, I knocked then tried the knob. As I'd expected, it was unlocked. I walked inside and stopped short, mouth agape.

Pine boughs glittering with twinkle lights festooned the doorways and rear windows. The wreath hung on the fireplace. My grandparents' antique tapestry in deep reds and greens hung on one wall. The nativity scene perched on an old cabinet covered in fake snow.

My breath hitched. The train chugged around a tree, the only thing in the room that hadn't been decorated.

Stunned and a little hurt, I made my way to the kitchen. Brik and my grandfather sat rosy-cheeked on the counter stools drinking eggnog.

The kitchen had been decorated too. Pine branches and a second, smaller nativity scene decorated the shelf above the sink. Christmas ornaments hung from the pot rack over the tile counter.

"Abigail!" My grandfather raised his glass in a toast. "Have some eggnog with us. We just finished."

On the tile counter, Peking quacked. The duck waggled his tail.

I set the carrier on the counter beside the mallard and moved to turn on the oven. It was already on. "What's—"

"We pre-heated it for you," Brik said.

Irrational anger heated my chest. Yes. I *know*. I said it was irrational, didn't I? It didn't help that I knew where it was coming from. A treat had been snatched from me, and I didn't like it.

And I guess... I guess I was feeling a little usurped by Brik as well. But I wasn't going to pout or cry or do any of those things that might blacken my name in Santa's book. I forced a smile and unbuttoned my coat. "I'll take that eggnog."

"We held off on the tree," Gramps said. "I know you have a special way of decorating it." He and Brik shared a look and grinned.

I *do* have a way of decorating the tree. It's not that special though; it's only common sense. The lights get wound around the branches inside the tree, to give it depth. And the larger ornaments go on the bottom and the smaller at the top to balance it.

I put the lasagna in the oven. Brik provided me with eggnog, and I went to survey the tree. It was a beauty, at least eight feet tall and well-shaped. I guessed Brik had something to do with the latter as well.

Gramps and Brik assisted while I decorated the tree and Peking watched. I let Brik put the star on top, because he was the tallest, and I could fantasize about kicking him off the ladder. Then we ate the lasagna, and Brik brought out a bottle of Cabernet.

When Brik stepped away to use the bathroom, Gramps asked, "Are you okay?"

"The holidays are making me think of the past." I reached across the dining table and rubbed his arm. "About how hard it must have been for you. You'd already raised your daughter, and then you and Gran took me on. And then Gran..." My throat closed.

"Nonsense. It was a joy."

I laughed. "I wasn't always a joy." Especially not during my sullen teenage years. *Yikes*.

He shook his head. "No, it wasn't always easy. But that was the point of it. It's the challenge, the responsibility, that gives life meaning."

"Then I must have an incredibly meaningful life, because the tearoom may kill me yet."

"Of course you do," he said seriously. "The harder the task you take on, the more reason you have to get up in the morning. Look. Taking care of you... Whenever I had a dark moment, whenever I asked myself what I was doing with my life, you gave me my answer. The difficult thing, the hard but right decision, that's where the meaning and beauty and joy lies. And I loved you."

My eyes burned, and this time not from lack of sleep. "I love you too." I cleared my throat. "And I'm glad you saved me the tree."

"Of course we saved it for you. But you're not upset I had Brik decorate, are you? I know we usually do it together, but you've been so busy at work, I thought it would relieve some pressure."

"Of course I'm not upset. The place looks terrific. Now I just have to do my own house."

His unkempt brows drew together. "You haven't decorated yet?"

"I haven't had time." But that wasn't true. I'd had the time, just not the motivation.

"Running a business takes it out of you," he said doubtfully.

"But it's worth it." It really was. Every disaster Hyperion and I had overcome. Every scone I'd baked. I couldn't imagine life without Beanblossom's. Gramps was right. The challenge did bring a sense of meaning.

Later that night, Brik and I caravanned home. He waited outside for me to unlock the door to my bungalow and step inside. I closed the door behind me and looked around my undecorated space.

Then I went online. I found the names of the owners of the restaurants that had shut down after their rent had increased. It took some time to locate them all.

Every one of them had left California for cheaper states. Two had restarted restaurants in Florida and Colorado. One was now managing someone else's restaurant in Texas. So they probably hadn't killed Callum.

Defeated, I went to bed.

The next morning, our first round of customers streamed into the tearoom at eleven. Jonasz Albrekt walked inside with them. He looked around and smoothed the gray scarf dangling from the lapels of his wool coat. Both looked a little motheaten.

"Hi, Jonasz." I walked around the hostess stand and frowned slightly. "How are you doing?" And why were all my murder suspects turning up in the tearoom?

"I'm looking for work, actually. Can we talk?"

I turned to the stand and scanned the open reservation book. Everyone with reservations had been seated. Waitresses were taking tea orders.

"I've got a few minutes," I said. "Come on back to the bar." I led him to the white counter, and we got settled on the barstools.

The slender man swallowed nervously. "I can see you're busy. Are you looking for any extra help over the holidays? I've had some experience as a waiter."

My heart pinched. Job hunting over the holidays was brutal. But I wasn't looking for extra help. And if I added a new waiter, I'd be cutting into someone else's hours and tips.

But I'd seen that look of desperation before. I'd *worn* that look before. But I didn't have anything for him.

"It's only... with the shop closed now..." He tugged on both ends of his scarf. "I can do part-time or full-time work."

I hesitated. "I'm not looking for waitstaff, no."

Jonasz grimaced and nodded. His hands curled on the quartz countertop.

I cleared my throat. "But do you have any experience with meal prep? It wouldn't pay as well, because no tips. But I could use an extra hand bussing tables, prepping food, that sort of thing," I lied. "Just for the holiday season. And if anyone got sick, you could step in to wait tables. But I can't promise any waitstaff work," I said hurriedly.

His fists relaxed. "Yes. Yes, I can do that. I assume you've got instructions, and—"

"I have recipes and manuals. You could start training today if you want. You can shadow Maricel and get up to speed."

"Yes." He leaned forward. "I can start now. How many hours can you give me?"

"Twenty a week?" I dragged my palms down the front of my apron. I hadn't budgeted for extra staff, and I wasn't sure I could pay for it. But I'd make it work somehow.

He smiled. "That will do. And your hours are just daytime, right?"

"Yes. We can come up with a schedule for you today."

"Thank you." He reached forward, and we clasped hands. His palm was damp. "Thank you," he repeated.

I walked behind the counter and handed him a menu. "Why don't you start familiarizing yourself with this. If you're hungry now, let me know what you'd like to try first. It's helpful if the staff knows what everything tastes like." And Jonasz looked too pale and thin.

His head bobbed. "I will. Thank you."

I found Maricel in the kitchen and explained. "I know training someone during the holidays is a challenge, but—"

"No, it's fine. I'll do it." She lowered her voice. "I hear his daughter is really sick."

I bit my bottom lip. And part-time work wouldn't get him onto our insurance program, dammit. I hadn't been thinking this through. But I hadn't thought any of it through. And I couldn't afford another full-time worker. I wasn't sure I could afford Jonasz.

But Jonasz shouldn't be off his old insurance plan yet. Usually that hung on for a few months. And he'd *said* he was okay with part-time over the holidays. Maybe he needed to keep money flowing in while he was looking for a full-time position? It's what I would have done. And yes, I was rationalizing again. But there wasn't anything else I could do.

"Hyperion's here." Maricel angled her head toward the door to the hallway.

"So early?" I asked, surprised. "Thanks." I walked to his door, surrounded by twinkle lights. It was cracked open, so I knew he didn't have a client inside. I knocked anyway and pushed the door wider.

In his high, carved chair, he frowned over a Tarot spread on the red-clothed table. He looked like a modern mafia don in a navy three-piece suit, his white shirt open at the collar.

"Come in," he said, not looking up. "I got hold of Merry. She wants us to come over today for another reading."

"Us?"

"I said we were doing a tea and Tarot special, and you'd be bringing by some goodies."

I should have busted his chops for volunteering me on such short notice. But I wanted to talk to her again too. "When?"

"Three o'clock," he said with an abstracted air.

I nodded. "I'll prep a basket. Ah, I hired Jonasz to help out part-time over the holidays."

He looked up and rubbed his long hands together. "Jonasz? Brilliant. We'll have one of our suspects right under our noses. Just think. He could be the killer."

Yeah. My stomach lurched sickeningly. *Just think...*

Chapter Eleven

I LOVE THAT MY job includes filling picnic baskets with goodies for holiday teas. It was what I'd imagined running a tearoom would be like.

But it wasn't my everyday reality. Neither were leaking sinks, guests locking themselves inside bathrooms, payroll reports and tax bills. Now we had the added challenge of training someone new during the busiest time of the year. It was all part of running a business.

But adorable baskets were some compensation. I tied a green bow on the wicker handle.

Jonasz stood beside the metal kitchen table and studied our operations binder. "Three seatings?"

"Yeah," I said. "Eleven to eleven-thirty, one-thirty to two, and four to four-thirty. We take reservations for those times, on weekends and during busy seasons. Other times, we're more flexible. The seatings give us a chance to re-set and re-count everything."

"And by re-count, you mean...?"

"Make sure we have enough scones and sandwiches." I angled my head toward the industrial oven. "It takes fifteen to thirty minutes to bake a batch of scones. There are three racks in the oven. That means three batches every fifteen to thirty minutes."

"I never realized things back here were so systematized."

"It does take some of the magic away, but it keeps things flowing out front." Dishes were stacking up in plastic bins by the industrial washer. I strode to them and began rinsing and setting them inside. "The cleanup goes on all day."

He set down the open folder and took the plate from my hand. "Dishwashing I can do." He smiled.

"May I ask... What was it like working for Emery Callum? I barely knew the man, and we were neighbors."

He scraped crumbs off a plate and into a big plastic waste bin. "He was a hard man with most people."

"But not with Merry?" I guessed.

He laughed. "He was hardest with his wife. I don't know how she put up with it. Or with—" His mouth clamped shut.

Or with what? Or whom? "Secrets are going to come out," I said gently. "They tend to after a murder." But they didn't always. Some stayed buried. And I felt a little guilty picking at this one, and at Jonasz. I'd put him in an uncomfortable spot, gossiping with the new boss about the old boss. But Hyperion was right. Jonasz was here, and it would be foolish not to ask.

"Maybe," he replied, his tone neutral.

"We're organizing a business watch. We spent most of yesterday inviting businessowners to attend. They were all interested after... It's worried people. But only one person had anything kind to say about Mr. Callum."

"Mrs. Henderson," he said in a flat tone. "She was at the store a lot."

"I understand they got their start in business at the same time."

He turned to me, humor glinting in his eyes. "They were having an affair. That is what you were getting at, wasn't it?"

I sucked in a breath. *An affair? Mrs.* Henderson? "I... Really?" I hadn't been anywhere *close* to thinking that, much less getting at it.

"When I found out the call about the hospital was a crank..." He shook his head. "I thought she might have done it to get some alone time with Emery. But of course, she wouldn't have. She was always kind to me. She would never have been that cruel."

"Wait. Are you saying...? Did Merry know?"

He nodded and closed the binder on the table. "They had an argument a couple months ago at the store. I was in the back room, doing inventory."

"I'm surprised Merry didn't leave him." California was a community property state. If Emery was the one cheating, I couldn't believe a prenup would have gone his way.

"He told her she would have a hard time proving it. And even if she did, she was only entitled to the half of his property that he'd earned during the marriage." Jonasz shook his head. "The problem was, he bought all his properties before they had married. He boasted about it to me. He was free and clear."

I winced. That couldn't have been comfortable to listen too. But it gave Merry a real incentive to get rid of her husband without going through a messy divorce.

"Who's the basket for?" Jonasz asked.

"Ah, for Merry." My face warmed. "She's a client of Hyperion's. It's sort of a condolence tea and Tarot thing."

He lifted his brows. "I see."

Yeah. That didn't sound very believable to me either.

An hour later, Hyperion and I were knocking at Merry's front door. She lived in a gloomy fairytale house of gray stone and crooked turrets. Moss grew on its uneven shingles. Overgrown juniper bushes stretched their dark branches toward us on the stone steps. I hugged the basket closer to my chest.

"How are we going to ask about Mrs. Henderson?" Hyperion adjusted the navy cap on his head.

I wanted to be one of those women who could wear hats. But I've yet to find a hat that doesn't make me look like a mushroom. It's one of the many curses of being height-challenged.

"I've got no idea," I said. "Maybe she'll bring it up?"

The door opened, and Merry smiled, wan. "Thank you for coming. Please, come in." She wore a sprig of fresh holly on her green sweater.

"Abigail insisted on setting out the tea things herself," Hyperion said. We followed her into a dark-paneled sitting room.

The carpet was beige and the furniture out of the nineteen eighties. But the Christmas decorations gave the room charm. Swags of sparkling faux-holly adorned the windows and curled around the wooden beams. Pillar candles burned on the coffee table. A fire crackled in the stone fireplace.

Merry tugged the hem of her sweater lower over her red slacks. "I know you said it doesn't make sense to have Tarot readings so close together. But I do have more, different questions."

"That'll work," he said, somber. "And I confess, I wanted to see you. I was a little worried about you after our last reading."

She laughed uneasily. "Whoever killed my husband has nothing against *me*. Why would they? I'm in no danger."

Hyperion shot her a quick smile. "Of course not. I only meant..." He shook his head. "Never mind. I'm glad to see you're well."

She sat on the couch and moved the candles on the low table aside. "Shall we set up here?"

Opening the basket, I pulled out the top layer of white and gold place settings. I set out cloth napkins, white plates, and a teapot. "Where's your kitchen? May I boil some water?"

"The kitchen's back there." She pointed through an arched entryway.

"Thanks," I said. "I'll give you two some privacy."

I found my way to the kitchen. The curved corners and stucco walls echoed the exterior's fairytale look. But the kitchen was depressingly tiny. It, too, hadn't seen any upgrades in the last decades. The brown counter tiles were chipped, and the counters themselves short and narrow. But I didn't have to live in it.

I located a teakettle and boiled water. My ears strained in an unladylike fashion for wisps of conversation. But uninformative wisps were all I got.

I abandoned the copper kettle and explored the kitchen, quietly opening cupboards. One was filled with medicines, much like in my grandfather's kitchen.

I found my way to the bathroom and found more medicine and the usual bathroom things. But nothing that implied criminality. So I guiltily slunk back to the kitchen.

It was a gas range, and the water didn't take long to boil. When I returned to the sitting room, three cards were already laid out on the table. The Seven of Cups: illusion. The Seven of Swords: betrayal. And Death.

Now the Death card doesn't usually mean a literal death. Typically, it refers to a change. An ending. But the hairs rose on the back of my neck anyway.

Hyperion swept up the three cards and shuffled them into the rest of the deck. It was an over-sized affair with blue and gray stripes on the back.

Merry looked up at me. "I was asking about my husband..." She trailed off.

I nodded soberly. It sounded like I was right on time.

There's something comforting about tea. I don't think it's the tea itself. I think it's the ritual. You can't drink tea quickly, because it's hot. You have to sip and slow down, and the world seems to slow down too.

I set out the scones and mini sandwiches and other food. Silently, I poured the tea into the elegant cups I'd brought.

"It was Ivette," Merry said abruptly. She motioned toward the stack of cards on the table by Hyperion's knee. "It was always her. She was always there, causing trouble. She was so... angry. All the time. She couldn't move on. It would have been better if she had. She couldn't let go of the past. But she couldn't have killed him."

Her gaze moved on to study the plate of mini scones and sandwiches. "I was so sure it was her, but the police said she couldn't have."

"Oh?" I asked.

She met my gaze. "He was killed while Jonasz was away. But I was..." She bit her bottom lip. Picking up a vanilla scone, she nibbled one of its corners.

"You were...?" Hyperion prompted.

She swallowed. "I went to her office that morning. It was stupid. I shouldn't have. I was just so angry. It's Christmastime, the holidays, and she was threatening another lawsuit. It would have wasted her money and ours. She knows she can't win."

"What time were you there?" I asked.

She sighed and took a sip of the tea. "I got there after nine-fifteen. Nine-twenty, I think. I left nearly an hour later."

But Ivette's office was only a few blocks away. It wouldn't have taken more than five minutes or so for her to get to Emery's store. Maybe Ivette didn't have an alibi after all, though the police seemed to be sure she hadn't done it. "Where—?"

A smiling Gino strode into the room. "Your door was open." He stopped short. "But I see I'm interrupting something." His dark brows drew downward.

Chapter Twelve

So. This was awkward.

Merry was the first to break the tension, rising from her couch and introducing us. "It was so kind of them to bring the tea and Tarot to me," she finished. Her image wavered in the paned windows swagged by holly. In the reflection, twinkle lights glinted off her flame-red hair.

"I'm not that surprised." Gino's coffee-colored eyes glinted dangerously. "I know Abigail and Hyperion well." He was wearing a navy suit, and since it was a weekday, I guessed he'd come from his office.

"You do?" Merry asked. "Would you like some tea? I think there's enough..."

"There is," I said. It didn't seem like Gino was about to bust us, but I felt weird and remorseful. And I guessed I deserved that. We hadn't exactly approached Merry directly.

"What did I interrupt?" The lawyer dropped onto the seventies-era couch beside Merry.

"We were revisiting the day of the murder," Hyperion said.

"Why?" Gino asked flatly.

"It's only natural to talk about it," Merry said. "I keep going over and over it in my head."

"Maybe you shouldn't," Gino said.

Hyperion shot me an expectant glance. If we were going to ask about Mrs. Henderson, we needed to do it now.

But I couldn't. First, with Gino here, Merry wouldn't admit she knew about her husband's affair. And second...

I shriveled inside. Gino was here. I just couldn't.

Hyperion's expression turned to disgust. He smiled and pivoted on his chair to face Merry. "Did Emery have any other *significant* relationships?" he asked. "Anyone else who would have wanted him dead?"

"I don't..." She swallowed. "I suppose... I don't think Jonasz would have... But he was so angry when he got turned down for that raise."

"When was this?" Gino asked.

"About a month ago," she said.

"No conflicts, er, closer to home?" I asked meekly.

She shook her head, a bewildered look on her oval-shaped face. "No. I don't think so. He didn't have many friends."

"I heard he and Mrs. Henderson were quite close." Hyperion's eyes widened with innocence.

Her face went from white to red. She whirled on me. "Where did you hear that?"

Gino glared. Hyperion raised his brows.

"Ah..." Why was everyone looking at me? "I don't... I didn't..."

She clawed a hand through her hair. "I'm tired. I'm sorry. This is too much to think about right now. I can't. I just can't."

"Of course." I stood hastily. Gathering up the plates, I jammed them haphazardly in the wicker basket. Without the food, there was plenty of space.

Hyperion rose. Smoothing his navy slacks, he whisked a Tarot card from the breast pocket of his suit jacket. He handed it to Merry and bowed. "For you."

She glanced at it. "Oh. Thank you."

"It's easier to meditate on when the card's in front of you," he explained.

Gino's frown deepened.

"Yes," she said. "Yes, I imagine it would be."

We made our way toward the front door. Hyperion stretched his hand toward it. The bell rang, three quick, insistent buzzes. He jerked his hand from the doorknob.

"Excuse me." Merry sidled past us and opened the door.

Ivette strode inside and stopped short in front of me. Since she was considerably taller, gold buttons and her forest-green dress filled my vision. "A party, Merry?" She cocked her gray head. "Consulting Tarot *and* an estate attorney? I see you haven't wasted any time. What did I miss?"

"I was coming to see you later," Gino said coolly, coming up behind me.

"Then there *is* something to see me about?" Ivette said. "How fascinating."

"What do you mean?" Merry asked. "Why would you need to see Ivette?"

"It's complicated," Gino said.

Ivette barked a sardonic laugh. "Emery didn't have a will, did he? I told him to do it, the fool. But what did he care? He'd be dead, and none of it would be his problem anymore."

"Emery wasn't a fool." Spots of color bloomed in Merry's full cheeks. "He has a will."

"Yes," Gino said. "But... it's complicated. And private."

"Our cue to be merry and bright somewhere else," Hyperion said. "Farewell." He bowed over Ivette's hand.

Grasping my shoulders, he steered me out the door. "What was that about?" my partner hissed when we were halfway down the walk and the door had slammed behind us. "You totally left me to ask about Mrs. Henderson. Talk about dropping the ball."

"She wasn't going to talk about it with Gino there." And neither was I.

He snorted eloquently. "I guess you're right, since she didn't, did she? But her reaction was interesting. She knew something was up between Emery and Mrs. Henderson. And what's the deal with the will?"

I crossed the damp lawn and told him what Gino had told me on the pier. "If he guessed right, Emery's will might be a mess." I stepped onto the sidewalk.

"Coming to the widow's house was a bold move on Ivette's part. What do you think she planned to accomplish?"

"Maybe the same thing Merry thought she'd accomplish when she stormed Ivette's office." Or when Merry had confronted Ivette later, in Beanblossom's.

"In other words, they weren't thinking?" He opened the passenger door of the yellow Jeep for me. "Ivette doesn't strike me as the spontaneous type. Though Merry does."

I set the basket on the floor of the car and climbed inside. "That's not fair. She just lost her husband."

"She hadn't when she went to Ivette's office." He adjusted his cap.

"What was the card you gave her?"

"The Two of Swords. Crossroads. Divided loyalties. Tough decisions."

"And Merry's supposed to meditate on that?" I knew Hyperion kept two decks for his readings. One to read with, and one that was "broken." The broken deck had missing cards. He gave away the meaningful cards to his clients to contemplate.

"It's the key card she drew, the card that has the answer to her problems."

We drove back to the tearoom and talked over the murder. But only half my mind was on the clues and the suspects. The other half wondered how annoyed Gino really was about our visit.

I didn't think we'd been too far out of bounds. But Merry was his aunt, and I couldn't blame him if he felt defensive about her.

Two hours in the tearoom finally managed to drive that concern from my head. For me, work always has been the best medicine. And working in a holiday wonderland could only boost my spirits.

The day waned. Guests trickled from the tearoom, and I moved to turn the sign in the window to CLOSED. The door opened, and I jerked my hand away. A slender young woman carrying a child who looked to be about seven edged inside.

"Hi," I said. "May I help you?"

"I am here to take Jonasz home," she said in an Eastern European accent. They both wore plastic raincoats. The woman's blond hair was plastered to her head. The little girl wore a polka-dot rain hat.

His wife and daughter. "Of course. Why don't you have a seat, and I'll get him?" I found them a table with a clean cloth on it. She set the girl down.

Movements uneven, the girl sat in the chair. She was pale and thin like her mother, but the girl's pallor had an unhealthy sheen. Her brown eyes wide, she stared wonderingly at the holiday lights and other decorations.

"I'll be right back," I said.

"Thank you. We only have one car you see, and Natalia had an appointment today." Smiling, she gently ran her hand over the girl's golden hair. "I am Anastasia."

The little girl pointed at the gingerbread house on the counter. "Mama!"

"Yes, Natalia. It is rude to point."

"It's nice to meet you both," I said. "I'm Abigail. Can I get you some tea or scones?"

"No, no," she said. "I do not want to bother you."

"You'd be doing me a favor. We can't sell the leftover scones and sandwiches tomorrow. I'll just be giving them away." A local homeless shelter came by every evening to pick up our extras.

She hesitated. "Then, yes. We did not have time for lunch today."

"You can hang your coats by the door." I pointed to the coat hooks and walked to the kitchen.

Jonasz sprayed dishes in the sink. He slid a plate into the industrial washer.

"Natalia and Anastasia are here," I told him.

He started and set another plate in the washer. "They're early. I'm sorry, Abigail. I didn't—"

"It's fine." I pulled out a tiered tea tray. "They can help us get rid of some of this food."

Sierra appeared in the doorway in a knit crimson duster, jeans, and a *Ho, Ho, Ho* t-shirt. "Is that your daughter, Jonasz? She's lovely."

"Thank you," he said.

"Do you think she'd like a Tarot reading?" Sierra asked.

He hesitated.

"I don't charge people in the tearoom," she continued. "And that includes family. It's good practice for me."

"Then yes, I think she would enjoy it."

Sierra grinned. "Excellent." She disappeared into the hallway, and I smiled. Sierra had been reading for at least ten years. She didn't need any practice.

I arranged food on the plate then returned to the dining area. The newcomers had discarded their raincoats, exposing matching blue sweaters that smelled of damp wool.

Sierra sat between the two and laid out cards. I set the tray on the table. "What sort of tea would you like?" I asked.

"Just black tea," Anastasia said. "For both of us."

I went behind the counter and made a pot of tea. I arranged a tray of cups and sugar, then brought everything to the table.

Crumbs lay scattered around the little girl's plate. Natalia picked at the crust of a tiny sandwich.

"Thank you," Anastasia said in a low voice. "For hiring Jonasz and for this."

"He's doing me a favor. I needed the extra help."

Her smile was wan. "Perhaps our luck is turning."

"I'm sure it is." I poured tea into her cup. "After all, Jonasz made it out of that accident on the freeway without a scratch."

Anastasia's expression hardened. "He would not have been in that accident at all if I had not..." She shook her head.

"Hadn't what?"

She clawed back a strand of blond hair stuck to her forehead. "I was on a video conference with one of Natalia's doctors. When Jonasz called me, I did not answer the phone. I did not think it was an emergency, and I... If I had answered, he would not have gone to the hospital."

"You couldn't possibly have known he'd received a fake call."

"I should have answered." Her lips compressed.

Jonasz emerged from the kitchen and strode to the table. He kissed his daughter on the head. "So much food for such a small girl."

Natalia shook her head and jammed a miniature scone into her mouth.

"These nice people will think I do not feed you," he said, laughing.

I shook my head. "I'll finish up in the kitchen. Take your time here."

"No," he said, "but—"

"It's fine. You're done for the day." I returned to the kitchen. The dishwasher was humming, and the counters had been wiped down. I got busy cleaning the refrigerators.

Jonasz stuck his head in the kitchen thirty minutes later. "Thank you, Abigail."

"No problem. I'll see you later."

He nodded and ducked out.

I finished cleaning up and returned to the dining area. The twinkle lights were the tearoom's only illumination, and I sighed, my spirits lifting. It was time to decorate my own place.

And when I got home, it seemed like the spirit of the season had approved my resolution and paid a visit. A massive Christmas tree leaned beside the yellow bungalow's front door.

Actually, it sort of blocked my door. I checked for a card between its branches, glistening with droplets. But I couldn't find one. Squeezing past the tree, I unlocked my door. I dropped my purse on the nearby couch and returned to drag the tree inside.

Have I mentioned I'm short? Well, I'm short.

I'm strong too, from lifting bags of flour and sugar. Professional baking isn't for wimps. The tree wasn't heavy, but it was big enough to be unwieldy for someone my size. The damn thing nearly knocked me flat the first time I tried to lift it.

Dragging it was a no-go as well. It was too big to get through the door without tying down the branches.

Whoever had left the tree had also overestimated the height of my ceiling. I could probably pull the tree around back and get it in through the French doors. But that seemed like a lot of work for a cold and foggy night.

That was no excuse not to deck the halls though. I abandoned the tree and hauled plastic bins of Christmas decorations from the back of my closet. The first was filled with bottle-brush Christmas trees in funky pastels. I lined them up on the mantel of the white brick fireplace. Unwinding a strand of colorful twinkle lights, I draped them around my front windows.

I was digging through a mess of knotted gold garland when someone knocked on my door. I checked the security camera on my phone. All I saw was tree.

"Who is it?" I called, striding to the door.

"It's me," Gino said.

Come to kiss me or to kill me? I took a deep breath, smiled, and opened the door.

Chapter Thirteen

"Hi," I said, glad he was here and a little worried about why. Gino was a good person. Smart. Funny. Solid. I didn't want to screw this up, but I suspected I already had. "I wasn't expecting you."

In my doorway, he grinned, his brown eyes twinkling. "I can tell. And I wasn't expecting you at my aunt's house today." Damp darkened his curling, near-black hair, and the shoulders of his navy suit jacket.

"Touché." My muscles relaxed. He wasn't angry, though he had every right to be. "Come in." I stepped away from the door, holding it wider.

He squeezed past the tree and kissed me. Then he pulled me closer and kissed me longer. Electricity spiraled inside me, my heart thumping, blood roaring in my ears.

We broke apart, and I swayed a little, gasping. "If this is a bootie call—"

"No." He angled his head, looking thoughtful. "Although..."

"No."

Gino laughed. He scraped his hand through his hair, scattering droplets onto the bamboo floor. "I was in the neighborhood. Ivette lives only a couple blocks away."

"Ah." I motioned him further inside and closed the door behind him. "How did it go at Merry's after we left?"

"It was a little tense."

I raised a brow. "Only a little?"

"It's complicated."

"The ex-wife and the widow?" I dropped onto the cream-colored sofa by the door. "I can imagine."

Gino sat beside me. "You and Hyperion think you're going to solve this murder, don't you?" he asked with an exasperated air.

"The police are on it," I said. "I guess I just don't trust the police after what happened in October."

"Your friend, that detective, was cleared though."

"Yeah." And there'd been a measure of luck in that which I hadn't liked. "After Hyperion and I tracked down the killer."

"Who then tried to kill *you*." He shook his head. "You really want to go down that path again?"

I pulled back to study Gino more closely. His smile had faded, the crinkles at the corners of his eyes smoothing.

"In fairness," I said, "he was trying to kill someone else. I just happened to be nearby." Fortunately, a cop had been feet away. And that was the lucky part that scared me.

I'd tried to help someone I'd believed in danger, not quite believing I might be in danger too. It was only after it was over, after the killer was sprawled on the sidewalk with a cop's knee on his back, that I'd begun to shake. It had worked out. I hadn't been hurt. And I'd told myself that I was fine, but none of it had been fine. It was, however, over. "That part wasn't fun," I said dryly.

"This isn't fun for Merry or Ivette either. It's their lives."

"Of course. It's not a game. A man was murdered. And it's important whoever did this is caught."

"I'm sure the police will catch him. At least, you were easier on Merry than Baranko."

I leaned closer. "He interviewed them?"

"Why wouldn't he? He's the lead detective."

Baranko had been at the crime scene. But I didn't know how involved he'd be. It looked like Santa Cruz was still managing murders for San Borromeo.

That made some sense. Our town was tiny in comparison to Santa Cruz. More and more police and fire stations were sharing resources across town lines. "Tony says Baranko's an honest cop, a good one." I pursed my lips. I had no reason to doubt Baranko's honesty. But I still didn't like him.

"But?" Gino prompted.

"But he's been blinkered before. He was so certain Tony was a crooked cop, he couldn't look beyond that." My hands curled on my thighs. "Maybe cops are his one blind spot, I don't know. But..."

"You don't trust him," Gino finished.

"No."

"He has a good record. I checked." His arm stretched along the back of the soft couch, his hand resting on my shoulder. "And he was thorough in his questioning of my aunt."

"Are you suggesting it would be better for me to stay out of this?"

"Would it matter if I did?" His thumb massaged a point in my neck, and my breath grew uneven.

I steeled myself. "No." This had been a sticking point with Brik. I can't say for sure it was the reason we weren't together, because we'd never had a chance. But it was the reason he'd given.

Maybe I was too stubborn about going my own way. But if detecting was something I was good at—and it was—and if it was something that mattered to me—and it did, I shouldn't give it up easily.

"Then I won't ask," Gino said lightly. "But these are people I care about. My uncle..." He shook his head. "He was the only family I had left, but he had no time for or interest in me. Both Ivette and Merry were different though. I want to make sure they're okay."

"I do too."

"I know," he said, and we kissed. We kissed some more. And then we did other adult things, and Gino left.

The next morning, Wednesday, was gray and drizzly. Jonasz came into the tearoom for a few hours. I demonstrated how to bake scones and prep sandwiches.

But I never got the chance to get him alone to talk about his old boss, Emery Callum. Every time I thought I might, a waitress would fly into the kitchen, and the opportunity went up in smoke.

Hyperion was no better. He had back-to-back private readings in his office all day.

It seemed obvious the next person we needed to talk to was Mrs. Henderson. But I figured Hyperion would want to be in on that. So even though I dearly wanted to run to her costume shop on my lunch break, I held off.

Finally, I saw him escorting one of his clients to the tearoom's rear door. He closed it firmly behind her, the metal door clanging.

I hurried to my partner. "Hey, how's it going?"

"Busy," Hyperion said. He checked the metal door, and it opened. "You need to be careful with this lock," he said, banging the door shut harder.

"I have two questions. First, did you send me a Christmas tree yesterday?"

He laughed and ambled toward his office. "I don't even have a tree yet. So, no, I didn't get one for you. Maybe Gino's upgrading from flowers."

"No, it wasn't from Gino. I asked him."

My partner stopped outside his door, twinkle lights blinking around his head. "Then it's a mystery. What's the other thing?"

"Mrs. Henderson."

Hyperion shook his head. "No way I can do it today. Maybe we can bring her a tea and Tarot package tomorrow or Friday?"

I smothered my disappointment. Talking to Gino should have cooled me on asking around, but I felt a weird sense of urgency. "I'll call and set something up," I said.

A man in a three-piece suit appeared in the hallway, and Hyperion smiled at him. "My next client," he said. "Gotta jet."

I returned to the kitchen. The dishwasher whirred, steam rising from its door. Jonasz cut dough into circles. A waitress loaded plates with sandwiches and scones. I called my grandfather.

"Abigail," he said, his tone pleased. "What's going on?"

"Weird question... Did you drop a Christmas tree by my place yesterday?"

"That was Tomas," he said. "He had an extra one and told me he was going to bring it by."

I relaxed against the long, metal table. "That's one mystery solved." I didn't know why I'd been so bothered by it. It's not like the tree was dangerous.

"Do you need help setting it up?" Gramps asked.

I flashed back to last year's tree raising. There'd been a lot of cursing involved, and not by me. "No, I've got it. But thanks for offering."

"Peking," he shouted. Wincing, I yanked the phone from my ear. "Get away from my cookies! I've got to go, Abigail."

I laughed. "Save the cookies." We said our goodbyes and hung up.

Seven hours and a half dozen failed attempts at quizzing Jonasz later, we closed the tearoom. We cleaned up, and I drove home, tired and frustrated.

Cars crowded beneath the eucalyptuses lining my street. Rock music pulsed, and I slowed, my stomach tightening.

Brik was throwing a party. It was a freaking Wednesday night, and Brik was throwing a party. And this wasn't even the party he'd bribed me not to gripe about. That was supposed to happen this weekend.

My annoyance shifted, morphing into another emotion, and a knot formed in my throat. I'd thought he'd gotten over this compulsion to keep crowds around him.

I shook myself. Brik didn't want my pity. And at least no one was blocking my driveway tonight.

I pulled in and tried not to stare worriedly at the blue house next door. Brik still hadn't bothered putting lights up. This surprised me, given the party going on there.

But... Stones and glass houses. I still had a Christmas tree outside my front door. Yawning, I edged past it and told myself I'd set it up tomorrow morning, when I had more energy.

I shut and locked the front door behind me. The bass beat pulsed through my bungalow and set my teeth on edge.

I turned on the twinkle lights in the darkened living area. They sparkled off the gold garlands. I switched on more holiday lights above the TV. They gave my Gran's collection of fortune-telling teacups a mystical glow. Satisfied, I collapsed onto the gaming couch.

My headset and controllers jounced. It had been weeks since I'd played. I turned on the TV and the game. It had the added benefit of blocking out the noise from next door.

My friend and ex-boss, Razzzor, had created a zombie-Nazis in space wargame on a lark. Razzzor being Razzzor, the game had taken off. There were space battles, and laser fights on exotic planets. The game was ridiculous and cathartic.

Tonight I prowled an enemy spaceship. I edged my character around the corner of a corridor. Three horned demons with lashing tails and wearing SS uniforms stormed toward me. "What the—?"

One of the creature's chests exploded. Red-black gore spiraled upward in the near-weightless atmosphere.

"Ho, ho, ho," Razzzor said in my ear. "I was wondering when I'd see you again."

"Thanks for the assist," I said, blasting the other two monsters. "What happened to the Nazis?"

His suited up character—a musclebound Santa in a space suit—appeared beside me on the screen. "It's the holidays, Abs. I uploaded a Krampus extension."

"That's Krampus?" The anti-Santa Christmas demon from Germany?

"That's lots of Krampuses. If you die, instead of just dying, they drag you to hell."

"Yeah..." No. "Is that *really* the Christmas spirit?"

"It is if you're Krampus. So. My therapist says I need to form more secure attachments. What's new?"

I tilted my head, my lips pursing. "Are you asking me what's new because you want to form a more secure attachment with me? Or are those two distinct ideas?"

"Uh... Both?"

A red alarm light started blinking high on the spaceship's wall. My shoulders tensed. I forced myself to ignore it. Knowing Razzzor, his Krampus hell would be impressive. When it came to programming, he was detail oriented. But the only way to see it would be for my avatar to die. "I just started decorating the house—"

"And you didn't invite me? I love decorating."

I shifted on the couch. "You hate decorating. You have a professional company decorate your mansion."

"That's only because they're better at it than me. And it's not a mansion."

It was a modern chateau with fourteen rooms. Big ones. "And we're starting a neighborhood watch for our business area. Between that and the December crowds, there's a lot going on." I decided not to bother him with news about the murder. He'd offer to help with that too, and I knew he was busy.

And maybe I was feeling a little professional—or amateur—jealousy? Razzzor could find out a *lot* about a person online. It was a mildly terrifying.

"I thought your tearoom was in a good part of town," he said. "Why do you need a watch?"

"It *is* in a good part of town. There aren't any bad parts of San Borromeo." I rubbed my thumb against the controller's plastic seam. Was I seeing the murder as something more because it made me feel safer? Anyone could be robbed. Murder by someone you knew was rarer.

"What's wrong?"

"Nothing. You're right." I blasted a Krampus crawling along the corridor ceiling and bit back a curse. I'd meant to get killed, but my instincts had taken over. Also, the blinking alarm light was getting on my nerves.

"Just put the watch thing off until January," he said.

The living area brightened. I frowned at the TV. Had something changed on screen? Because the spaceship corridor looked exactly the same.

"Abigail?" Razzzor asked. "You there?"

My foot twitched, and I uncrossed my legs. "Yeah..." My pale blue walls flickered. The spaceship alarm light hadn't caused that. That was more of a constant strobe. And the light in my living room...

I twisted on the couch. Flames blossomed outside my front window. I sucked in a breath, my heart constricting in a quick jab.

"Fire!" I wrenched off the headset and leapt from the couch. The headset cord tangled around my foot. I tripped, half fell onto the arm of the couch, kicked off the headset, and ran to the front door. I placed my hand against it. It was hot. I knew enough from that old movie about firefighters not to open a hot door.

Racing to the kitchen, I grabbed the fire extinguisher and hurtled out the kitchen door to the narrow side yard. I ran down the brick path and through the open gate.

The Christmas tree blazed, flames licking the yellow bungalow's eaves. Fumbling, I pulled the pin on the extinguisher. I ran to the other side of the porch steps to get a better angle on the tree. Uneven waves of heat struck my skin.

There was a rushing sound behind me. Before I could turn, icy water drenched my head and cascaded down my back. My shoulders jumped to my ears. "Gagh!"

There was a loud cheer.

I sputtered, turning. "What the—?"

Brik stood bare chested in his yard and trained a hose on the flaming tree. A crowd of people in party clothes whooped drunkenly behind him. A blond tossed a red plastic drink cup at the tree. It missed by a mile and bounced off my hatchback.

I moved to the opposite side of the stairs and hit the tree with my extinguisher. The flames lowered and died. Brik walked closer, keeping the jet of water trained on the tree. A woman in a gold sequined dress hooted.

"Did I hit you?" Brik asked.

Really? I brushed the hair from my eyes. "Yes," I gritted out. Smoke rose from the smoldering tree.

"Sorry," he said, curt, and turned to the spectators. "Show's over, folks."

The partiers applauded half-heartedly and trickled back into his modern house. Water dripped down my nose.

Brik dropped the hose, which had stretched to its limit, and climbed the steps. Picking up the smoking tree one-handed, he tossed it into my front lawn. Brik studied the bungalow. The front and the door were blackened, the yellow paint blistered.

He shook his head, expression grim. "This could have been a lot worse." His gaze raked me. "You okay?"

"I'm fine." Aside from the adrenaline spurting jerkily through my veins. My hand holding the extinguisher trembled. I clutched it to my chest so I didn't drop it on my foot. Because knowing my luck, that would happen.

"What happened?"

"I don't know. I was in the living room..." I sniffed. My front yard smelled like an airport. *Kerosene*. "Do you smell that?"

He inhaled. "Smells like kerosene."

"Yeah." My body curled inward around the extinguisher, my head lowering. The tree hadn't spontaneously combusted. But I wanted to believe it was an accident. It wasn't.

Someone had set it on fire.

Chapter Fourteen

SIRENS WAILED. A FIRETRUCK crept down the street, making its way past the parked cars. Its red and blue lights strobed sickening shadows over the eucalyptus trees. A few people emerged from Brik's house to wave at the firemen.

And someone had tried to burn down my house. With me in it. Someone had come to my house. Someone knew where I lived. And I needed to stop thinking these thoughts or I'd start crying.

"Did you call the fire department?" Brik asked. He shifted on his bare feet. "Because I didn't."

"No." I straightened and hugged the extinguisher more tightly. "Maybe someone at..." I sucked in a breath. "Razzzor. I left him..." I retreated down the narrow brick path to my kitchen door and ran inside. Jogging into the dining area, I reached over the back of the couch. I grabbed the headset, pressed it to my ear.

"Abigail," Razzzor bellowed.

I winced and yanked the headset away. "I'm here," I said shakily. "It's fine. Look, the fire department's here—"

"Good. I called them."

"Thanks." I clawed a trembling hand through my wet hair. "Thanks," I repeated. I was lucky to have friends like Razzzor. And Brik. This could have been really bad. The whole house might have caught fire with me in it. It could have spread to other houses.

My hand tightened on the headset. "I'd better go deal with them."

"You sure you're okay? What happened?"

Truck brakes squealed outside. I glanced toward the front window. It was black. "There was a Christmas tree..." I shook my head. "I'll explain later. The fire's out, and I'm okay. But I've really got to go. Bye."

Dropping the headset I strode to the front door and stepped outside. A chill wracked my body. The night was colder without the fire blazing. Hugging my wet blouse closer, I trotted down the steps. Three firemen clustered around Brik.

"...a prank," Brik was saying. "I smelled kerosene."

"That's no prank," said the tallest firefighter, in a canvas coat. "In California, it's a felony." He turned to me. His green eyes widened slightly. "Are you the homeowner?"

I nodded, my teeth chattering. "I didn't see anything. I was inside on my headset when I noticed the fire."

"How'd you, uh, see it?" He stared hard at the house.

"It was visible through the front window." I pointed. The window frame was blackened, and the side of the window covered in soot.

A fireman poked at the remains of the tree. A second inspected the house.

"Looks clear," the latter shouted. Another shudder rippled through me.

"You're freezing," Brik said to me. "Go inside. I'll take care of this."

"Yeah," the fireman said. "It's fine."

"You must be cold too." I pointed out. My neighbor was bare chested. But Brik must have been one of those superhuman types who didn't get cold. He only shook his head and smiled.

"I'm fine," he said.

And since I really was freezing, I scuttled inside the house and peeled off my sopping blouse. My face heated. The blouse had gone semi-transparent after the soaking. This might explain why the lead fireman hadn't been able to look me in the eyes. Though since my arms had been crossed the whole time, he wouldn't have been able to see much anyway.

I took my time, thinking over what had happened. *Kerosene. Arson.* Nausea swam in my throat. The odds that this had been a dumb prank were depressingly low.

In a soft sweater and jeans, I returned outside. A police officer had arrived, and he took my statement. I didn't bother mentioning this might have been connected to Emery Callum's death. Someone would ask why, and then I'd have to admit I was part of an amateur detecting duo.

That sort of thing never goes well.

Brik and I saw the emergency crews off. At some point, he'd put a jacket on. I'm ashamed to admit this was mildly disappointing. He stared after the departing firetruck. "What was a Christmas tree doing on your porch?" he asked.

"Tomas brought it over as a surprise. I couldn't get it inside without some serious tree trimming. I was going to, but I just didn't have the time."

He jammed his hands into the pockets of his jeans. "You should have asked me for help. I'd trim your tree."

We stared at each other. His face colored, and I started laughing. I couldn't help it. Maybe I'd been spending too much time around Hyperion and his double entendres. Or maybe it was a post-fire hysterical reaction. "Thanks for putting out the fire," I choked out.

He shook his head. "It's what neighbors do."

But I still appreciated it, and warmth expanded in my chest. Irritating parties or no, Brik had acted fast. He might only be a friend, but he was a good man to have around in a crisis.

And I should be grateful for what we had, not wondering about what might have been.

"What's wrong?" Brik asked.

"Nothing." I forced a smile. "Thanks again." I returned inside to my earplugs and an uneasy sleep.

Fog wrapped San Benedetto in cool liquid mercury the next morning. But that didn't slow the stream of holiday diners to the tearoom. Our windows glowed cozily, inviting, and the tables and bar were packed.

During a break between seatings, I called Mrs. Henderson at her costume shop.

"Henderson Costumes," she trilled. "How may I help you?"

I leaned against the white counter. "It's Abigail Beanblossom. Is this a bad time?"

"No, not at all. What can I do for you?"

"Actually, we were... I feel so bad about Mr. Callum. Hyperion and I were hoping to bring you a sympathy tea, maybe tomorrow?"

"Oh, you don't need to do that, dear. But it's very sweet of you to think of it."

Drat. "We'd really like to," I said. "Tea, scones, maybe a Tarot reading..."

She sighed. "I would like to try a Tarot reading someday, but this just isn't the time."

It was the first time a tea basket had failed to get me through a door. I was stumped.

"What about Saturday?" she asked.

My pulse quickened. "This Saturday?"

"Why don't we do it in the tearoom though? You don't need to come here. And I confess, I'd much rather take a break from the shop."

"Of course," I said heartily and sped around the counter to the hostess stand. Frantically, I flipped through the reservation book. As I'd feared, we were fully booked on Saturday. "What time?"

"Lunch?"

"No problem," I lied. So what if lunch was our busiest time? Beads of sweat broke out on my forehead. I'd make it work. "I'll see you then."

I hung up and scanned the tearoom. Maybe if we shifted tables around, I could jam a two-top in the corner. But then where would Hyperion sit?

The phone rang on the hostess stand, and I snatched it up. "Beanblossom's Tea and Tarot. How can I help you?"

"Um, hi. This is Frank Perth from Perth Jewelry? I'm RSVP'ing to the business watch on Monday."

Perth Jewelry wasn't on Main Street. It was two blocks over. I rubbed my temple. How many people had Hyperion invited? "Great," I said. "I'll put you down."

"Thanks for organizing this," he said. "Ivette was in here yesterday—poor woman. This has really shaken her. It's shaken all of us."

I pressed the receiver tighter against my ear. What was Ivette doing in a jewelry store? "I heard she had an eye on one of your bracelets," I hazarded, chuckling. "Did she get it?"

"No," he said, "a sapphire ring. Hey, would it make sense if I brought some jewelry to the watch? Some people might be interested in last-minute shopping."

A plate crashed somewhere in the tearoom, and my shoulders hunched to my ears. "Sure. That'll be fine. I'll see you Monday. Bye." I hung up and searched out the disaster.

But Jonasz was already busy sweeping up the mess in the hallway. I relaxed. Maybe hiring him for the season hadn't been such a bad idea after all.

The cell phone rang in my frilly apron's pocket, and I pulled it out. *Tomas*. I winced. I hadn't told him about the fire yet. Since he was my landlord, I should have. "Hi, Tomas."

"What happened to the house?" he roared. "I came by to cut that tree down to size, and—"

"Someone set it on fire last night," I said quickly, my stomach lurching. "There's a police report. Sorry, I meant to tell you sooner. That's on me."

"Who the hell did that?"

"Ah..." I leaned against the hallway wall. "I don't know. I didn't catch them." A woman slipped past me and into the restroom.

"If that party of Brik's last night got out of hand, we're going to have words."

"You knew about his party?" I shouldn't have been surprised. Somehow, my grandfather and Tomas had gotten onto Brik's invite list.

And then Tomas's words penetrated. *Could* it have been some drunk from Brik's party? Was I overestimating my importance to the killer? Because that would be nice. "I don't know, but the police are investigating."

"I'll call them for the report. My insurance will want it. Are you okay?"

"Yes, I'm fine. Brik actually helped put it out." And why did I feel the need to defend him? Okay, yes, Brik did help put the fire out. But... I didn't want to think about that either. "Thank you for the tree though. It was really thoughtful."

"Huh. I'll get you another one."

"No, you don't have to."

"Now it's just a matter of pride. I once killed a man with a bottlecap. No one burns down my Christmas tree and gets away with it."

I glanced toward the hallway's white ceiling, hung with glittery snowflakes. *Oh, boy.*

"Besides," he continued, "I figured you could put it in that spot by the French doors. It would be perfect."

That spot *would* be perfect—prominent but out of the way. "That's a good idea."

He sighed. "I'll take care of the bungalow. Not sure if I'll be able to get it fixed up before Christmas though," he warned.

"That's okay. I'm really sorry."

"It's not your fault if someone set it on fire."

But *had* it been my fault? I gnawed my bottom lip. Had I brought this on myself, and on Tomas's rental?

Tomas coughed. "I should have brought the tree around to the back instead of leaving it on your front porch. But I thought you might not see it there. It was a good tree," he said dolefully.

"It really was."

"Perfectly shaped."

"Yup."

We mourned the tree for a bit longer, then said our goodbyes and hung up. I hurried to Hyperion's door. It stood ajar. I knocked.

"Come in," he said.

I pushed open the door and leaned inside the frame. "I got a call from Perth Jewelers. They're coming to the meeting on Monday."

"Good." He looked up from his laptop on the table.

"I thought we were only inviting businesses on Main Street, ones who might have actually seen the guy who broke our window."

"I sent Ivette an invitation—guess why."

I grimaced. I should have thought of it myself. If we were going to use the meeting for our own selfish purposes, we may as well do it right.

Hyperion shut his laptop. "It would look odd if she was the only business owner from that area we invited."

"Oh." That made sense. "How many people did you invite?"

"Fifty."

My eyes bugged. "I need refreshments for fifty people?" I'd been planning on serving leftovers, but not with that number of guests.

"They're not all going to come. We'll be lucky if we get ten."

"Ah, I've already had fifteen RSVPs." I walked inside and pulled out the chair opposite to take a load off. On its red-velvet seat, Bastet meowed up at me. His furry face had a don't-even-think-about-it expression. I rested my arms on the chair back instead. "How many have you collected?"

My partner leaned back in his high-backed chair. He slipped his hands into the pockets of his charcoal skinny slacks. "Uh... Another ten? Most people who are going to come have probably already RSVP'd."

I sure hoped so. "Ivette bought a sapphire ring from Perth Jewelers yesterday," I said absently.

"To celebrate?" He arched a brow.

"I don't know, but his stuff isn't cheap."

"It *is* the holidays," he said.

"Yeah. I suppose."

Merry staggered into his office and slammed the door behind her. Spots of color darkened her cheeks. "I need a reading." The damp had turned her red hair frizzy. A too-tight black blazer strained against her chest.

Hyperion rose from his chair and motioned to the one I gripped. Bastet dropped from the cushion. The tabby hopped onto the altar, making space between its crystals and driftwood.

"Has something happened?" Hyperion asked Merry.

"It's that Henderson woman." She gulped, her stare glassy. "She did it. She killed Emery."

Chapter Fifteen

HYPERION AND I GAPED like beached guppies. My partner pulled the look off better than I did, snapping his jaw shut a second or two before I realized mine was hanging open. Bastet, unimpressed by Merry's announcement, hopped onto the driftwood altar and licked his paw.

"I don't know how she did it." Merry slumped into the red velvet chair Bastet had just vacated. Her manicured hands dangled limply off its arms. "But somehow, that Henderson woman did it. She killed Emery."

"How do you know it was her?" I asked. The police had arrested Mrs. Henderson?

"It's because of Emery's will," she said. "She gets everything."

Whoa. I had not seen that coming.

"She what?" Hyperion said.

"Maybe not everything," she said. "It's confused."

So was I. Was this conjecture on Merry's part or an actual arrest? "Would you like a cup of tea?" I asked.

"Yes." She nodded. "Yes."

I hurried into the kitchen and brewed her a pot of Earl Grey. While the water reached a boil, I set up a tray of vanilla scones and tiny sandwiches and did some hard thinking.

It was unusual for suspects to drop in for interrogations. Granted, I still fell on the amateur side of the detecting game. And all these visits to the tearoom certainly made life easier. But in my limited experience, I normally had to chase suspects down.

Jonasz walked inside and dumped broken crockery into the big waste bin. *Suspects like Jonasz.* I glanced away and got back to arranging the tray.

"Was that Merry Callum I saw?" Jonasz asked.

"Yes," I said neutrally. "She's here for a reading."

He nodded toward the plastic bins of plates and cups. "I'll get started on these dishes."

"Thanks." I grabbed the tray. Jonasz, Ivette, Merry... Even Mrs. Henderson was making things easy by coming to the tearoom. What was going on? I walked into Hyperion's office.

"...need a reading," she said. "I know you said too many readings aren't helpful, but the situation has changed."

"Yes, of course," Hyperion said.

I set the tray on the table and organized the tea things. "What's happened?"

Hyperion steeped his fingers, looking like a plotting prince on his pseudo-throne. "Apparently, Emery did his own trust. He put it in Audrey Henderson's name. It appears to have been an accident."

"He told me he was going to make her the trustee," Merry wailed. "But instead he made her the trustee *and* the beneficiary. She's not just managing the estate. She *gets* the estate."

Oh boy. I poured tea into a cup. "What does Mrs. Henderson say?"

Merry rocked in her chair, her hands twitching on the tablecloth. "She acted surprised. She said she thought she was the trustee too, and it must be some mistake. But the fact is, she's also on the trust as beneficiary. Which means there may be a legal battle."

Hyperion's dark brows sloped thoughtfully downward. "I suppose it depends on how honest Mrs. Henderson is."

Merry made a small, miserable sound and brought the teacup to her lips. She banged the cup on the table. It tipped, spilling, a dark stain spreading across the red cloth.

Whipping a towel from the waistband of my red-checked apron, I blotted at the mess. It wasn't the first disaster I'd cleaned up today. I had a feeling it wouldn't be the last.

"I'm sorry." Merry pressed a hand to her cheek. "I'm so sorry."

"It's fine," Hyperion said. "It washes."

I lifted a brow. "You don't believe Mrs. Henderson's honest?" I straightened and poured her another cup.

Merry sniffed. She grabbed a tissue from a box that had appeared on the table while I'd been in the kitchen. "Not by a longshot."

"Why?" I asked.

Her face worked. "It's just a feeling I have."

"It does appear that your husband and Mrs. Henderson *were* close though," Hyperion said. "Close enough he'd make her trustee. Or beneficiary. Or whatever."

"I think..." She reached for the cup, then drew back. "I think they were having an affair."

"Get out of town." Hyperion's brown eyes widened, guileless. "Why would you think that?"

"I saw them together," she said bitterly. "In the back room of his shop. There was no doubting what was going on."

"Did you confront your husband?" I asked.

Merry brought a shaky hand to her forehead. "He denied it, of course. And then Ivette—" She winced and looked away.

"Ivette?" Hyperion prompted.

She exhaled slowly. "The problem isn't just Audrey Henderson. Emery's trust is nearly three inches thick. It has dozens of amendments. Many of them contradict each other."

"What does that have to do with Ivette?" I asked, puzzled.

"Nothing, it's only... She was left on one of his brokerage accounts as the beneficiary. It's worth over half a million dollars."

Hyperion whistled and met my gaze. That was one heck of a motive. No wonder Ivette was out buying jewelry. Her hated ex dead, and she five-hundred thousand richer. Why not throw down? Bastet sneezed.

"It was just another accident that wouldn't have happened if my husband had seen a lawyer. But no, he insisted on doing it all himself to save money," Merry said. "And then for him to go to Audrey of all people..." Her head lowered. She breathed heavily. "She knew. She must have known. Your reading. That card, the swords, the betrayal. She must have..."

On the altar, the cat washed his face with one paw. Hyperion drummed his fingers on the table.

"If the will was such a mess," I began, "it could be... I mean, *couldn't* it be possible Mrs. Henderson didn't know?"

"What?" She twisted in her chair to look at me. "How? How could it be possible? I just... I can't do nothing. I have to do something. I'm *going* to do something."

Hyperion's fingers stilled on the tabletop. "Do what?"

"I don't know." She leaned forward and pressed one hand to the table. "So will you? Do a reading for me?"

"Yes, of course," he said smoothly.

Backing from the room, I shut the door behind me. I swiped my damp palms down the front of my holiday apron. Aside from hire a good lawyer, I didn't know what Merry could do. And she had already had Gino.

Merry left half an hour later. I knew because I was watching his office door. I hurried inside.

Hyperion, brow furrowed, gathered the cards from the table. The giant tabby sat upon it, his striped tail flicking.

"Well?" I asked.

"I don't like this," he said. "Not at all."

Oh, damn. I rubbed my arm. "What happened?"

"The reading wasn't significantly different from the last, if that's what you're asking. Betrayal, deceit, endings."

"I'm not sure what I'm asking." I jammed my hands in my apron pockets. But—also in my limited detecting experience—the more I asked, the more I learned. This seemed true even if my questions were vague and lacking purpose.

"Merry Callum is a wreck," Hyperion said flatly.

"Her husband *was* murdered. And now with this mix-up with the trust... It would rattle anyone. Does she have any money of her own?"

"No. And this certainly opens up the motives for murder."

No kidding. Mrs. Henderson and Ivette both benefited from Emery Callum's death—and both at Merry's cost. "Assuming Ivette or Mrs. Henderson knew how mixed up that trust was," I said.

"Mrs. Henderson might have," he said, "as executrix. I do love the feminization of professional titles, don't you? They just have a certain ring to them. *Executrix. Beneficiar...x*?" He shook his head. "That's not as elegant."

"Technically, she was a trustee and not an executor." I collected the plates from the table and set them on the tray. "How *would* Ivette find out about being beneficiary?"

He eyed me. "You do know you've got an estate attorney on speed dial?"

"Ye-es."

He arched a dark brow. "And the problem is...?" the cat dropped from the table and vanished beneath its long cloth.

"He—It's— Gino's protective of Merry, and rightly so. She's his aunt."

"So's Ivette."

"He's protective of her too." I stacked the cups, making more room I didn't need on the tray. "And as an attorney, he's bound by confidentiality." I didn't want to use Gino for favors any more than I wanted to do that to Brik. I wanted us to be in it for each other, not for what we could "get."

"Preventing you from asking a general question? Like, I don't know, how would someone find out if they're a beneficiary on an account?" He pursed his lips.

"He'll know exactly why I'm asking." And I was still feeling uncertain in the relationship. It had been so long since I'd *been* in a relationship. While everything was new and exciting and fun, it was also awkward.

"Why's that a problem?" Hyperion laced his fingers together and propped his chin on his hands. He batted his thick lashes. "Trouble in paradise?"

I crossed my arms. "No. I just don't want to put Gino in an awkward position."

"Really?' His smile turned lascivious. "You don't?"

Ignoring that. "Fine. I'll call." I pulled my phone from my apron pocket and dialed.

"Abigail," Gino purred. "I was just thinking about you."

My heart gave a little jump. "Good things, I hope."

Hyperion pivoted in his chair and groped his shoulder blades while making kissing noises. I turned away from him.

"Very good things," Gino said. "There's a new restaurant in Santa Cruz I'd like to try this Friday. How do you feel about a Brazilian steakhouse?"

"Never been to one." I smiled, warmth bubbling inside me. "But I hear it's basically all-you-can-eat meat."

Hyperion choked back a laugh, and I winced. My partner had an unholy aptitude for making innocent comments seem dirty. "I'm in," I said.

"Pick you up at seven?" Gino asked. Bastet emerged from beneath the table and made for me.

"Better make it seven-thirty." I bent to scratch behind the cat's ears. "Fridays are pretty busy here."

"Gotcha. So why'd you call?"

I hesitated. "Merry was here for another Tarot reading. She seemed pretty upset."

"She told you about the trust," he said flatly.

I swallowed. Why did I feel guilty about this? I hadn't asked her to come to the tearoom and unload her problems. "Yes."

"I really can't talk about it," he said.

I grimaced. "I know," I said. "It's confidential. But I just have a general question."

He sighed. "I'll see you tomorrow night, Abigail." Gino hung up.

"*That* was a disappointment." Hyperion examined his nails. "By which I mean *you* were a disappointment. By now, you should have that man wrapped around your pinkie."

"I wouldn't want a man I could wrap around my pinkie," I said tartly. Maybe I'm old-fashioned, but a relationship like that seemed boring. "But I do have another source." I called my grandfather.

"Abigail," Gramps said cheerfully. "What are you up to this fine Thursday afternoon?"

"Is it fine? That's good news." It was still pretty foggy here, near the water. But we were in the land of microclimates. It could well be eighty degrees and sunny at his house.

I sat on the arm of the empty chair. "Gramps, how would someone find out if they were a beneficiary on a brokerage account?"

"The brokerage company would inform the beneficiary after the firm received a death certificate for the account owner."

"What about before the account owner died?" I asked. Bastet coiled around my ankles.

"The owner would have to inform the beneficiaries themself," he said.

My brow furrowed. It didn't seem likely Emery would tell his ex he'd kept her as a beneficiary. "And there's no other way?"

"Short of the beneficiary seeing the documents—no."

"Okay, thanks," I said, disappointed. Maybe Ivette wasn't such a great suspect after all.

"What's going on?" my grandfather asked.

"It's the Callum murder," I said. "It seems his trust was a real mess."

He laughed shortly. "I'm not surprised. I hear Callum did his own bookkeeping too. He was probably better at that though. He was always good with money."

There was a quack in the background, and a crash. "I'd better go," he said. "Peking's trying to roost in the Christmas tree again."

Again? "Thanks, Gramps." We said our goodbyes and hung up.

"Well?" Hyperion rose. Setting the tea tray on the chair, he whipped off the stained tablecloth.

I shrugged. "The brokerage company would inform Ivette only after they received the death certificate."

He opened a low cabinet and pulled out a fresh, crimson cloth. "So she probably wouldn't have known about the half-mil before Emery died. I mean, if she was left on by accident, he wouldn't have told her."

"What if it wasn't an accident?" I ran my hand along the top of one of the tall chairs. "What if he intended to leave her the money and had told her?"

"That doesn't jibe with what we know of his character. Plus, wasn't she suing him for more money? If someone was suing me, I wouldn't leave them a *centime*."

"Me neither. But half a million is a motive." Especially if you had a grudge against the murder victim.

"Would you kill someone for half a million dollars?" He arranged the cloth on the table.

"I wouldn't kill for any amount. But people have killed for less, and for other reasons."

"Depressing but true." He checked his watch and tossed me the dirty tablecloth. "And I've got another reading in five minutes. Throw this in with the other wash, won't you?"

Since I could take a not-so-subtle hint as well as the next person, I collected the tea tray and left his office. The tearoom hummed with chatter and laughter and brimmed with holiday scents. And this time, work *did* manage to drive thoughts of murder from my mind.

Jonasz left at three to get to another seasonal job he'd picked up. I caught myself thinking it would have been nice to have him around for the evening cleanup. Maybe hiring him had been less a favor to him than I'd told myself.

Finally, I locked up at seven. Hyperion walked me to my Mazda in the parking lot. "Er, I got three more RSVPs for Monday's meeting." He shot me a guilty glance.

I sighed. *More people to feed.* What had we gotten ourselves into? "We'll make it work." The phone rang in my purse, and I dug it out, glanced at the screen. *Gino.* A sense of warmth and light spread through my chest.

"Mind if I take this?" I opened the car door and pressed the phone to my ear. "Hi, Gino. What's—"

"It's Merry." His voice was jagged as a coral reef, and I flinched. "She's dead."

Chapter Sixteen

"Dead?" My hand gripped the phone more tightly. It was impossible. We'd just seen Merry here, alive. She'd had a Tarot reading. Bastet had watched from the altar. I'd gone to the kitchen, and... I'd heard wrong. This was wrong. "She can't be dead."

I winced. It had been a stupid thing to say. Gino wouldn't joke about something like this, and he didn't respond to my inane denial. I braced my hand on the top of my hatchback, its metal cool and damp beneath my palm.

"Who's dead?" Hyperion gripped my arm. "Abigail, what's—"

"It's Merry," I told him, stunned. It didn't make any more sense when I said it out loud. A fog phantom swirled beneath a nearby parking lamp. My body convulsed in a shiver.

"When did she leave Beanblossom's?" Gino demanded. "How did she seem?"

"She left sometime after one o'clock," I said.

"You said she was upset," Gino said. "Why didn't you stop her?"

"I didn't know someone would... Gino, what's happened? Where are you?"

There was a long silence. He sighed. "Sorry," he said shortly. "It's not your fault. I'm at her house. Outside it, actually. The police are here."

"I'll be right there," I said.

"No," Gino said. "You don't—"

"I'll be right there," I repeated and hung up.

"What the hell's going on?" Hyperion clawed a hand through his thick hair.

"I don't know. Gino's at Merry's house. He says the police are there. He wanted to know when she left Beanblossom's."

"How did he know she was here?" His jaw set, his forehead wrinkling.

"I told him on the phone," I snapped. "You were there."

"Oh. Right. I'm coming with you."

"Good."

And for once, Hyperion didn't insist on driving us in his Jeep. We drove in my poky hatchback to Merry's fairytale house. Red and blue emergency lights flickered across its stone walls and crooked turrets.

Police cars surrounded the house, and a uniformed cop waved us past. We parked up the street and hurried back toward Merry's. Groups of neighbors clustered on the sidewalk. We stopped to ask an elderly couple what was going on.

"Suicide, I heard," the silver-haired man said sadly. Hyperion paled and stilled.

"Oh, no," I breathed and pressed my palm to my chest. "Are you sure?"

The man shook his head. "I'm not sure of anything. It's what people are saying, but that's all I know. The police aren't exactly giving us updates."

"No," I said, "I don't suppose they would." I scanned the yard and spotted Gino talking to a policewoman. His dark gaze met mine. He said something to the policewoman, and she nodded.

Gino strode toward us. "What happened?" he barked. "What did you say to her?"

I took a step backward. "I don't—"

"I told her she was facing a difficult time," Hyperion said, "but she wasn't alone. There were people who could help her."

Gino's jaw hardened. "Bullshit. Abigail told me she was upset when she left you. I told Merry not to waste money on a Tarot reading. But you had to lure her in with your tea and scones and sympathy."

"Gino," I said, blinking rapidly. "That's not... What happened?"

"I found her with her head in the oven," he said, his voice taut with anger. "That's what happened." He pointed at Hyperion. "You did this."

Hyperion swayed, looking sick. "She didn't... She told me she was going to put Christmas lights on her house tonight. She said Emery didn't want a high electric bill, he refused to put them on the house. But she thought she needed to put them out now."

The elderly couple watched wide-eyed, their gazes ping-ponging between Gino and us. The woman clutched her husband's arm. Absently, he patted her hand.

The cold of the sidewalk seeped through the soles of my shoes. "If we had any idea Merry was..." My throat closed. "This is awful. Gino, I'm so sorry."

"This has nothing to do with you, Abigail." Gino glared at Hyperion.

"Of course it does," I said. "And Hyperion's—"

"Stop defending him," Gino shouted.

Hyperion laid a hand on my shoulder. "He's right. You don't need to defend me." He turned to Gino. "Merry was upset. She was upset by her husband's death and by the confusion surrounding his estate. When she left, I thought she was less upset. I thought she'd determined a plan to go forward."

"She killed herself," Gino said, low and intense. "That was her plan."

"That wasn't..." Hyperion swallowed. "I had no idea that was in her mind."

"Right," Gino said acidly. "Because you're not a psychic."

That wasn't fair. Hyperion made clear to all his clients he wasn't psychic. But Gino was hurting and in shock, and ten minutes ago I'd snapped at Hyperion for no good reason too. So I wasn't much better under pressure. I cleared my throat. "Are the police sure she—"

"Don't," Gino said warningly. "Just don't." He glared at Hyperion. His hands fisted. "We're not done." He turned and strode back to the policewoman.

I watched him go, mist chilling my face. "This wasn't your fault," I told Hyperion. He didn't respond. "It's not," I said sharply. "I know how you work. You would never—"

"Never what? Misread a client's intentions? Gino's right. I'm not psychic."

"Exactly. You couldn't have known what she was planning."

"I knew she was in dark waters," he said quietly.

"What's going on here?" a man drawled behind us.

I turned, relieved. Blond and tall and lean, Tony stood on the sidewalk in jeans and a button-up shirt. He'd found us. I had no idea how the ex-detective had found us, but in the moment, I didn't care.

"Merry Callum," I said. "They're saying it was suicide. There was a gas oven..." I'd made tea on that range. Bile swam up my throat, and I briefly closed my eyes. She'd been a prime suspect then. And now...

"Hyperion?" he asked.

"Merry Callum was a client," my partner said. "She came for a reading today. She was upset. I didn't think... I didn't think," he finished heavily.

"How did you find us?" I asked.

"Hyperion wasn't answering his phone," Tony said. "And then I heard there was a death here. Hyperion told me about your investigation." He put the final word in air quotes. "I figured you two would be—I figured you'd be here."

The arched door to Merry's house opened. Baranko strode outside. The policewoman hurried to him, and they spoke. He studied the clusters of people on the sidewalk. His gaze landed on us.

The detective strode across the lawn. Eyes flinty, he stopped in front of Tony. "You're not a cop anymore, Chase."

"Nope." Tony shoved up the front of his cowboy hat with his thumb. "Just an ordinary civilian gawking on a public sidewalk."

The burly detective's lip curled. His gaze lasered in on Hyperion. "You. I hear you saw Mrs. Callum this afternoon at your little Tarot con, and she left in distress."

"She came to us in distress," I said. "And it's not a con. Tarot is a tool for self-development. The cards depict archetypes from our universal unconscious and allow us to tap directly into our subconscious and superconscious knowledge."

"Abigail," Hyperion said in a low voice. He smiled at me. "Shut up."

I folded my arms. "Well, it is."

"You spoke to Mrs. Callum?" Baranko asked me.

"Yes. Briefly."

The detective jammed a meaty finger in my direction. "You. Wait here." To Hyperion, he said, "You. Come with me." He angled his head toward the house. The two men moved away from us and out of earshot onto the lawn.

I gnawed my bottom lip and glanced at Gino, standing alone near the front door. "This isn't right."

"Hyperion's a big boy," Tony said. "He can handle himself."

"I know." But I also knew that he was wondering if he was somehow to blame. And Gino... To find someone like that, your aunt, someone you knew and cared about... What he'd said to Hyperion hadn't been right, but he wasn't thinking straight. If Gino was the person I thought he was, he'd realize that eventually.

An iron band tightened around my chest. I really hoped he was the person I thought he was.

Chapter Seventeen

HYPERION EMERGED FROM THE mist. He came to a halt beside me on the sidewalk outside Merry's home. "Your turn." Expression bleak, he nodded toward Baranko. The burly detective waited outside the fairytale home's lead-glass windows, lit from within.

I studied my partner for a long moment, then nodded. Limbs heavy, I walked across the lawn to the house. Maybe it was the fog clutching its turrets. Maybe it was the sickening strobes of red and blue emergency lights across its front. Maybe it was just me, but the house now seemed a gothic nightmare.

Baranko glowered down at me. "You saw Mrs. Callum today?"

I hugged myself against the chill. *Keep it brief and accurate. Don't embellish. Don't get defensive.* "Yes, she came to the tearoom sometime between twelve-thirty and one. She left about thirty minutes later."

"Did you speak?"

"A little."

"How did she seem?"

"Tense. She told us her husband's will or trust was confused. Mrs. Henderson was on the trust. Emery's ex-wife was still a beneficiary on one of his brokerage accounts."

"Was it a will or a trust?" he asked sharply.

I shifted my weight. The grass was damp, chilling my feet through the canvas shoes. "I think she said a trust." But what did my opinion matter? He could find out easily enough on his own which it was.

"Was it a living trust?" he demanded. It wasn't quite a shout, but his tone was enough to make me start. "In California," he continued, "a will goes through probate. A living trust doesn't. There's a big difference. Which I'd think you'd know, since you were raised by a CPA. Don't they deal with estate law?"

Heat flushed my face. Why was he taking this out of *my* hide? "Ask Merry..." I bit my bottom lip. He couldn't ask her. Merry was dead.

My anger shifted to shame. "Her nephew, Gino Redmond, was helping her with the estate. He'd know the details."

"And you know this because...?"

"Gino told me he was helping her. We're dating." Or we *were*. I glanced across the lawn at him, talking to a policewoman. I wasn't so sure we were staying together after tonight.

"When you say she was upset, what do you mean?" the detective asked.

"Upset. Confused. Worried. Angry."

"Depressed?"

"She lost her husband. Of course she was—" *Don't guess*. "I don't know."

He grunted. The detective asked me more questions. It was clear he thought my responses were sub-par. Finally, he let me go.

I trudged across the lawn to a waiting Hyperion and Tony. The Texan adjusted his hat.

"How'd it go?" Hyperion asked.

I glanced over my shoulder at Gino, still talking to the cop. "He asked a lot about Merry's state of mind." I kicked a weed growing through the sidewalk crack. "I don't know. I didn't think she would do something like this."

Hyperion's head dropped. "Me neither," he said in a quiet tone.

"I hate to bring this up now," I said, "but it's possible she didn't commit suicide."

"It's also possible she did," Hyperion said bitterly. "That Merry was more overwhelmed by the loss of her husband than I thought. Or that she killed him and then killed herself out of remorse, or out of fear of getting caught."

"It happens," Tony said, noncommittal. "And the holidays are rough for some people."

Not helping. Annoyed, I shot the tall Texan a look. Couldn't he see Hyperion was wracked with misplaced guilt?

"Tony's going to give me a lift home," Hyperion said. "Are you going to be okay?"

"Yeah. I'm fine." I hesitated, glancing around the scene. Cops milled on the lawn and strode purposefully in and out of the house. Gino had vanished, and a hollow space opened beneath my ribs. Returning to my Mazda, I got inside and pulled from the sidewalk.

I glanced in the rearview mirror. Tony and Hyperion stood close. Tony put a hand on Hyperion's shoulders. And then I rounded a bend in the treelined road, and the scene vanished.

My hands tightened on the wheel. *Suicide*. It was possible. But I didn't want it to be true. I didn't want it to be true because I knew Hyperion would blame himself.

And Merry hadn't *seemed* hopeless. The last thing she'd said in my hearing was she was going to do something. I'd never dreamed that action might be taking her own life.

And Gino... A knot tightened in my gut. What an awful thing to find. Someone you cared about, dead, and not a peaceful death.

Because torturing myself is my favorite activity, I let those thoughts revolve as I drove home. Turning onto my street, I slowed and sucked in a breath.

Cars lined the sidewalk. Music vibrated my car. *Brik*. Of all the nights, he had to... Now? *Now*? My hands twisted on the wheel, knuckles whitening.

Lights shone from the windows of his narrow, two-story house. I edged around the cars partially blocking my driveway and parked. And when I stomped up my stairs to my blistered front door, I managed not to kick it open. I also didn't slam it when I strode inside. Much.

Music pulsed through the bungalow's pale-blue walls. I turned on the Christmas lights and turned off the overheads. The soft glow against the tinsel lifted my spirits for all of thirty seconds. Then the volume next door increased.

I unclenched my jaw. I was angry because being angry beat worrying about Hyperion or thinking about Merry and Gino. Brik needed this right now, or he wouldn't be doing it. And his other neighbors weren't bothered. They were older and hard of hearing. And if Brik and I were really friends, I could live with this.

The doorbell rang, and my stomach butterflied. *Gino*.

I hurried to the door and opened it without checking the security camera. There was no point. That had been wrecked in the fire too.

Razzzor stood on my doorstep in a Santa hat. In one hand he held a wicker basket with a wine bottle. A fire extinguisher stuck from the basket along with Christmas cookies on sticks. In his other hand, he held an insulated pizza carrier. "Merry pre-Christmas."

Razzzor is tall and lanky. His hair and eyes are brown. His skin is pale from too much time in front of a computer monitor. He's also one of the best people I know. If his tech gazillions hadn't turned him rotten by this point, I didn't think they ever would. Razzzor was rotten-proof. And he was exactly the person I hadn't known I'd needed to see tonight.

I leaned against the doorframe and smiled. "Pre-Christmas isn't a thing, but I'll take it. What are you doing in San Borromeo?"

"I got an invite to Brik's party." He angled his head toward the blue house next door and grinned. "But I figured after the fire and with all the noise, you could use some solace. Also, I want to hear about our latest case."

I straightened off the doorframe. "*Our* case?"

He strode past me and looked around my bungalow's pale blue living area. "I like what you've done with the place." He plucked a pastel Christmas tree from the mantel. Hastily, I flipped on the overhead lights.

"Now you've ruined the mood lighting." He strode to the dining table and set down his basket and pizza.

My stomach growled. The pizza smelled fantastic.

Razzzor adjusted his glasses. "You can't call me in the middle of a Christmas tree arson and not expect me to take an interest. You could have PTSD."

"How do you know it was arson?"

He cocked his head and raised a brow. "Do you seriously have to ask?"

Right. He'd probably hacked the police department's database. I wouldn't put it past him, and I didn't really want to know.

"You could have been killed, burnt alive," he said cheerfully, and I felt my smile waver. "But it's okay to feel your feelings," he said. "I'm here to listen, no judgment." Razzzor was also permanently in therapy. Psychobabble was his second language.

"Right now," I said, "all I'm feeling is hungry."

He unzipped the pizza carrier and pulled out a cardboard box. "I'm here for that too. Now, I take it the tree business has to do with the murder of Emery Callum?"

"How did you—?"

"Come on." He set the pizza box on the table and opened it. "He was killed right down the street from Beanblossom's. Of course you and Hyperion are on the case." He pressed a hand to his chest. "And I'm a little hurt you didn't tell me about it the last time we talked."

"I didn't want to bother you," I said. "I know you're busy with the zombie game."

"Yeah," he said glumly.

"What's wrong?"

"The Krampus extension is a huge success."

"And?" I asked.

"That's it."

Ah. Now Razzzor would have to spend more time building the company. My old boss preferred to start new projects and walk away once he got bored. That was easier to do if the projects were failing. Unfortunately for Razzzor, his rarely did.

I shook my head and grabbed the wine bottle. I didn't bother to check the label. Razzzor had his own vineyard with a team of crack viticulturists.

And yes, the wine was excellent with pizza.

After we killed half the pizza, we relaxed on the couch with our goblets and stared at the blank TV. "So," he said brightly. "Murder?"

The wine soured in my mouth. "Suicide." I set the goblet on the arm of the couch.

"Huh?"

"Sorry." I propped my feet on the coffee table. "There's been another death." I told him about Merry.

Razzzor's frown deepened. "Are you sure it was suicide? Because it sounds kind of sketchy to me. Merry learns that two women have grabbed a big chunk of her inheritance. But there's going to be a legal battle. I mean, there had to be. She was Callum's wife. And now she's dead, and there won't be. Those other two women had everything to gain by her death. Maybe they did it together."

"Unlikely." Pensive, I sipped the Cabernet. "But you're right. There's no one to fight them for the money." Their path would be free and clear. Unless Gino had been included in the trust, and I didn't think he had been. But I didn't know. I studied the blank TV.

"What does Gino have to say?"

"Eh?" I looked up from my wine goblet. Ears hot, I cleared my throat. "Oh. I didn't really get a chance to talk to him. He was pretty upset tonight." I hoped once he got past the shock and pain, he'd realize Hyperion wasn't to blame.

"Yeah." Razzzor put his feet up beside mine, knocking my game controller to the carpet. "I'd imagine he would be. But it wasn't okay for him to take it out on you."

I studied him. He sat with his eyebrows raised inquiringly. If that comment had been a shot in the dark, it had landed. "How did you...?"

He made an airy motion with his free hand. "I have an instinct for these things."

He really didn't, and my eyes narrowed. Did he have a source? "He took it out more on Hyperion," I said slowly.

"Who's no doubt feeling guilty about not stopping Merry's suicide, even though it probably wasn't a suicide. But Hyperion can't admit it's not a suicide, because he just thinks he's trying to evade the blame for it."

I stared, and he shrugged modestly. "Ten years of therapy. I'm chock-full of insight. The thing is, this is murder. *You* know it's murder. *I* know it's murder. We just have to prove it." His brow wrinkled. "No, that's wrong. Hyperion has to prove it if he's going to really get over this. It's gonna be tough though, what with all the denial and guilt going on. Where's your laptop?"

I pointed at the dining table.

He laced his fingers together and stretched his arms overhead, palms out. His knuckles cracked. "Let's do some digging."

Razzzor migrated to the dining table. He opened my laptop, and his fingers flew across the keyboard. In my bedroom, the printer whirred. He angled his head. "That's for the murder board."

"I don't have a murder board."

Head down, he tsked. "Seriously? What kind of amateur sleuth are you?"

"A frustrated one," I muttered, rising. I walked into my bedroom and strode across the dark bamboo floor to my printer on its stand. Pages flowed from its mouth.

I knew you were supposed to keep business and electronics out of the bedroom, and I tried. Other than the printer, my bedroom was calm and lovely, in tones of browns, whites and blues. A chandelier hung from the ceiling. The silhouette of a tree was painted on the wall behind my bed. Sitting on the edge of the bed, I started to read.

Press releases from the opening of Ivette's business. A wedding announcement of Merry and Callum. An article on Mrs. Henderson's costume shop. The obituary of Mrs. Henderson's husband, Saul, in 2006. Social media photos of Merry and Ivette...

"I take it Emery wasn't on social media?" I called through the bedroom door.

"No," he said. "Aside from his business license, he's a ghost."

Another piece of paper spat from the machine. A business license. Property records... Lots of property records.

I whistled. "Holy Hannah. Emery owns about a third of Main Street."

"And your Mrs. Henderson owns the other third."

"She does?" More pages whizzed from the printer. She *did* own a bunch of property on Main Street.

I frowned down at the whirring printer. Mrs. Henderson was cannier than I'd thought. She and Emery would have made the ultimate power couple if someone hadn't killed him first. And now... Mrs. Henderson inherited everything, lock, stock, and barrel.

Chapter Eighteen

THE DOORBELL RANG. I dropped the papers Razzzor had printed onto my bed and hurried to the bungalow's front door.

"That'll be the murder board." Razzzor didn't look up from my laptop at the dining table.

"Murder board?" How did he get one here so fast? All this efficiency was unsettling. When I'd worked for Razzzor, I'd been his Girl Friday. He'd been mostly helpless when it came to day-to-day stuff. Now he was making murder boards happen? I opened the door.

A man in a black ZNS jacket (Zombie Nazis in Space) looked warily at my siding's blistered paint. "Uh, delivery for Razzzor?" He leaned on an oversized cardboard box.

"In here, Phil," Razzzor shouted. "You can set it up wherever."

"Not wherever," I grumped. This was still my house. "Razzzor, you can't just order me murder boards."

"Who said its yours? We're borrowing it from ZNS."

My face heated. "Oh. Well, you can't just order murder boards to be set up in my house."

"We can't do it at mine. You know what that's like."

He lived in a freaking mansion. Last I checked, he had room for a dozen murder boards. "You can set it up... there." I pointed to a spot in front of the ivory couch by the window. Phil edged past, dragging the oblong box.

"And I can't put it up at my office," Razzzor said. "You and I won't be able to work on it together there."

Oh, boy. He wanted to do more than internet research? This was going to get interesting.

"Good. You're home." Tony strolled through the open front door and removed his cowboy hat. "Nice decorations."

Belatedly, I shut the door. "Thanks. Ah, what—?" The bell rang, and I opened it again.

Tomas frowned in at me. "You okay?"

I ran my hand across my hair. "Sorry. Did I close the door on you? And yes, I'm fine."

Phil pulled out a box cutter and neatly slit open the box. The cardboard sides fell outward.

"Hi, Tomas." Razzzor waved from the table.

"Hiya, Razzzor. I'm here to see if there's any interior damage." The older man stepped inside the door and squinted at the ceiling. I thought so." He unzipped his Giant's windbreaker and pointed. "Smoke."

"Huh?" I looked up. The ceiling by the door *was* a little darker than the ceiling in the rest of the living room. I guess I hadn't noticed with all my holiday mood lighting.

"I'll have to repaint the ceiling," Tomas said.

My grandfather huffed up the steps and adjusted his cabby hat. "Tomas told me it was bad, but I had no idea. You were lucky." Gramps pulled a pocketknife from the rear pocket of his baggy khakis. He scraped it across the exterior paint. My grandfather studied the knife blade and shook his head thoughtfully. "Hm."

Tony frowned at Phil, who maneuvered a bulletin board from the remains of the box. "What's going on?" the Texan asked.

"Murder board." Razzzor looked up and blinked. "You're that cop, Tony Chase."

"Ex-cop," Tony said.

Razzzor grimaced. "Sorry, man. You got screwed on that case."

"In fairness," the Texan drawled, "it was an excellent frame-up. Abigail, can we talk?" He strode into my kitchen without waiting for an answer.

Exasperated, I shot Tomas and Gramps an apologetic look and followed Tony. Honestly, my house usually doesn't get this much traffic. "What's wrong?" I asked.

He dropped his cowboy hat on the butcherblock work island. "What makes you think something's wrong?"

"Because you didn't come here to play video games with me and Razzzor."

He leaned against the gray granite counter. "Fair enough. What have you found out about the Callum murder?"

"Nothing that Hyperion doesn't know. Didn't he tell you?"

"I'd like to hear it from you."

Because I couldn't think of a reason not to tell him, I told him. Everything. "And then I got a call from Gino—"

"The victim's nephew."

"Yes. And Hyperion and I went to Merry's house, and you know the rest."

"We need to figure out what happened," he said.

"I know. That's what—wait. We?" My breath caught. "You're helping?" This was amazing. He was a real detective. Or he had been. If Tony was helping, we had the killer in the bag.

"I don't have my PI license yet," he said warningly.

"Are you getting one then?" This was even better news. I'd been worried he'd leave the state for a job with a different department.

Something crashed in my living room, and my shoulders shot to my ears. I edged toward the kitchen door. "I just need to—"

"They'll fix whatever it was," Tony said, halting me. "And yes. The PI application is in process."

"But I thought you didn't want to get involved."

"I didn't. Now I do. Hyperion needs to know the truth."

My pulse slowed. Then we'd been right. Hyperion *was* blaming himself. "He believes it was suicide," I said heavily.

Tony shook his head. "Let's see your murder board."

I spent the rest of the night tacking up the articles Razzzor had printed on the murder board. Tony unpinned and read them. Gramps and Tomas discussed repairs and finished off the pizza with Phil.

By the end of the exercise, I had more questions than answers. And if Tony had reached any stunning moments of clarity, he didn't tell me. Razzzor and I didn't get anything more out of him that night than a few grunts.

Eventually, everyone left. I absolutely did not slam the door behind them.

The weekend passed in a whirl of holiday tearoom madness. Hyperion had canceled all his readings and didn't appear. This worried me, but Hyperion was an adult. If he needed some time off, I wasn't going to mother hen him.

But I was a little worried when I checked our RSVP list for Monday's watch meeting. Ivette's name wasn't on it. Restraining myself, I didn't call Hyperion to ask about her invite. I was going to respect his privacy, even if it was killing me.

My patience was rewarded late Monday morning with a knock on my front door. I looked through the peep hole, which Tomas had cleaned last night. Hyperion's brown-eyed gaze filled it like the Eye of Sauron.

I opened the door. "Hey."

It was a little irritating he could make brown shoes work with near-black skinny jeans. He'd pulled it all together with a charcoal turtleneck and a brown thigh-length coat. If my partner ever gave up Tarot, he could become a fashion consultant.

"Hey yourself." Hyperion walked inside and stopped short at the murder board. "Redecorating?"

"Razzzor. He's on the case."

He laughed hollowly. "Of course he is. I suppose he's created an Abigail algorithm to figure out when you've gotten involved in a murder investigation."

I stilled, startled. That was actually... possible. And disturbing. "He's the one who got me that nifty murder board."

"How charmingly low-tech of him." He dropped onto the couch and studied the board's suspect photos and pinned articles. "The board's not really seasonal. Maybe add some of that gold garland, or at least a bit of holly."

"Yes," I said dryly. "That will make all the difference."

"I'm sure Razzzor will be a help. Neither of us are the masters of technology that he is."

"How was your weekend?"

"I got done a *ton* of procrastinating. But don't worry, I'll be back in the saddle—to use a Tonyism—tomorrow."

I released a slow breath. "And the watch meeting tonight?"

"Oh, I'll be there with bells on. Seriously. I have bells."

"Great." I sat on the arm of the couch. "But I noticed Ivette wasn't on the RSVP list."

He crossed an ankle over his knee. "That's because I didn't invite her."

What? Then what was the point? I shifted my weight. "I thought you said you'd invited people in Ivette's neighborhood."

"Yes, but not Ivette. Don't you know the best way to encourage someone to come is to make them think they've been left out? And then, oh, the horror! I made a mistake. Here's your invite. Plus, now we can talk to her in person and hopefully alone."

It was a cunning strategy. It was a good thing we'd become partners rather than adversaries. "Meaning we need to drop by today with an apology and an invite?"

"Exactly."

Ivette might not be able to make it on such short notice. But the odds she'd reveal something in a group setting had been low anyway. "And I think I'd like to talk to her receptionist, too," I said slowly.

"To confirm Ivette's alibi?" The corners of his lips whitened. "Merry already did that."

I grabbed my purse. "It might be too soon to start assuming we've got the right answers."

It was one of those odd, sunny December days. The temperature was already in the high sixties. It was expected to hit the seventies that afternoon. Though it was a Monday, the sidewalks downtown were crowded. People in shorts and t-shirts ambled toward the beach.

We found Ivette's office on the first floor of a two-story office building. The receptionist, a young woman with titian hair, looked up at us and frowned. "You don't have an appointment."

A fern hung in one corner of the room. A low table with children's books and plastic letters stood in front of a pale green, leather sofa.

Hyperion beamed. "No, we're here with an invitation—"

"No solicitors." She pointed to a sign on her desk. The desk was modern and impersonal, with only a computer, inbox, and phone. The inbox was empty.

"Ugh," Hyperion said. "*Hate* them. No. Somehow, Ivette's invitation to the business watch meeting didn't make it to your office."

He rolled his eyes. "The meeting's tonight. We wanted to make sure Ivette got it." He handed her an envelope.

"Oh," she said in a bored tone. "I heard something about that." She tossed the envelope in the in-box. "I'll give it to her when she arrives."

"She's not in?" Hyperion asked.

"That's what I said."

"We wanted to do something after Mr. Callum's murder," I said. I was tired of standing around like a plank of wood.

Hyperion stuck out his hand. "Hyperion Night. Tarot consultant."

The receptionist looked at it like he'd offered her a moody scorpion. Her lip curled. "*Consultant*?"

"There'll be a detective at the meeting tonight," I said hurriedly. "If you have any information from the day of the murder, you should come."

"Why would I have information?" she asked. "I was here. The murder was on Main Street."

"Yes, but..." Hyperion sidled closer. "Of course the police have already spoken with you."

"Yes," she said. "They did."

"To confirm when Merry Callum was here." Hyperion drummed his fingers on the thigh of his black skinny jeans.

I lowered my head to study the gray carpet. One of Hyperion's many talents was his ability to get people to gossip. But she seemed to be one of those rare people who Hyperion couldn't crack.

The receptionist folded her arms. "What's this about?"

"Merry Callum's dead," I said bluntly.

She paled. "What? But she was..." She blinked. "Was she murdered too?"

"We don't know how she died," I said. "What happened when she was here?"

"A lot of shouting. She got here around nine-twenty and stormed into Ivette's office. I tried to stop her, but Ivette told me it was fine. I could hear her through the door though."

The receptionist motioned toward the closed office door. "She accused Ivette of trying to ruin her marriage and all sorts of..." She blinked. "But what do you care?"

Answering that question was going to get me nowhere. But bulling forward seemed to have been moderately successful, so I asked another question. "What time did she leave?"

"A quarter after ten."

Then Merry might have had time to sneak over to the store and kill her husband. But Merry was dead, and odds were that Callum's murderer had killed her too. Still, we had to be thorough. "Was Ivette very upset?" I asked.

"Annoyed. She complained to me about her for a good thirty minutes afterward. Why?"

"Someone told me they saw Ivette on Main Street around ten," I lied. "I just wanted to clear it up."

"Well, they were wrong. I should know."

"Right. Thank you." I edged toward the door.

Hyperion followed me into the open hallway. "That was as useless as a fractured, evasive, obscene oval."

"What?" Usually his Lovecraftianisms made more sense. Had that even *been* Lovecraft?

"I don't know. I don't know what I'm saying anymore." He flipped up the collar of his brown coat.

"It wasn't useless. We got their alibis confirmed until ten forty-five. Now we just need to know the time of Emery Callum's death."

He bared his teeth. "I'm talking about that woman. My charm had zero effect on her. She's one of those frank skeptics. The paradox should eventually force them to self-destruct, but they never do."

"Paradox?" A breeze flapped my jacket, and I pulled it closer.

"She thinks she's being frank, telling it like it is, and she assumes everyone's just like her and can take it. But as a skeptic, she doesn't believe in anyone. This is a paradox because she believes in herself, and thinks everyone's just like her."

I laughed. "And you got all that from our conversation?"

He stepped onto the sidewalk and scowled. "They're the only type of people my charm doesn't work on. It's super, super irritating."

At least Hyperion was back to normal—or as normal as he could be. But I wondered about the timing of Merry's visit. Why had she chosen that day to storm Ivette's office? Had something been coming to a head with Ivette's lawsuit? Or was it something more?

I shook myself. Hyperion was right. Merry wasn't a suspect. But I glanced over my shoulder as we walked down the brick sidewalk, as if I might catch someone watching.

Chapter Nineteen

THE FOG CREPT IN after dark, a hallmark of California coastal winters. It pressed damply against the tearoom windows, studding them with droplets.

Unusual for a Monday night, Beanblossom's was hopping. Business owners from up and down the street filled the dining area. They mingled between white-clothed tables, beneath dangling snowflakes, and amidst holiday lights.

Hyperion had brought pomegranate champagne. I suspect he'd hoped the alcohol would loosen people's tongues.

Detective Baranko was the only one who drank tea (Earl Grey). But he'd made it clear he'd have preferred coffee. There's always one.

From behind the counter, I searched the crowd for Ivette. She wasn't among the other businessowners. Maybe her receptionist hadn't given her the invite. Or maybe we'd shot ourselves in the proverbial feet with the short notice.

A round-faced woman edged toward the big gingerbread house on the counter. My eyes narrowed. I'd already driven off three people who'd thought the house was an hors d'oeuvre. Granted, it smelled and looked delicious, but come on, people.

Besides, tonight I was serving my Killer Gingerbread Scones. I'd baked them with pieces of candied ginger. The ginger was strong enough that I kept the scones small. They were delicious, but some people found the ginger overpowering in large doses. Not me. But some people.

Hyperion clinked a champagne glass with a spoon. "Hear ye, hear ye. The introductory business watch meeting is about to begin." The crowd quieted.

The heavy, metal door down the hallway clanged shut. Ivette tiptoed into the dining area and looked around. She found a free seat at a table, and I relaxed.

"I'd like to introduce Detective Baranko." Hyperion motioned to the detective. "Detective, would you like to explain how a business watch works?"

The round-faced woman edged closer to the house. She reached for a green gumdrop.

I tensed. "That's for display only." I smiled.

"Oh! Sorry." Flushing, she sat on one of the counter stools. It was suspiciously near the gingerbread house.

Baranko glowered at me, and I clamped my jaw shut. "It's simple," the detective said. "It's a group of business owners who agree to work together to watch their community and liaise with the local police department to keep it safe. If you decide to create a watch, I'll be your liaison with the San Borromeo PD."

Oh, terrific. Fortunately, this business watch had about as much chance of getting off the ground as I did of going to the moon with a devil-may-care billionaire who owned his own spaceship.

Mrs. Henderson raised her hand, and the blood rushed from my face into my gut. *Ivette.* I glanced uneasily from the costume shop owner to Ivette. Mrs. Henderson had been having an affair with Emery Callum *after* he'd divorced Ivette. If we were lucky (and when did *that* happen?) there wouldn't be any hard feelings between them.

And if a catfight broke out, Baranko could deal with it. This time, I was staying put behind the counter. I glanced again at Ivette, seated at a table near the back hallway.

"But what do we actually *do*?" Mrs. Henderson asked.

The round-faced woman leaned her back against the counter. "It's just that..." She angled her head toward me. "I always wanted a gingerbread house as a child and never had one," she whispered.

"I've got smaller ones for sale," I said.

Baranko turned to glare again. I smiled weakly and shriveled inside.

"The most important thing is to stay active by coming to meetings," the detective said. "That helps you stay informed and keep others in the group informed. In the first meeting, members usually discuss concerns. From there, an action plan is developed." His narrow eyes glittered. "What concerns do you have?"

Mr. Jamison stood and brushed back his damp, blond hair. Was the damp from the fog or had he gotten in some surfing before the meeting? The surfboard in his shop had looked well loved.

"Emery Callum was killed in a robbery just down the street," the shop owner said. "That concerns me." The crowd muttered in agreement.

Baranko nodded. "Has anyone seen any suspicious activity that might have been connected to that? It would have been two Saturdays ago."

"There was a car parked behind my shop that didn't belong there," Mr. Jamison complained.

"What kind of car?" the detective asked.

"A red Tesla."

"Probably from one of those tech companies," a sparse, gray-haired woman who ran an apothecary shop said. Her narrow face creased with annoyance. "They're ruining the town. My rent went up fifty percent last year. How are we supposed to compete?"

"I heard a new tech company is taking over two of Callum's places on Main Street," Mr. Jamison said. "At least, that's what he told me." The buzz of the crowd rose.

A redheaded woman raised her hand. "Someone's cat keeps getting into my garbage bins."

"You sure it's not a raccoon?" a man asked her.

"It's definitely a cat," the redhead said. "I've seen it, and it makes a real mess. People should control their cats."

"That's impossible," the man scoffed. "They're cats."

"It's possible if their owners keep them indoors." She shot Hyperion a dark look.

He pressed a hand to his chest and bowed. "I assure you, Bastet does not roam about willy-nilly."

The tabby wandered into the room and meowed. Hyperion hurried to the cat and scooped him up. "He's an indoor cat." He vanished down the hallway with the tabby.

"Any *other* suspicious activity that may have been related to Mr. Callum's death?" Baranko asked wearily.

Hyperion eased into the dining area. An older blond woman raised her hand.

"Yes." The detective nodded to her.

"I thought there was going to be a secret Santa?" the blonde asked.

"I thought so too," another woman said, and I smothered a laugh.

Hyperion sprang in front of Baranko. My partner shook a goldfish bowl filled with strips of white paper. "Yes, that's correct. The secret Santa is on, never fear. We'll have the drawing a bit later. Now, who's seen anything sus?"

The crowd stared blankly at him. "That's short for suspicious," Hyperion clarified.

"Have you noticed how those young engineers move down the street in packs?" the redhead asked. "I've been forced to step off the sidewalk for a gang of them more than once."

"They're good eaters though," Mr. Salazar said.

"Nice," the redhead snapped. "The tech companies are great for the restaurants, but what are the rest of us going to do? We don't want to become like San Mateo."

The crowd fell silent. A chair squeaked against the floor.

"What happened in San Mateo?" I asked.

"Haven't you been there lately?" the redhead asked. "It's almost all restaurants now. The tech companies moved in, and the shops were driven out."

"They've got some great places to eat though," Hyperion muttered.

Baranko glared at him. "Any other sus— suspicious activity you'd like to report?"

A man cleared his throat. Barry, who ran the wine bar that backed onto our shared parking lot, raised his hand. He was dark haired and balding and had a good-sized mustache.

"Yes?" Baranko said, voice tinged with impatience.

"I'm not sure if this is suspicious or not." Barry's gaze darted around the room. "But I saw a delivery person at Callum's back door Saturday morning. The morning he died. Was killed, I mean."

I leaned forward, my stomach pressing against the counter. Egads, blimey, and jeepers. Was this business watch going to actually pay off?

"What time was this?" Baranko asked.

Barry squinted. "Around ten, I think?"

"What did he look like?" Baranko asked.

"I didn't pay much attention to him, quite honestly. We were prepping to open. I'd gone out back to take out some trash. I can see the back of his shop from there. I run the wine bar."

"What can you tell me about the delivery truck?" the detective said.

Barry shook his balding head. "I didn't notice a truck, but I wouldn't have. It was a busy Saturday."

"Why'd you notice the deliveryman?" Baranko asked.

"Because I was waiting for a delivery myself, and he wasn't it. A big crowd had reserved the wine bar for a lunch party—"

"Engineers?" the redhead asked. "I'll bet they were engineers."

"They might have been from one of the local tech companies," Barry admitted.

The meeting devolved from there. It was obvious Baranko was using it for the same reason we were—to investigate. And I didn't believe for a minute he was investigating a common robbery. Not after Merry's death. Which meant we were on the right track.

Or at least, we were on the same track Baranko was on. He must have figured that too, because he lingered after the meeting to get in some looming.

"Forget it, Baranko," I said as he towered over me by the blue front door. "I'm not telling you who my secret Santa is."

His broad face spasmed. "I heard about the fire at your house. If I find out it's somehow connected to my case—"

"The police on the scene seemed to think it was teens playing a very bad prank," I said. "Did you learn something different?"

His nostrils flared. "Your involvement in this case is over," he said. "If I catch you doing anything more than organizing a phone tree, I'll smack handcuffs on you so fast it'll make your head spin. Got it?"

"Mm, hm," I said meekly. "Handcuffs. Spanking. Spinning. Got it."

One elbow braced on the hostess stand, Hyperion made a choking sound. Baranko reddened.

"Sorry," I said. "Smacking. Smacking not spanking."

He stormed out the blue door. It slammed behind him, the bell jangling overhead.

"I'm not sure which one of us is the bad influence anymore," Hyperion complained. "But it's supposed to be me. Stay in your lane."

Weary, I looked around the tearoom. Twinkle lights blinked balefully. Used plates and glasses littered the tables. Most of the food was gone, so at least that was *something* I didn't have to clean up.

"I don't suppose we could put off the cleanup until tomorrow morning?" Hyperion asked.

My gaze flicked to the paper snowflakes dangling from the ceiling. "You mean when you're not here?"

"Yeah."

"No."

He sighed. "Let's get this over with."

Thanks to the power of my industrial dishwasher and the expedient of replacing the tablecloths, the clean-up wasn't awful. The floor could have done with a mop job, but I decided to take pity on Hyperion. I could squeeze that in tomorrow morning before opening.

We exited through the heavy metal door in back. Hyperion and Bastet watched while I locked it. The lock made an echoey click.

I cleared my throat. "There's something I need to tell you."

"No, you don't. I know it's not my fault Merry died. So I'll stop acting like a drama queen over it. But I have to tell you, I can't stop thinking over Merry's last reading. Maybe I *did* say something to her, or she said something—"

"No," I said. "You didn't." We walked toward my car.

Hyperion blew out his breath. "Sorry. I guess I should tell you that Tony's sniffing around our case. He's too by-the-book to admit he's investigating though."

"I figured. He came by my place last night to find out what I knew."

"I *told* him you knew what I knew, but he believes in..." He stopped short. "Uh. Was that there when you parked?"

Pieces of broken glass glittered on the pavement beside my hatchback. "No, no, no..." I muttered and hurried forward. My shoes crunched on the glass, and I stopped short, swaying. My driver's window was shattered, glittering pebbles strewn across the seat.

Chapter Twenty

My hands clenched. "Another broken window?" This was just getting repetitive. Not to mention expensive. Brik had given me a break on the tearoom's front window. But replacing it had still cost the GDP of a small Latin American country.

"Uh, you've got insurance." Hyperion picked up the cat and examined his paws for glass. "Right?"

I shifted on the pavement, and a piece of glass crunched beneath my tennis shoe. "Right." But my shoulders slumped. I wouldn't report this to the insurance company. They'd just jack up my rates. *Again*. In the long run, it would be cheaper to fix it myself.

A flash of white sailed through the darkness and landed on a nearby phone booth, which the town or phone company had somehow overlooked in the age of cellphones. It had actually become a hot selfie spot. The seagull fluttered its wings and sat on the closed lid as if it were settling in for the night.

Beneath Hyperion's arm, the tabby hissed at the bird. My partner pulled his phone from the pocket of his slacks.

"Who are you calling?" I asked.

"I'm not. I'm making an online police report. Didn't you hear Baranko at the meeting? We can make reports for petty crimes online now. It sounded like the police preferred it to talking to us plebs."

And that way we could do our duty and make a report while avoiding Baranko. *Clever.*

Hyperion frowned, thumbs poised above the phone screen. "Was anything taken?"

I hurried to the passenger side of my Mazda and unlocked the door, opened the glove box. My favorite pocketknife was still there, and the car docs looked undisturbed. "No..."

My gaze traversed the seat, littered with broken glass. "Hold on. My Valentine's file is gone."

Hyperion arched a brow. "You keep files on Valentine's Day? Keeping track of your exes or already plotting a romantic evening with Gino?"

My stomach lurched. I still hadn't heard from Gino since that awful night. "No," I said shortly. "For the tearoom." I looked under the seats and checked the back in case I'd put it somewhere else. "It's definitely gone."

"It was in one of your manila folders?"

"This one was red." Sue me. I'd gone thematic. But it made it easier to keep track of holidays.

"What kind of thief steals a file folder and leaves a cool pocketknife?" he asked.

Our gazes locked, and I swore. It was getting harder to believe this had been a random crime. Not when everyone knew we were investigating a murder.

Murders, I mentally corrected. Because I didn't believe for a minute Merry had taken her own life. In a way, the theft was proof that someone connected to the crimes was still out there.

Hyperion shook his head. "I know what you're thinking. This doesn't prove anything about Merry's death."

"But it's suggestive."

His brow furrowed. "It is." He pocketed the phone. Shifting the cat under his arm, he scanned the parking lot. "Okay. Let's say I'm a thief. I've just smashed into your car and gotten away with a promising looking file. Except when I open it, it's not so promising. Unless I'm a rival tearoom owner desperate for Valentine's ideas. And we don't have any rivals in San Borromeo."

"Thankfully." I shuddered. I wasn't sure I could handle the competition.

"What do I do next?" he asked.

"Toss it."

"You take that side." Hyperion nodded to my right.

We turned on the lights on our phones and paced through the parking lot, our heads lowered. Since it was a Monday night and most restaurants were closed, there were only a few cars to maneuver between.

After ten minutes, I'd finished my side. "Anything?" I called.

"Nope." Transferring Bastet to his other arm, Hyperion raised his flashlight. It illuminated the garbage bin behind the wine bar.

Half-hearted, I shrugged. We had to take a look. If my file was in one of the bins, it would give us an idea which direction the thief had left in. And at least we wouldn't have to dumpster dive. If someone had tossed my file in a bin, it couldn't have been too long ago. The file should be near the top.

Standing on his toes, he peered inside the high bin. "I don't see it here."

I trailed after him as he circled the lot, looking inside the bins. Finally, we reached the bin nearest to Beanblossom's back door. The seagull had migrated from the phonebooth to the top of the dumpster. Atop its black lid, the bird's eyes glinted eerily. Bastet growled.

Hyperion flapped his hand at the bird. It made a dangerous sound in its throat. "Beat it. Vamoose. Scat."

The bird pecked the bin's black plastic lid warningly. Bastet's growl rose.

"Uh, you got any scones on you?" Hyperion asked.

Yes, and they were for me. "Why?" I asked, suspicious.

"A bribe for birdbrain here." He nodded toward the seagull.

"It's only a bird. Just shoo it away."

"Haven't you watched any Alfred Hitchcock? It's never only a bird." He shuddered. "That movie still gives me nightmares."

Resigned, I dug a wrapped scone from my purse and handed it to my partner. "Fine."

His mouth twisted. "You keep scones in your *purse*?"

"It's in plastic wrap. And why'd you ask if you didn't think I had any?"

Hyperion unwrapped the scone. "I thought you'd go get one from the tearoom." He broke off a piece and tossed it to the bird. The crumb bumped across the dumpster lid and fell behind it. The bird didn't react.

"You need to get it closer," I said.

"I have never seen such a lazy seagull. It's because people keep feeding them. It's outrageous."

"*We're* feeding it."

"Thanks for including yourself in that." Hyperion tossed another crumb to the bird. It sailed high over the seagull's head.

I sneered. "You couldn't hit the broad side of a barn, could you?"

Hyperion scowled and broke off a third piece. "Here, birdy. Here's a nice snack. Don't—"

The seagull bulleted from the garbage bin straight at Hyperion. Squawking, the bird flapped around his head. "Oh, my God," my partner shrieked. He flailed his arms. "Get it off. Get it away!" Bastet howled and climbed on top of Hyperion's head.

"Give him the scone," I shouted.

In a blur of motion, the scone bulleted from Hyperion's hand. There was a thud, and the bird dropped to the pavement.

Hyperion peered from beneath one arm and opened his eyes. "Is it gone?"

"You..." I stared, incredulous. "I think you killed it."

"What?" He looked down at the lifeless bird. "Dammit. That has *got* to be bad luck."

"It was for the bird."

Hyperion nudged the seagull with the toe of his shoe. "Maybe he's sleeping." He bent. "Does it look like it's breathing? It—"

The seagull burst into the air. Hyperion shrieked and stumbled backward, dropping Bastet to the ground. The bird flapped away.

Bastet huffed. The cat pulled a white feather from his paw with his teeth.

"Check the bin before it comes back," I said.

Hyperion staggered and clutched his chest. "No sympathy for me at all. Where's your milk of human kindness?" He raised the lid and drew in a breath. "Got it." He snapped a picture with his phone and stepped back, his eyes watering. "The file's there," he said. "Go for it."

"Ah... It's okay. Everything's on my computer. I don't really need the file."

He brushed off the lapel of his brown coat. "It may have fingerprints."

Oh. He was right. It might. "We could call Baranko," I said, without much hope.

He shot me a look. "Do you think he's going to come out for this?"

No. I really didn't. I shuffled my feet. "Can you reach it?"

He raised his chin. "It's in a dumpster. I'm not touching it. Bad enough I had to open all those lids. Besides, it's your file."

"Nice," I said acidly. "How am I supposed to get it? I can't even see inside." On very rare occasions, being short has its advantages.

"Maybe you can stand on a box." He looked around. "Here." He grabbed a cardboard box and turned it upside down.

I stepped on it. The box collapsed beneath my weight. The cat huffed. Atop the flattened box, I folded my arms. "Just get the file."

He scowled. "Fine." He stood on tiptoe and reached inside the dumpster. "I can't reach it. It's right in the center of everything. On the positive side, there's nothing moldering, undigested, or parasitic on top of it."

"More Lovecraft?"

"Natch. That means naturally, for you luddites. Here. I'll boost you."

"What do you mean, boost me?"

"So you can reach the file." He laced his hands together and held them low.

"Look at what I'm wearing." I motioned to my ivory slacks and sweater. "I don't want any part of my clothing touching that garbage bin."

This wasn't me being as much of a princess as it sounds. I've cleaned up plenty of disgusting messes in my time. You wouldn't believe the things that have gone on in the tearoom bathroom, or the mess a woman giving birth there makes. It was enough to make me rethink the entire process.

But the sides of that garbage bin were truly terrible. They were an antediluvian, infected abomination, to steal words from Hyperion's calendar. My budget, home dry-cleaning kit wouldn't cut the cleanup. And the real dry cleaners were horribly expensive.

"What if you draped your scarf over the edge?" he asked.

I clutched the crimson scarf against my chest. "My grandfather gave me this scarf. Its cashmere."

He rolled his eyes. "What if your hands only touched the sides of the bin? Would that work?"

Wary, I nodded. Like I said: not a princess. It was still gross, but hands I could wash. Bastet lashed his tail.

"Get on my shoulders." Hyperion got on one knee. I stared at him. "Get on my shoulders," he said, "and we will never speak of this again."

"Fine. Let's get this over with." I got onto his shoulders, and he lifted me up. I swayed and grabbed the side of the dumpster for balance. It was revoltingly damp, and I told myself that was just from the fog. *Yeah. Just the fog.* I reached for the red folder.

"Careful," Hyperion said, and I straightened.

"You don't want to smear any prints," he continued.

I stretched forward, hanging onto the side of the bin so I didn't pitch inside.

"Oh, hey," Hyperion said brightly. "I've got gloves. I forgot Tony gave them to me."

I straightened and glared. This was lost on him since my view was the top of his dark head. But he could have remembered the gloves before I'd had to touch anything.

He waved the gloves high in the air. "You don't want to smear any prints."

"No," I ground out, snatching them from his hand. "I don't." I snapped on the sheer, rubbery gloves and stretched forward.

The parking lot lights went out, plunging us into darkness. I swore. Bastet's eyes glowed.

"Got your phone?" Hyperion asked.

"In my pocket," I caroled through gritted teeth. I pulled it out. It took three attempts to turn on its flashlight with the gloves on, but I finally managed it.

Golden hair flashed near my hip, and I yelped.

Brik looked up at me. "Uh, what are you doing?"

"I'm trying to get my Valentine's recipes back," I snapped. Why did the universe hate me? What other humiliations did it have in store for tonight? There was no reason for my neighbor to be here. And I looked like an idiot.

Hyperion turned to face Brik, and since I was on his shoulders, I turned with him. "It may be crucial evidence in a murder investigation," my partner said. "Fingerprints, you know. Someone stole it from Abigail's car."

Brik was silent for a long moment. "You want a plastic bag for that then?"

Hyperion shrugged, and I grabbed his hair to keep from tumbling off his shoulders. He yelped.

"I'll take that for yes." Brik walked away, presumably to get a bag of some sort. I finally retrieved the damn folder and opened it. "Everything's still there."

"Great." Hyperion grunted. "Will you get off me now?"

"Oh," I said. "Right."

He lowered to one knee again, and I clambered off his shoulders. Brik returned with an oversized sandwich bag. I slid the file inside and peeled off the gloves, tossing them in the dumpster.

Brik had also brought a rag and hand sanitizer, bless him. I cleaned off my hands while Hyperion called Tony.

"...thought you might be able to help us with the prints." Hyperion yanked the phone from his ear and winced. So did I. I could hear Tony's shout from where I stood.

Hyperion returned the phone to his ear. "Do you really think he would have come for a car break-in...? We used your gloves, and it's in a plastic bag... But I don't want to... But... Are you *sure*?" He hung his head. "Fine." He hung up and pocketed the phone. "We need to call Baranko."

"I don't want to call Baranko," I said.

"But if this folder has the fingerprints of a killer, we have to," he said.

It *was* the only responsible thing to do, dammit.

We called Baranko.

Chapter Twenty-One

"You shouldn't have touched that file." Baranko glowered in his rumpled suit and folded his arms. At his ankles, Bastet batted playfully at his brown shoelace.

The twinkle lights in the tearoom windows made a cheerful frame around the big detective. Since they were on batteries, they were the tearoom's only illumination. Power hadn't only gone off in the parking lot. The whole block was out.

But the tiny lights had impressive wattage. I could see the blot of tomato sauce staining Baranko's tie. We'd caught him in the middle of a late dinner.

"So I've been told," Hyperion said wearily. "Repeatedly." He crossed his legs and propped his elbow on the table, rumpling the fresh, white cloth.

"It was probably a petty thief," the detective said for the third time.

"Then why are you here?" I leaned against the counter beside Brik. He sat on a barstool eating a leftover Killer Ginger Scone from my purse.

"Because you called me," Baranko snapped, edging away from the cat. "And what's he doing here?" He jabbed his thumb toward Brik.

"I was in the neighborhood," Brik said easily.

"All right." Hyperion stood and stretched, arching his back. "Then if we're done—"

"Sit down," the detective said.

Hyperion sat.

Baranko's eyes narrowed. "Why do you two think there's something more to this than a random car break-in?"

I stiffened, glancing at Hyperion. The question was a trap. I could hear it in his voice. Also, who would break into a car just to steal a file folder?

"It seems a little too on the nose," Hyperion said. "Don't you think? A car break-in outside a neighborhood watch meeting?"

I relaxed. Hyperion had seen it too. Baranko wanted us to admit we were involved in the investigation, i.e. interfering. And of course, we were. But we weren't dumb enough to admit it.

"Business watch," the detective corrected. "And that wasn't what I was asking. Why would someone breaking into your car be connected to Emery Callum's murder? What connection do you two have to him?"

"I barely knew the man," I said quietly. And we'd been neighbors. Even if he had been a miser and a hard-ass, I should have made the effort to know him better.

"What was Ivette Callum doing here tonight?" Baranko asked.

Hyperion raised his brows. "We invited her. Her office isn't far."

"And Merry Callum?"

"Uh, we didn't invite her," Hyperion said. "And she couldn't have broken into Abigail's car. She's dead."

Baranko fixed me with a long, uncomfortable stare. "I meant, what's your connection to her? Aside from your boyfriend."

"We told you before," Hyperion said. "She was a client. Both she and Ivette came to the tearoom the day of Emery Callum's murder."

"Why?" Baranko repeated. "Why you two?" Bastet meowed and pawed at the detective's brown loafer.

"Because it's a tearoom," I said, frustrated, "and it was nearby. Or at least that was what they told me. Merry showed up after Ivette, and they argued. Hyperion took Merry into his office for a reading, and Ivette left."

"Why is this the first I'm hearing about an argument?" the detective asked.

Hyperion shrugged and leaned back in his chair. "It's the first time you asked."

The tips of his nostrils whitened. "What did they argue about?"

"Merry was upset that Ivette was suing Emery," I said. "Something to do with the alimony, I believe."

Baranko strode to the counter and loomed over me. "And?"

My jaw hardened. Using his height was a cheap intimidation trick. "I think that was all," I said tightly.

His face reddened. "Bull. You know more. Do you think I'm an idiot? You two have been playing detectives again. A murder down the street was too much for you to pass up. Withholding evidence in a murder investigation is a crime."

"We don't have any evidence," I said. "I mean, maybe the stolen Valentine's file, and we gave that to you."

"What do you know?" He leaned closer, and I didn't edge away, even if his breath did smell like garlic.

My hand flattened on the counter. I was not going to be bullied in my own tearoom for doing the right thing.

"Nothing," Hyperion blurted. "We know nothing, I mean, we know Emery owns a lot of property on Main Street, and he might have been having an affair with Mrs. Henderson, who's also some sort of local property magnet. He made her trustee, but the will or trust is a mess, so it looks like she might have inherited everything. Merry was pretty salty over that. Oh, Ivette got some money too—she was still a beneficiary on some brokerage account, a cool half-mil, but Ivette and Merry alibi each other. They were arguing all morning at Ivette's office when Emery died. The receptionist overheard them. And then after Merry left, Ivette complained to the receptionist about her for another thirty minutes or so, which leaves Jonasz, who seems like a decent fellow and is hard up for money. He's working part-time here for Abigail now, because you know Abigail, she's a sucker for a hard luck story, and his daughter's *really* sick but he needs to get a full-time job though with good insurance, so this is just a temporary thing. And that basically leaves Jonasz and Mrs. Henderson as the prime suspects, unless one of his tenants killed him. Callum's been raising the rent and driving people out so he can rent to tech companies. See? We don't know anything you don't know. It's all just gossip."

Baranko blinked. He grabbed the plastic bag with the folder off the counter and strode out the blue door. The bell jangled over his head. Bastet loosed a mournful howl.

"Good going," Brik said through a mouthful of scone.

Hyperion sagged in his chair. "He knew I was the weak link," he muttered.

"You don't say?" I braced my fists on my hips.

"This is a good scone," Brik said. "It's got some serious ginger."

"Yes," Hyperion said. "It's very manly, puts hair on your chest. And it's haunted."

"It's not haunted," I said. "How can a scone be haunted?" Why did everything with him have to be supernatural?

"But there's a totally supernatural history of gingerbread." My partner shifted in the gloom. "Didn't you know? There's an old story that gingerbread men were actually poppets." He lowered his voice. The twinkle lights flickered.

"What's a poppet?" Brik asked.

"It's like a voodoo doll," my partner said. "Witches would bake them in the form of their victim and then eat them to kill the person. They were actually made illegal in parts of Europe for that reason. Gingerbread was so closely associated with witchcraft that the Germans began making Hexenhuts, or witch huts, out of gingerbread."

"So why do we have them at Christmas?" Brik asked.

"Everything got mixed up when so many Germans emigrated to Pennsylvania and brought the tradition with them." He nodded to my enormous gingerbread house on the counter. "That's a witch hut."

"It's not a—" I hissed a breath. The peppermint above its front door was gone. "Someone stole a peppermint."

"You should get right on that," Brik said. "It was probably the same person who broke into your car."

"Ha," I said flatly. "Ha ha. You're hilarious."

"Hilarious comes from the Latin," Hyperion said. "In fact, there was an ancient roman festival called Hilaria—"

"Oh, shut up." I marched into the kitchen, found a bag of peppermint rounds, and whipped up some frosting.

When I returned, both men lounged companionably at the counter in the dim light. Brik finished the last Killer Ginger scone. My stomach grumbled. I'd been so busy serving food, I hadn't gotten a chance to eat. It was why I'd pocketed all those scones in the first place.

"...thought Abigail had organized her notes on the crime in that folder," Hyperion was saying. "Little do they know she's got a murder board in her living room."

"Really?" Brik swiveled to face me. "You've got a murder board?"

I scrubbed a hand over my face. "Razzzor was at my place this weekend." And I should have asked him if he had any job openings for Jonasz. Razzzor's company had a great benefit package. I'd ask him next time we spoke.

"Cool." Brik stood. "I'll see you home. I've got a broom in the truck. We can clean up the glass."

"Oh my GOD!" Hyperion leapt to his feet, and we started.

"What?" I asked. He'd figured out the murders?

"Gingerbread Tarot cards! They'd sell like crazy to my clients and to yours. It's genius. I'm a genius." He grabbed my arm. "You can do it, can't you?"

"Sure, if I had a frosting printer, which I don't."

"Frosting printer. Got it." Hyperion jogged down the hall. He returned, grabbed the tabby, and hurried away. The back door clanged shut, then clanged shut again, Hyperion double-checking it was closed.

Brik grinned. "Because you're not too busy or anything."

"It is a great idea," I admitted. I should have thought of it myself.

I locked up again. Brik and I swept the glass from inside and around my car and dumped it in one of the garbage bins. Brik taped clear plastic sheeting over the broken window. "That'll get you to a garage to get it repaired."

"Thanks," I said, meeting his gaze. "For sticking around. I know you hate all this mur—police stuff." Being falsely accused of a heinous crime would do that.

He clipped the broom into a metal fastener in the side of his truck bed. "It's okay. I don't like it, but I've built a sense of distance."

A dark, empty pit opened in my gut. *Distance from murder, or from me*? "Oh," I said. "Good."

The phone rang in my purse, and I answered it without checking the number. "Hello?"

"It's Gino."

My heart jumped. "Oh. Hi." I straightened my spine, bracing myself. At least he was reaching out. That had to be a good sign.

"I wanted to apologize. I was a jerk the other night. Merry... I was a jerk, and that's on me."

"No," I said, and my legs wobbled a little with relief. This was going to be okay. "I mean, yeah, but your aunt. It would have shaken anyone."

"And we had a date on Friday. I didn't even cancel."

Brik slammed the door of the truck bed shut.

"Yeah," I said. "But it was kind of obvious that was a no-go."

"Monday's your free day, isn't it? I don't suppose I can make it up to you tonight, if it's not too late."

I glanced at Brik. "It's not too late," I said.

"Great," Gino said. "Um... Should I come by your place?"

"I'm actually in town. Why don't I meet you at that Chinese restaurant? I think it's open on Mondays."

"Perfect. I'll see you in thirty minutes. Bye."

"Bye." I hung up.

"A date?" Brik asked, expressionless.

"You don't have to sound so surprised. It's demoralizing."

He smiled faintly. "I'm not surprised at all."

Something squirmed in my chest. "Well. Thanks again."

He watched while I walked to my car. It was ridiculous to drive to the restaurant. It wasn't far. But I didn't want Brik to offer to escort me there, and I suspected he would if I started off on foot.

Or maybe he wouldn't have, and that would have been even more demoralizing.

Chapter Twenty-Two

I PAUSED IN FRONT of the Chinese restaurant's arched red door. The restaurant must have been outside the zone of the power outage, because the golden lamps bracketing the entrance were on. They made dim globes in the nighttime fog. I pulled my cranberry scarf closer around my neck. My usual pre-date butterflies changed to something darker, heavier.

I reached for the gold-painted door handle, then let my hand drop. I liked Gino. He was a good man with a moral code. But I wasn't sure I fit inside it anymore, or if I ever had.

I knew I tended to be pricklier than maybe I should be about boundaries and independence. Both were important, but they could be taken too far.

Here's the thing. I'd once been inflicted with a cyber stalker. Razzzor had rescued me from the situation. After that, it was hard to know where a healthy boundary ended, and the Great Wall of China began.

I also knew I tended to hang onto relationships maybe longer than I should. In short, my instincts regarding relationships weren't always the best.

I pushed open the tall door and walked inside. A miniature Christmas tree stood beside the cash register on the high, wooden counter. Delightful warmth blossomed around me, and I relaxed, scanning the crowd. As one of the few restaurants open Monday night, it was packed.

The manager, Mr. Chen, hurried to meet me. "I'm sorry I couldn't make the meeting tonight. How was it?"

"We agreed to meet again next month. I'll send you an email about it if you want."

"Yes, please. Can I get you a table?"

"For two. I'm meeting someone."

He found me a quiet corner table, and I sat facing the door so I could hail Gino when he walked in. I ordered a beer and studied the menu. It hadn't changed since the last time I'd been there, but pretending to read killed time while I waited.

Gino arrived on time five minutes later. He handed the hostess his long coat and hurried to the table, bending to kiss my cheek. "Am I late?"

I smiled. "No, I was early." And I really hoped I didn't smell like dumpster.

"Good. You look great."

He didn't look so bad himself in his charcoal business suit and tie. With his dark hair and eyes, it made him look dangerous in all the right ways.

Fabric rustled behind me. Jonasz, in a black vest and slacks and white shirt, appeared beside our table. "Good evening. I'll be your waiter tonight. Can I get you something to drink?" he asked Gino.

Gino stiffened. I did a doubletake. "Jonasz?" I said. "I didn't know you worked here."

"Since last week," he said. "Nights only. But it won't interfere with my job at the tearoom."

"I wasn't worried about that," I said. "I'm glad you found other work." Feeling warm, I pulled off my scarf and folded it, laying it by my arm on the table.

"I'll have what she's having," Gino said, curt. Jonasz nodded and left.

"Is this why you suggested the Chinese restaurant?" Gino asked me.

"No. I just knew it was open tonight. Had I known Jonasz worked here too, I would have suggested another place. The poor man's got to be sick of me ordering him around."

Beneath his well-fitting suit, Gino's muscular shoulders loosened. "You really didn't know."

"He told me he had other jobs. I didn't ask where. I could only offer him part-time work at the tearoom."

Gino studied me. "Why *did* you offer?"

"Well, he asked, and I… I know what it's like to not know where your next paycheck is coming from." But unlike Jonasz, I'd always had a backstop—my grandfather. I'd known that no matter what happened, I'd always have a place to go, a roof over my head. And I didn't know what it was like to be responsible for a vulnerable, sick child. But I could imagine. "He's been a real help."

"The tearoom's doing well?"

"We're on budget." I wasn't sure how, but we'd made our first year projections. Barely. "It's a Christmas miracle," I joked, then turned serious. "How are you holding up?"

He looked down at his empty plate. "I'm not sure. I don't have to deal with my uncle's estate anymore, not with Merry…" He quirked his head and grimaced. "It's a relief and a horror all at once."

I laid my hand on his. "I'm so sorry about your aunt." He swallowed and didn't respond. "Have the police said anything?" I asked.

His expression turned bleak. "She took pills first. The same pills Emery had taken before he was killed."

"What?" I withdrew my hand. I hadn't known Emery had been drugged before being attacked. The fact was, I didn't know many of the details at all. And that was a problem.

He nodded. "The police think this was a murder-suicide."

"But wasn't Merry with Ivette when your uncle was killed?" I didn't actually know this was true, since I didn't know the exact time of his uncle's death. But maybe Gino had more intel than I did.

"She left Ivette's office after ten. She could have gone to my uncle's office and... There was time."

I shifted in my chair. It was possible. But something about it didn't seem right. "Or maybe the same person who drugged your uncle drugged her," I said slowly.

"No." He shook his head. "The drugs were from his own medicine cabinet. How could anyone else have known what he was on? He didn't advertise it."

"Murder suicide... That's..." *Strange*. When I heard about them on the news, they seemed to happen in quick succession. Murder first. Suicide immediately after. The killer didn't commit suicide days later out of remorse.

"I know."

And I wasn't an expert in murder suicides. "I learned a bit about California estate law from my grandfather," I said. "It's been over a week since your uncle's death. Wouldn't Merry's share of your uncle's estate go to her heirs, not his?"

"Yes. A friend of Merry's is her executor, and I..." He exhaled slowly. "I—"

Jonasz set a glass of beer in front of Gino. "Have you had a chance to look over the menu?"

"I'll have the egg rolls and the Mu Shu pork with brown rice," Gino said.

"May I have the crispy sesame chicken with white rice?" I asked.

Jonasz bobbed his head. "Sure thing." He strode toward the kitchen.

"Sorry," Gino said. "I'm just not comfortable talking around that guy."

I wrinkled my forehead. "Why not?"

"Merry told me he wasn't honest, couldn't be trusted."

"Oh." My chest hardened. I crossed my arms, uncrossed them. Was I defensive on Jonasz's behalf? Or was I defensive because I'd hired him without checking references? Usually, I *did* check references. I couldn't afford problems in the tearoom. "Anything specific?"

"No," he said. "She wouldn't tell me anything more. But why would she lie?"

"She might not have lied. She might have just been wrong."

"Merry may have been a killer, but she had a pretty good head on her shoulders. Don't let her running to a fortune teller at the end color your opinion."

"Versus my opinion of her possibly killing her husband?" I asked, incredulous. And I *worked* with that fortune teller.

He held up a hand. "Yes, I know that fortune teller is your partner and friend, and he is a good guy. I'm just saying, she obviously wasn't operating at her best."

That much was obvious. I unfurled my cloth napkin with a snap and changed the subject. "But who's going to deal with Emery's estate now? Mrs. Henderson?" I arranged the napkin in my lap.

"Looks that way. And Merry left everything to me, so—"

"Wait. What?" I gaped. *He* was Merry's beneficiary?

"Yeah." He laughed shortly. "Can you believe it? With the mess Emery's estate is in, I'm not sure when or if I'll see anything."

"Do the police know this?"

Gino rolled a shoulder in a shrug. "I just found out. I'm sure they will too."

I plucked at my scarf, lying on the table. If they weren't so certain Merry was the killer, Gino would have to be a suspect. "Hold on. Who called Jonasz at nine-thirty to tell him his daughter was in the hospital? Merry and Ivette were together at that time."

"I'm sure the police have figured that out."

"I'm not." I'd gotten the sense from Tony that ego and laziness could get in the way of an investigation. Sometimes the urge to close cases trumped ensuring the correct person was arrested. Tony would never do such slipshod work. But Tony wasn't a cop anymore.

"The phone call probably had nothing to do with the murder."

"That doesn't seem likely," I said, appetite gone. "The timing was pretty convenient for the killer."

Laughter rose at a nearby table, and I glanced their way. A family of five celebrating a birthday.

"Look, let's not talk about it," he said. "It's been a rough couple of weeks. I'd rather just relax."

"Sorry. It's gotten a little personal. You know that Christmas tree that was beside my front door the other night?"

"I meant to ask you about that." He took a swig of his beer. "Do you need help setting it up?"

"Not anymore," I said. "Someone set it on fire."

He set down the beer. "You're kidding me. Was there much damage?"

"No. I mean, we're going to have to do something about the door and the paint. But the house itself didn't catch fire."

"You were lucky." He shook his head. "Idiots. Teens don't understand the ramifications of their actions."

In violation of the rules of etiquette, I braced an elbow on the table. The crimson cloth rumpled beneath my arm. "It wasn't a teen. Someone broke into my car tonight, smashed the front window. The only thing they took was a file folder."

Gino frowned. "What was in it?"

"Plans for our Valentine's tea." I wondered what Baranko would make of my rose-petal scones.

"Do you have copies?"

"Yes, but that's not the point. They didn't know what they were stealing. They probably thought they were taking case notes."

"Maybe someone really wanted your scone recipes." He smiled slightly.

My hand clenched on my scarf, crumpling its fine fabric. "Well, they must have been disappointed by what was inside. We found the file with the recipes in the dumpster by Beanblossom's back door."

Gino shook his head. "Petty criminals aren't known for their thinking skills. It's why they're petty criminals."

"Detective Baranko thinks there's more to it. He took the file for fingerprints."

"You're working with Baranko?" He sat back in his chair. "That's a relief." A waitress carrying a tray bustled past.

"I'm not working with him," I said sharply.

"You ought to. Otherwise you might get arrested for interfering in his investigation." He leaned forward. "Look, I know you like to do things on your own, and I admire that about you. But there's a reason we have police. We train them and pay them so they can devote their time to chasing criminals. They're professionals."

Augh. "Yes," I said with forced calm. And why was my heart thumping, heat rushing to my face? Was I that insecure? "It's a pretty good system. But it's full of people, and people are flawed."

"You think Baranko's a dirty cop?"

"No," I admitted. Even Tony had told me that he was one of the better ones. But that didn't make Baranko right.

"The system's here for a reason," Gino said. "We voted for it. We support it with our tax dollars. We're a part of it. And the police are the experts. They have information you don't."

"And I have information they don't. Or I did. We've told Baranko everything we know. But the cops don't always get it right. Innocent people get convicted. The system isn't perfect."

"Neither are you."

My shoulders tightened, my anger rising. The menu on the table felt cool and plastic beneath my fingers. Beside the small white vase, a poinsettia leaf lay on the crimson tablecloth. Voices rose and fell around us, people having normal conversations that weren't straying into dangerous territory.

"Fair enough." I nodded. "But if I fail, it's on me. If the system fails and I could have prevented that, that's on me too. I prefer the first option."

"That's on you?" Both his brows lifted. "Really," he said, his tone disbelieving. "I just walked out of a situation where my uncle figured he could ignore the experts and draw up his own trust. And he had a fairly complex estate with multiple properties. He left a disaster for his widow to deal with, at a time when she didn't need any more disasters. So excuse me if I'm just not feeling it for the plucky amateurs right now."

"Fair enough again. If I ever had an estate of any value, I'd see a lawyer. But the situations aren't the same. Cops do rely on citizens to assist in solving crimes. That's what neighborhood watches are for. And Hyperion and I have solved murders. More than once. We may not have all the resources the cops do. But we have our own individual knowledge and skill sets."

"Then you should get a license and become a private investigator. There's a reason they require licenses."

I crossed my arms and kept them that way. "Oh? And what's that?"

"So you don't have amateurs claiming they can solve crimes and wasting people's money."

"You think a PI license automatically means the PI is competent? *Hairdressers* in California need licenses, and trust me, I've had some bad cuts." And the only person who's money I was wasting on this investigation was me.

"It means they've attained a certain level of knowledge."

"And so have I."

"No, Abigail," he said flatly. "You haven't. And your obsession with murder seems borderline unhealthy."

At a nearby table, waiters in black and white gathered and sang the birthday song.

"It's not unhealthy to want to—to take up the responsibility to put things right."

"It is if it's none of your business."

"Do you think I'm delusional or just overconfident?" I asked when the song finished.

"I don't know what to think."

I dug through my purse and set two twenties on the table. "Well, when you figure it out, let me know."

And I left.

Chapter Twenty-Three

I WASN'T PROUD ABOUT walking out on Gino last night. I didn't like walking away from arguments. It was cowardly. But I hadn't seen ours going anywhere useful—my temper had been too hot. And I also didn't like arguing in public.

Also, Gino hadn't been entirely wrong.

From an outsider's perspective, an amateur trying to solve a murder *was* nuts. The police had more training and resources, not to mention authority.

But Hyperion and I weren't inexperienced. And the murders had been hard to ignore. Merry and Ivette had come to us, in a sense, by coming to the tearoom. And then Merry had become Hyperion's client.

And then Merry had died.

And yes, I was rationalizing as I made scones in the tearoom kitchen. I hate being wrong in a fight as much as the next person.

"Morning, Abigail." Jonasz strolled into the kitchen, the first to arrive.

"Hey." I looked quickly away as he tied on an apron.

To my relief, he didn't mention last night's hasty exit when he came to work at Beanblossom's. I didn't know if he was just being polite, or if Gino had made a good excuse for me. And I didn't want to ask.

So I baked scones and served tea. And then I ducked into Hyperion's empty office to call Razzzor. I could at least do *something* besides rehashing last night's argument.

"Hey, Abs. Did you solve the murder?"

"Not yet," I said. "You?"

He released a gusty sigh. "Nope. What's going on?"

I dropped into Hyperion's high-backed chair. "I was wondering... I told you about Jonasz, he's working for me right now?"

"Yeah?"

"He needs a better job. But I'm not sure where, and I'm not sure he sees all the possibilities either. How would you feel about an informational interview with him? To try and figure out if any of his skills might fit in a tech company? Not yours," I said. "I'm not trying to guilt you into anything—"

"Especially since he's a murder suspect."

"Right," I said slowly. I'd just suggested one of my best friends sit down with a possible killer. And Razzzor had already done so much for me. I was starting to feel like I was abusing our friendship. This was a bad idea. "You know—"

"Actually," he said, "an informational interview could work."

"It could?"

"Sure. It gives me an excuse to interrogate him. And if there's a place at one of my companies, I can sign him up for a background check."

"Ah..." *Background checks*? I mean, yeah, that would be useful. But it all seemed so official. What had I gotten Jonasz into? "Okay. Thanks. I'll talk to him about it, see if he's interested. I wanted to talk to you first, so I didn't get his hopes up."

"No, no, no. This is great. I've got forms." He hung up.

I wasn't sure what that meant, but I hurried into the kitchen and found Jonasz. "Hey, would you be interested in doing an informational interview at a tech company?" I asked him.

Jonasz turned from the open industrial washer. "An informational interview? What is that?"

"You wouldn't be interviewing for a job. You'd be trying to figure out if your experience and background fit in somewhere at a company like Razzzor's. It would help with designing a resume, figuring out what to say in interviews, and maybe get you some contacts. There are so many tech companies opening up around here. I suspect they pay better than tearooms and Chinese restaurants."

"Why not? Who is Razzzor?"

"That's a longer story. I used to work for him. He owns a few companies." *In the Fortune* 500. Pulling an order pad from my apron pocket, I scrawled the name of one of his operations on it. I handed it to Jonasz. "You can find out more online. If you decide you want to talk to him, I'll set something up."

"Of course, I want to talk to him. I need work with better pay. No offense."

I smiled. "None taken."

We served lunch and re-set for the next cleanup. I'd just opened the industrial washer when Hyperion staggered into the kitchen. His head was hidden behind the two cardboard boxes he carried. He set both on the metal counter and braced his hands on his hips. "Hey, girl. Got the printer."

I pulled a steaming rack from the dishwasher and blinked. *Printer?* Then I remembered the gingerbread Tarot card idea. Did I have time for another project? I dropped the rack on the counter. The cups inside clinked.

"The best part," Hyperion said, "is we don't have to limit this to the holidays. We can print on sugar cookies the rest of the year. Or whatever." He ripped open the big box.

I set down the heavy plastic rack of clean plates. "That's an edible ink printer?" The picture on the box looked like the printer I had at home. A waitress bustled into the kitchen and grabbed a tray of scones.

"No," Hyperion said. "It's a regular ink jet printer. It's the ink and paper that's edible. I sent you links to online videos about the process. Didn't you watch any of them last night?" The waitress strode into the hallway.

"No. I was..." I smoothed the front of my holiday apron with a quick, forceful movement. "I was busy."

"So was I. And I have news. The police think Emery was killed sometime between nine-forty-five and ten-thirty."

I glanced at the open kitchen door. "And Jonasz left the store at nine-thirty. How did they get the time of death narrowed down?"

"There was a witness. A vendor called the store and spoke with the victim around nine forty-five. Have you been able to get anything out of Gino about the will imbroglio?"

My neck tensed. "Good word, imbroglio," I said lightly. "No."

Hyperion rolled his eyes. "He's a prime source, Abigail. I know you don't want to take advantage—"

"Now that Merry's dead, he's no longer involved." The words came out in a rush. "He was only helping her out because she asked. And she has her own executor."

"So you have talked to him? What else did he say?"

Heat rose to my cheeks. "He's..." I leaned against the metal table in the kitchen's center and folded my arms. "Merry left everything to him."

"Whoa. That—"

"Makes him a suspect," I said testily. "I know."

"Hm." He gave me a sharp look. "Something else going on I should know about?"

"No," I said shortly. "How's Tony?"

"Tony's totes on board with our investigation. How do you think I got the intel from the police?"

Totes...? Ah. Totally. Got it. I relaxed my arms. "How did he get the intel?"

"He's still got a few friends with the SBPD. The edible paper and ink are in the other box. Ta." He strode from the kitchen.

I scowled at the boxes. Something told me gingerbread Tarot cards were going to be a lot of work, even with a printer. But I was too busy to worry about that now.

I got back to unloading dishes. The next seating swarmed in, and I eased back into the regular ebb and flow of the tearoom.

But when I drove home that night, I was already thinking about the cards. A Death card gingerbread cookie was out, and so was the Devil. They didn't represent evil per se. The cards were more warnings against destructive behavior. But they didn't exactly scream holiday spirit.

I turned onto my street, and the thud of bass vibrated through my car. I muttered a curse. My hands tightened on the wheel. *Patience.* Brik needed this.

I slowed to a stop in front of my driveway. A strange BMW blocked it. Swearing some more, I drove down the street until I found a spot. My easygoing compassion evaporated, and I stormed to Brik's blue house.

I didn't bother to ring the bell. The door was open. I would have strode inside, eyes blazing. But the house was too packed with people for striding, even with my short legs. I squeezed past construction workers and CEOs and popped out near the kitchen bar.

"Abigail!" My grandfather swiveled on a barstool and raised a beer stein in my direction. "You made it."

Beside him, Tomas grinned. "Have a beer?"

"I'd better." If I didn't calm down, I was going homicidal. *Patience.* Maybe the universe had sent Gramps and Tomas here to remind me to listen to my own better angels. "What are you two doing here?" I shouted over the music.

"Eh?" My grandfather put his hand to one ear and shook his head.

"Your grandfather wanted to take another look at the fire damage," Tomas shouted.

Someone handed me a red plastic cup, and I took a swig, coughed. It was a margarita strong enough to make me sway.

"Someone will be by tomorrow to strip the paint," Tomas continued.

"Okay," I hollered back. The usual twinkle lights above the bar were gone. And then I realized there weren't any holiday decorations inside the house either. I'd have thought Brik would have had some to make the party more festive. "Where's Brik?"

My grandfather pointed to the wall of glass that made up the back of the house. "Outside."

I nodded and wound made my way through the crush. The glass doors were open. Eagerly, I stepped outside and sucked in a gulp of fresh air. It was an unseasonably warm night, still in the high sixties or low seventies. There were even more people on the patios.

I walked down the wide concrete steps to the seating area beneath a modern pergola. Usually it had white lights on it as well, but those, too, were gone. Brik stood by the smoking barbecue with a trio of younger men.

I didn't wait for a break in the conversation. "Someone's blocking my driveway."

"Whoa," Brik said. "Sorry. What kind of car is it?"

"A blue BMW."

"That's Parker's. I'll take care of it."

"Thanks," I said. Maybe that gulp of margarita had mellowed me. "What happened to the lights?" I motioned toward the pergola.

"I thought we could use a break from Christmas," Brik said. "It gets to be a little much."

One of the other men grinned. "Brik hates Christmas. Didn't you know?"

Brik stiffened, the muscles in his neck cording. "I don't hate it. It's just not my favorite time of year. There's too much of it. Sometimes you need a break. I'll find Parker." He strode away.

I stared after him. He'd been protesting a little too much, and something unpleasant slithered in my gut. "Why does he hate Christmas?"

The man who'd spoken shrugged. "Beats me. What do you think? Is *Die Hard* a Christmas movie?"

I glared. "Don't even start." I stalked back inside the blue house, said my goodbyes to Gramps and Tomas, and went home.

I opened my computer on the dining room table and watched videos about printing on cookies. I'd been right. It wasn't as simple as just printing on cookies.

I'd have to frost the cookies with royal icing. After the icing dried, I'd need to paint clear piping gel over the frosting. The clear gel would work as glue for the printed image, fitted over the cookie. Then I'd have to put some sort of border around the image. Otherwise, it would look like something I'd stuck onto the cookie. In other words, it would look cheap.

At least the Rider-Waite-Smith Tarot deck was out of copyright. We could legally use those classic images, which I loved. And if I got a multi-rectangle cookie cutter... That would save some time. I was willing to bet the Lovers would be hot sellers in February.

My thoughts returned to Brik. It was perfectly respectable not to be that into Christmas. Complaints the holiday had been too commercialized were valid. I loved the season, but Beanblossom's was also enjoying the extra holiday income.

But to remove the lights as an anti-holiday statement seemed like a lot of unnecessary work. And Brik's parties had started up again in December...

That unpleasant something wriggled again inside me. I hesitated, then typed some names into the search engine. I clicked on an article, and a lump hardened in my throat.

So. That was why he hated Christmas.

Feeling slightly sick, I shut my laptop and went to bed.

Chapter Twenty-Four

WEDNESDAY SPED PAST IN a blur of clotted cream and lemon curd. When I returned home that night, the blistered paint had been stripped from the front of my bungalow, exposing bare, dark wood planks.

Music blasted from Brik's house. More in sorrow than anger, I stuffed in my earplugs and went to bed.

Gramps ambled into the tearoom the next day just before our one-thirty seating. He claimed a place at the bar.

Smiling, I poured him a cup of Earl Grey. "Are you here for a late lunch?" I asked.

He removed his checked, cabby-style hat and set it on the white quartz counter. "What have you got?"

"How about some spicy beet and carrot soup and a tea-smoked chicken salad sandwich?"

"How do you tea smoke a chicken?"

"In a wok with a steamer and brown sugar and rice."

"Sounds fancy," he said suspiciously. "Okay. I'll try it."

In the kitchen, I prepped his lunch, then I returned with it to the counter. "Here you go."

"Thanks." He lifted the top slice of bread and peered at the contents. "How are things going with, uh...?"

I adjusted my apron's square collar. "Gino and I aren't seeing each other anymore." I hated admitting it, and I hated that I hated admitting it. The breakup felt like a failure on my part.

"You're not?" He returned the bread to the sandwich. "I was going to ask about Brik. You didn't seem too happy about his party the other night."

"Oh. No," I said, relieved. "The party was fine. There was just someone blocking my driveway."

"What happened with Gino?" He braced his elbows on both sides of his plate. "He wasn't the person you thought?"

My hands fell to my sides. "No. He wasn't happy Hyperion and I were asking about his uncle's murder. And he has a perfect right not to be happy. So I guess I wasn't the person *he* thought."

"You'd think he'd be asking the same questions about those murders." Gramps took a bite of the sandwich.

Maybe now that he'd inherited, he didn't want to ask. I shook my head at the unfair thought. "He was closer to Merry than to his uncle."

"Ah, well," he said. "That's the breaks. Better you found out sooner rather than later. People don't change."

"Are you talking about Gino or Brik?"

"Both. It's no surprise he'd restart his parties for the holiday season."

I shifted my weight. "It isn't?" How much did my grandfather know about Eureka?

"It's the holidays," he said. "Everyone's having parties."

A tiny bit of tension released inside me. "Oh. Right." So Gramps didn't know about what I'd discovered two nights ago. It was all there, online. I don't know what had stopped me from making the connection before.

Eureka. Brik's girlfriend had been killed in December, on December twenty-first.

The parties were about more than not wanting to be alone. They were a distraction. He'd eased up on them over the year, making progress. But for Brik, the holidays had to be a horror.

The thought made me a little sick. I poured my grandfather more tea.

His blue eyes sharpened. "Unless there's something more going on?"

My pulse accelerated. "No," I said. "Nothing. Just Brik being Brik." I laughed lightly.

"Well," he said, "I know breakups are hard on the heart. But don't let it ruin your holidays. Romance might add to the Christmas spirit, but that's not what it's about. Now, what are we doing for Christmas?"

We made plans for Christmas Eve and the day itself. Then my next seating of customers flowed into the tearoom, and I was busy again.

By three o'clock, my stomach was howling, and I realized I hadn't had a chance to eat. I grabbed a chicken sandwich for myself and slipped it into a plastic bag.

"Maricel," I said, "I'm going to take a break and step outside. I'll be back in an hour."

My assistant manager nodded. "Enjoy your break."

I hurried out the back before someone could stop me, and I walked to the beach. It was another cold, foggy day. The sun was already lowering in the sky, and the lights along the pier had come on. I sat on a warm concrete bench on the beach and ate my chicken sandwich. The steady crush of the waves unknotted my shoulders.

When I finished, I ambled toward the giant Christmas carousel. The Weihnactspyramide's giant electric candles glowed. Wise men and wooden animals revolved in their tiers in a stately procession. I braced my hands on the barrier of blond-wood pickets around the rotating carousel.

On a nearby bench sat a curvy woman, her wavy, mahogany hair streaked with gray. Her head was bent to a slim, green hardback.

"Allyson?" I asked.

She looked up, and her face broke into a smile. "Abigail! I've been trying to get a reservation for your tearoom, but it's always full when I want it. You must be doing well."

Allyson was a writer and a friend. It had been too long since we'd hung out. "It's great to see you again." Guiltily, I stuffed my hands in the pockets of my slacks. "What are you reading?"

She turned the book's cover to face me. "A *Christmas Carol*. I read it every year around this time to get me in the Christmas spirit. Or to remind me of what that spirit is. Mankind was my business," she quoted. "Charity, mercy, forbearance, and benevolence, were, all, my business. The deals of my trade were but a drop of water in the comprehensive ocean of my business."

"Scrooge?" I asked.

"Marley's ghost." She smiled. "Or these things *should* be our business. But all this hustle and bustle sometimes make me forget." She smiled at a child holding a red balloon.

He pressed against the picket fence and watched the animals and shepherds go round. His mother beamed down at him.

"It's all about others," Allyson finished, "isn't it?"

Yes, it was. Was that what I'd been missing lately? "Speaking of which, next time you call the tearoom, talk to me. I'll make sure you get a table. And let's grab lunch, sooner rather than later."

"I'd like that. Thanks."

"I've got a question. If you wanted to take a bunch of say, blog posts, and turn them into a book, how would you do it?"

She pressed the book to her ample chest. "You mean self-publishing? There's a bit of a learning curve, but it's not that hard. And you can get help. You just have to be careful who you ask. There are all sorts of companies that charge ridiculous sums, promising the moon. They can rip you off. But I know someone who can turn what you've got into a book, get you a reasonably priced cover designer... Are you thinking of a cookbook?"

"No, though that's a good idea. I'm thinking of a Christmas gift, and I'd love the name of your person."

"I'll email it to you." Allyson rose and stretched. "And now I have to get back to work. Let's have lunch soon." She wandered down the fog-bound beach.

I turned to watch the Weihnactspyramide go round. Had I gotten too caught up in holiday rituals and busyness? Had I failed to connect with the people I cared about? Was that why I'd been feeling off?

My grandfather would remind me that Christmas is first about meeting the divine. But Allyson might be right too. I suspected love for others was one path to experiencing that great mystery.

If I wasn't feeling any Christmas spirit, it wasn't because of work or Brik or murder. It was because of me. And it was up to me to get it back.

A red balloon floated upward. The Pacific breeze caught it and drove it into the Weihnactspyramide. The balloon snagged in a shepherd's wooden crook. A child's wail rose on the breeze.

"It's okay," his mother said, soothing. "It's only a balloon."

"I'll get it," I told her. I unhooked the picket gate, letting myself inside the enclosure. I'd watched the men assemble the spinning carousel one Monday. They'd all taken a brief ride on it. And they'd been big men, at least twice my size. So I wasn't worried about doing any damage. I clambered onto the first tier and waited for the shepherd to come my way.

The thick board I stood on vibrated. Alarmed, I grabbed a nearby post for balance and steadied myself.

The shepherd trundled around the bend, the red balloon hooked in its crook. I blinked. Had the carousel sped up? I shook myself. It had to be an illusion.

I extended my hand. Another shudder trembled through the carousel, and the shepherd lurched toward me.

I stumbled forward, grasping wildly for a handhold. The crook trapped my wrist and sped onward, twisting my arm. I yelped and jumped onto the moving track before my arm was yanked from its socket.

"What's happening?" the mother shouted.

I pulled the balloon free and turned to step off the track. But it was moving too fast. Posts blurred past. I clung to the shepherd, my hands damp. This wasn't an optical illusion. The carousel *had* accelerated.

A familiar head of dark hair flashed past. "Abigail?" Hyperion's voice floated up to me, but he was already gone. Ocean and town rapidly switched places in sickening flashes of grays and pastels. My stomach bobbed and weaved, nausea clutching at my throat.

Hyperion waved his arms. "What— Are— You— Doing?" he shouted with each rotation.

"Turn it off," I shrieked. "Turn it off!"

"How?"

I pressed my forehead to the shepherd's brawny wooden chest. This was a nightmare. Not only was I about to throw up all over a beloved holiday attraction, I'd broken the damn thing. I closed my eyes.

The merry-go-round lurched to a halt. The sudden stop whipped me backward so fast I let go of the shepherd. I staggered, the world tilting sickeningly, and I stepped into space.

A woman screamed, but it wasn't me. It had happened too fast for me to yell. And then strong arms yanked me close.

My head lolled. "I'm gonna be sick."

The arms hastily released me. Still holding the balloon, I staggered to a nearby garbage bin. I heaved up tea-smoked chicken sandwich. It did not taste anywhere near as good on the way out as it had on the way in.

Dizzily, I straightened. The little kid stared up at me and pointed to my hand.

I looked down. Somehow, I was still holding the balloon. I handed it to the boy.

"Ah, thanks?" his mother said and hurried him away.

"What the devil?" Hyperion glowered at me. "You broke a cherished holiday attraction."

"*You* saved me?" Still feeling dizzy, I sat on the sand. It was cold, but it beat hanging off a garbage bin. I seemed to be doing that a lot lately.

"Not me. Him." Hyperion nodded toward the Weihnactspyramide.

Inside the fence, Brik squatted at the carousel's base. The camels and sheep resumed their sedate circuits around the wooden pyramid. He stood and closed a small door in its side.

Tingling swept across my face, and I closed my eyes. *Cursed.* I was freaking cursed.

"We were meeting for lunch," Hyperion said quietly. "I think he's feeling a little dark. The holidays get to some people that way."

And Hyperion had taken the time to do something about it. Unlike certain other tearoom owners. "Yeah." Clambering to my feet, I staggered to Brik. I braced my hands on the carousel's picket fence.

Brik stepped outside and closed the gate behind him. "You okay?"

"Fine." My stomach knotted. "Did I break it?"

"No. But you could have burned out the motor if you'd left the speed on high like that for much longer. What were you thinking?"

What was I thinking? "The speed was on high? I didn't know it would get faster when I stepped onto the carousel." My grip tightened on the pickets. What idiot would make something like that?

"No," Brik said, "it got faster when you pulled the lever to high speed."

"But I didn't pull any lever."

Hyperion joined us. "Give her some credit. Abigail's crazy enough to risk her neck getting a balloon for a kid. But she wouldn't fiddle with the motor. She's practically a luddite."

"Do you mean to tell me someone sabotaged that thing while I was on it?" I scanned the beach. There weren't many people out on a foggy Thursday afternoon. Someone could have gotten inside the carousel without anyone noticing. I certainly hadn't noticed. The interior panel had been on the opposite side where I'd been standing.

"You know what this means?" Hyperion asked.

Someone had sabotaged the Weihnactspyramide, a beloved holiday attraction. My jaw hardened.

I knew *exactly* what this meant. This meant war.

Chapter Twenty-Five

"We have signage!" Hyperion squeezed past a waitress and strode into our industrial kitchen. Triumphantly, he raised a cardboard box over his head.

I set a round of scone dough on a cookie sheet. "We already have signage," I said. "What's that?"

"Business watch signage," he said. "You know, with the spy hat and binoculars?"

"We're not even sure if we *have* a business watch," I said. "We've only held one meeting."

"But the signs are cool, and I thought we could drop them off personally," he said, his voice dropping on the last word.

I whisked the sheet full of scones into the oven and set the timer. "That *is* a good idea." It made an excellent excuse to interrogate Mrs. Henderson and Ivette.

"I'm chock full of them. Have you tried out the frosting printer yet?"

I hadn't, though I'd had time last night. I just hadn't had the energy or interest after the Christmas pyramid incident. I'd been slightly nauseated all night. "I watched some videos," I hedged. "We'll need to get a food-safe cutter for the designs."

"I'm on it. How much is it?"

"About three hundred and fifty bucks." Which I had not budgeted for, and I didn't believe Hyperion had either.

He winced. "Ugh. Can't you cut them by hand?"

"It will take longer, won't be as neat, and will end up costing us more."

Hyperion sighed. "Fine. I'll see what I can do." He slouched into the twinkle-lit hallway.

I looked around the kitchen. Everything and everyone was working as they should. Pulling a bag of trash from the plastic bin, I took it into the parking lot. I tossed it into the nearest open dumpster. The nearby phonebooth rang once and fell silent.

An ancient gray Honda Civic pulled into a nearby spot, and Jonasz stepped from the car. "Hi," he said.

"Hi, back." I glanced at the phone, but it didn't ring again. "You're here early on a Friday."

"I know." He smiled. "I hate being late, so I am always early."

"That's not a bad thing. We're about ready to open anyway. Why don't you take the hostess—I mean host stand this morning? It's going to be busy today."

"Will do." He bustled into the tearoom. I followed more slowly, then detoured into Hyperion's office.

"You came in early today." Eyes narrowing, I shut the door behind me. Hyperion was never here at this hour, something I should have cottoned onto sooner.

My partner looked up from his laptop. "I'm working on a new blog post."

"Oh." But Hyperion could have done that from home. He was keeping something from me, and I didn't think it was my Christmas present.

"Why?" he asked. "Do you need the computer? Because I'm at a good stopping point."

All right. If he wasn't going to tell me what was up, that was his business. "Is there anything online about the accident on 101? You know, on the morning Emery Callum was killed?"

His long fingers flew across the keyboard. "Oh yes, there is." He turned the laptop to face me. I pulled one of his high-backed chairs close and sat.

SAN BORROMEO—CA

Six people were hospitalized following a multi-vehicle crash on the southbound 101 in San Borromeo according to the Santa Cruz Sheriff's Office.

Around ten AM, deputies were dispatched to a multi-vehicle crash with injuries in the area of the Sunset Beach exit. Sheriff's deputies arrived and located five vehicles, four with major damage. One, in the center of the pile-up, was miraculously unscathed.

Initial reports say the driver of a 2012 Toyota Corolla, driven by a 44-year-old man of Santa Cruz, California, was traveling southbound. Witnesses say the driver of the Corolla was driving recklessly at a high rate of speed.

The driver of the Corolla attempted to pass a southbound 2006 Jeep Cherokee, driven by a 55-year-old man from San Francisco. While passing, the Corolla struck the Jeep causing both vehicles to lose control.

101 Southbound was closed for nearly two hours. The crash remains under investigation by the Santa Cruz Sheriff's Office Technical Crash Investigations Unit.

There was an overhead picture of the pile-up, which I guessed had been taken by a drone. Jonasz's gray Honda Civic sat in the middle of the disaster.

Tension released from my shoulders. "Jonasz's alibi seems to check out," I said. "He couldn't have been anywhere near the store before ten-thirty. Not stuck in that mess."

"Huzzah. Your employee isn't a murderer."

"Yes," I said, "that *is* the bright spot."

"So if the killer's not Jonasz, and it's not Ivette or Merry, that leaves Mrs. Henderson or..." He trailed off. His gaze cut away from me toward the driftwood altar.

My insides tightened. *Or Gino.* "Or maybe someone we haven't pegged yet," I said smoothly. "A tenant or business owner with a grudge."

He drummed his fingers on the scarlet tablecloth and glanced at me. "I don't want to think it's Gino either," he said in a low tone.

I slumped in the chair, and my heart throbbed once, a tight ache. "We broke up. At least, I think we did. We had a big argument, and I stormed off like a child, and we haven't spoken since."

"You? Storming off like a child?" Hyperion raised a brow.

"I know. I'm not proud of it." I was embarrassed. I must have a faulty high horse, because I never stayed on it for long.

"What did he do?"

I ran my palm along the velvety arm of the chair. "It wasn't so much what he said as the way he said it."

Hyperion arched a brow. "Oh, I totally get that. How'd he say it?"

"He told me I should either leave investigating to the pros or get a PI's license."

He lurched forward in his chair. "What? He did not."

"I *know*. Right?" We contemplated that outrage for a minute or so. I'd never been one for long gab fests with friends about—well, much of anything. But it felt good to unload to Hyperion. He was a good listener. And he'd become a good friend.

"You know what would make you feel better?" Hyperion asked.

"What?"

He bent over the arm of his chair and picked up the cardboard box with the signs. "Not leaving it to the pros and interrogating Mrs. Henderson."

"You know me so well." Doing the opposite of what I was told usually *did* improve my mood. I checked my watch and rose. "Give me an hour."

I returned to my actual job. We got the first seating seated and orders taken and delivered. Then I ditched my fancy holiday apron, put on my green wool coat, and walked with Hyperion to the costume shop.

"We need Mrs. Henderson's alibi," I said. "For both Emery *and* Merry's death."

"Why both? We only have Jonasz's alibi for Emery's death."

"I know. But I just can't see him going after Merry. Killing an irritating boss would be..." I cocked my head. How irritating *was* it that I kept leaving the tearoom to investigate crimes? "I won't say killing the boss is understandable, but it's a motive." Maybe I should up the holiday bonuses. "But why kill Merry?"

"She knew too much?"

"Maybe. Jonasz told me he was going to another job the afternoon Merry was killed. I'll follow up on that."

We turned into a cobbled alley. Hyperion knocked on the arched, pink door, and grasped the costume shop's brass doorknob. He frowned. "It's locked."

I studied the window. A miniscule CLOSED sign hung crookedly from the pane. "Maybe we should have called first?" I said.

"What's the fun of that?"

"Let's try Ivette's," I said. "She might not be the killer, but she still knows more than we do about the victims." We strolled to Ivette's office, knocked on the door and let ourselves in.

Behind her sterile desk, the titian-haired receptionist arched a brow. "You again. You don't have an appointment this morning either."

"No," I said. "We're just dropping by signs for the business watch."

Hyperion pulled one from the box with a flourish. He handed it across the desk.

She sighed and picked up the phone, pushed a button. "Ivette, some people from the business watch are here... Yes, I'll tell them." She hung up. "She'll be with you in a moment, if you'd like to wait." She motioned to the green leather couch.

"Sure," I said. "We'll wait." I sat on the couch.

Hyperion bounced onto the cushion beside me. "Anything you'd like to report to the watch?" he asked the receptionist.

"No."

"Then we're doing our job," Hyperion said. "Achievement unlocked."

The receptionist squinted at him. He smiled benignly.

The door to the inner office opened. Ivette, in a cream colored skirt and matching suit jacket and red blouse, stepped into the reception area. "How nice to see you both. Please, come in."

Hyperion sprang from the couch and swanned inside. I followed.

Ivette's office was cozy, with a colorful corner nook with children's toys. The rest of the office was in elegant sandy tones. A purple orchid bloomed on her desk. Floor-to-ceiling windows looked out on an alley mural of a garden. Someone had bracketed the mural with topiaries strung with twinkle lights.

"One of our better alleys," Ivette said dryly and motioned toward the windows. "It's fortunate, since I prefer the natural light. How's the watch going?" She sat behind the desk and crossed her legs.

"We're still in the organizational phase," Hyperion said blithely. "But everyone who attended Monday night's meeting left us with numbers and emails. I'm taking that as a positive. And we have signs." He raised a sign and flapped it in the air.

"The signs at least may be something of a deterrent," she said.

I wasn't so sure about that, but they couldn't hurt. "How are you holding up?" I asked, sitting in a tan leather chair opposite. "We heard about Merry."

Hyperion set down the box and sat in the chair beside mine. He crossed his legs and bounced one foot.

The lines around her eyes deepened. “Poor Merry.” She ran her hands along the edge of the desk, as if she could smooth the wood. “The stress...” Her mouth flattened. “I added to it. Or at least I didn’t help it. I should have been more sensitive. And now...” She shook her head. “Now it’s too late.”

Hyperion’s foot stilled. “You can’t blame yourself. The only person responsible is the murderer.”

“If they catch him,” she said bitterly, “I doubt they’ll be able to charge him for her suicide.”

“Unless it wasn’t a suicide,” Hyperion said. “And I don’t think anyone really believes it was.”

I shot him a sharp look. If Gino was right, the cops believed it. But I hadn’t told Hyperion about that.

“Why do you say that?” Ivette pressed a hand to her chest. “This might make me a terrible person, but I hope you’re right. I hope she didn’t kill herself. I’ve been blaming myself for... What have the police told you?”

“It’s not what they told me,” he said. “It’s what Merry told me. She came for a Tarot consultation the day she died. She wasn’t suicidal. She was determined.”

A chill trailed across my neck. I shivered and pulled my wool coat closer. The orchid on the desk trembled.

“Sorry.” Ivette rose and went to the tall windows. She closed the open one, bracing both hands on the panes and shoving it closed the last inch. “Since this was repainted recently, I haven’t been able to completely shut it. It’s maddening.”

“It’s fine,” I said. “Ivette, can you think of anyone else who might have had a grudge against Emery and Merry?”

“Aside from me?” She shook her head. “Possibly that Henderson woman. Everyone knew she was having an affair with Emery.”

“I didn’t realize.” *That you knew about it too.* I leaned back in my chair, and the leather cushion squeaked.

"Some people are saying Merry killed herself out of remorse," Hyperion said.

"For killing Emery?" Ivette's brows rose. "That doesn't make much sense. She was with me when Emery died."

"What time, exactly, did she leave?" he asked.

She returned to her seat behind the desk. "I couldn't say exactly, but it was around a quarter after ten, I think?"

"Did you happen to see her last Thursday?" I asked.

"No," she said. "I took the afternoon off and went for a hike in Santa Cruz. I wish... I'd like to think I could have changed things, but I was in such a mood. There are so many things I'd like to take back. But we can't, can we?"

No, we couldn't.

Chapter Twenty-Six

OUTSIDE IVETTE'S OFFICE, WE stopped on the brick sidewalk. "You know," I said, "I don't think I've ever been down that alley." I motioned toward the wide arch between the two blue stucco buildings.

I should have been racing back to the tearoom. But I'd been rushing around too much lately. I wanted to take a breath, to explore for no other reason than my own pleasure.

"That's because nice girls don't walk down dark alleys," Hyperion said.

"It's not dark. It has a mural. Come on."

We started through the alley. Hyperion squinted. "Is that an ice cream truck?" He raced forward into a covered parking lot.

I followed more slowly, pausing to examine the twinkle-lit garden mural and its topiaries. It was lovely. Not high art, but lovely. The tension between my shoulders relaxed. Maybe there was something to all that New Age stuff about being in the present.

Passing through the covered lot, I met Hyperion on the sidewalk beyond.

He handed a fiver through the window of the ice cream truck. "What one?" he asked. "My treat."

I folded my arms. He *knew* I was lactose intolerant. "No," I said. "But thanks for your generous offer."

He shrugged. "Satisfied with your alley-cat tour?" Hyperion asked.

"Yes. I am." It had been a silly, small thing, but I'd gotten to explore an unfamiliar feature of the town. If I'd been down that alley before, it must have been pre-mural.

We returned to the tearoom, and Friday continued in its typically busy way. Tea was served, gingerbread was baked. Tarot readings were told, watch signs were distributed.

The weekend, however, passed in a blur of holiday teas. Mrs. Henderson didn't appear for lunch on Saturday. I was equal parts worried about her and relieved I wouldn't have to jam in an extra table. And then Monday came and I slept in, because I could.

That lasted until eight AM. Then I got up, got dressed, and walked into my kitchen.

I studied the iced gingerbread rectangles on the gray granite counter. It was time to try some printing. I lined up an icing sheet in the printer, went to my laptop on the dining room table, and pressed PRINT. Through the wall, the printer in the kitchen hummed.

I jogged into the kitchen and muttered a curse. I'd put the icing paper in wrong-side-up. I flipped it over, reinserted it, and repeated the process. A grid of Tarot cards slowly emerged in glorious color.

I left the icing to dry and returned to my laptop. The Rider-Waite-Smith Tarot cards had given me an idea.

The RWS deck had been designed by Pamela Colman Smith at the behest of Arthur Edward Waite. They'd both been members of The Golden Dawn, a magical secret society from the Victorian era.

The society was probably the basis for the collaboration. I didn't know for sure.

But I did know Smith had gotten stiffed on the credit side. For decades, the deck had been known as the Rider-Waite deck (Rider being the publisher). Now, Tarot readers included her name in the title, because it was only fair. She'd illustrated the deck.

The point is, the deck was old, published in the early 1900s. It had recently gone out of copyright. At my computer, I found a copy of the RWS Eight of Swords from *The Illustrated Key to the Tarot*. The RWS images in that book were even more out of copyright. I got to designing.

When I'd finished, I leaned back in my wooden chair. It was the finishing touch on Hyperion's Christmas gift, and it looked pretty good.

My partner might find something better—I was sure there was better out there than what I'd come up with. But my design might at least inspire him.

Then I returned to the kitchen and cut out the frosted Tarot cards. I carefully lifted the images free. Brushing the cookies with clear piping gel, I set the images on each cookie. I whipped up a batch of royal icing and piped it around the edges. Then I dipped each cookie in pearlescent white sprinkles to make a border.

Decorating food is not my forte. It took several tries and a frustrating amount of wasted icing and sprinkles to get it right. A lot of both ended up on my fingers.

Finally, I stepped back from the tray. The cookies looked like three-D Tarot cards. It *had* been a good idea.

But the process was still a little time consuming. Fun, but time consuming. I'd have to consider if it made sense to make the cookies a regular item. And to think about how to much to charge for each.

Someone knocked at my bungalow's front door. Wiping my sticky hands on my apron, I hurried to answer.

I peered through the new peep hole. A brown eye stared back at me. I opened the door. "Good morning, Hyperion."

He strolled inside and frowned at my murder board beside the sofa. "You haven't added anything to it."

"Not yet, but I do have something to show you." I led him into the kitchen.

He admired the tray of cookies. "These look good enough to eat. Can I? Can I? Can I?"

"I'm not going to sell them." They hadn't been baked in a commercial kitchen.

He snatched up the Star and bit into the gingerbread. "This is good, Abigail." He wiped the corner of his mouth. "How much are we going to charge?"

"I need to figure that out."

"We've got to get them in the tearoom. 'Tis the shopping season. OMG, you made a Death card?"

"I don't think they'll be huge sellers." But I'd been too lazy to edit the card out of my grid of Tarot images, and these were only test cookies.

"You never know. There's always the Goth contingent." He picked it up, pivoted and flashed it like a badge at my refrigerator. "Gingerbread *dead*." He straightened. "Because gingerbread *death* doesn't have quite the same ring. How are we going to package them?"

"Clear cellophane." *Ugh, packaging.* That was another step to slow the process and add an expense. I'd have to find some bags, and maybe ribbons to tie them with.

He picked up the Empress cookie and set it aside on the butcherblock work island. "So. Mrs. Henderson. By a process of elimination, it has to be either her or..." He set the Hierophant beside her. "Gino."

"It's not Gino," I said sharply.

He studied me. "At the risk of getting my head bitten off, did you get his alibi?"

My face heated. "No." I hadn't spoken to him since that night at the Chinese restaurant. And if I called to apologize... Did I want to apologize?

My stomach hardened. I did want to, dammit. And I wasn't even sure if I was the one at fault. But I was certain he was no killer.

"But it's not him," I said. "I refuse to believe that my instincts about people are that far off. And why did you make him the Hierophant?"

"He *is* all about rules and regulations and telling people with less knowledge what to do."

I winced. That had hit a little close. "So's the Emperor."

He shrugged. "Fine. Gino can be the Emperor." He returned the Hierophant to its spot and put the Emperor beside the Empress.

"It's not Gino."

"He did find Merry's body. The police always look at the person who found the body."

Reaching behind me, I gripped the kitchen counter's cool edge. It was the wrong move, because the feel of it brought back a memory of Gino and I in this kitchen. My low back pressed against the counter, my hands gripping its edge, and Gino...

I glanced toward the window above the sink. A hummingbird, jewel wings shimmering, hovered on the other side of the glass. The bird darted away.

"It's not Gino," I repeated stubbornly and folded my arms.

"Then it has to be Mrs. Henderson. I called her, and we have an appointment to bring the watch sign by her store this afternoon."

A spot between my shoulders loosened. She was all right, even if she had ditched our planned lunch at the tearoom. "Good."

"Now we just have to figure out how we'll break her down."

My gaze flicked to the white ceiling. "We can't exactly give her the third degree. She's nearly seventy."

"Ageist. What's wrong with you? We've got a killer on the ropes."

"I don't know. This just feels too easy. Something's not right. Let's go over everyone again."

"Fine. Ivette." Hyperion plucked the World cookie from the tray on the gray counter. Pivoting, he set it beside the Emperor on the work island.

"Why that card? Cookie. Whatever. You know what I mean."

"She's got it all now, doesn't she? A cool five-hundred thou, and her rotten ex and his new wife dead. She doesn't have an alibi for Merry's death. But her mortal enemy gave her an alibi for Emery's. I'd say that's pretty solid."

"As his ex, she probably would have known what sort of prescription drugs Emery was taking," I said.

"So did Merry, but she's dead. We're not believing that nonsense that she killed Emery then took her own life. Are we?"

My throat tightened. We'd failed Merry. She'd come to us for help, and she'd died. And telling myself she'd gone to the police as well didn't make it any better.

"No," I said. Though it was better than believing Gino had done it. "No," I said more forcefully. "I suppose Jonasz might have known about the meds, but he was stuck in that car accident."

"He could have had an accomplice."

"Yeah, but that accident..." I shook my head. "He couldn't have known about it. Jonasz didn't cause it. He was just lucky enough or unlucky enough to get caught in the middle."

"But if he set up that fake call to pull him away from the store..."

A crow cawed outside. I glanced again at the window above the sink.

"Okay," I said. "Assuming Jonasz didn't kill Callum and then drive away, pretending he'd been called to the hospital... The earliest the murder could have happened was around nine forty-five, yes?"

"Right you are. Jonasz went to the hospital at nine-thirty. He immediately turned around, and under normal circumstances would have been back by ten. So if Emery had been killed at nine forty-five—and we can't say for sure that he was—then he might have been the one to find the body instead of Sierra."

"But why?" Frustrated, I picked up the Devil and bit his head off.

"Am I sensing some repressed anger?" Hyperion rubbed his throat.

"You can't go at the Devil sideways," I mumbled through the gingerbread. "The shadows, the self-deceptions, the back alleys are all his territory. The only shot you've got is to face him head on."

"Hm. You're sounding a tad defensive. But I'll give you this. You really *do* get Tarot."

I swallowed. "Emery may have been a tyrant, but by killing him, he loses his job and his insurance. He could have just quit."

"And if Jonasz had killed him, I'd expect it to be a crime of passion. I mean, Jonasz might have lost his temper and bashed him over the head one day. But I can't see him plotting an elaborate murder involving drugging his boss first."

"The drugs point straight to Merry." Straightening off the counter, I set the Strength cookie beside the others. "She left Ivette's office at a quarter after ten. She could have made it to Emery's shop by ten-thirty and killed him within the right window of time."

Hyperion shook his head. "But Jonasz might have been back by then. She had no way of knowing how long it would take him at the hospital. Let's say fifteen minutes to figure out there'd been a mistake. But he could have gotten in touch with his wife and found out sooner that his daughter was okay. Why didn't he?"

"She was on a video call with a doctor and didn't pick up the phone." I walked to the pantry and closed its louvered white doors. "Sorry. I forgot to mention they came by the tearoom. Sierra gave his daughter a reading."

"Okay, maybe that's true. But Merry would have no way of knowing that."

"Maybe she figured if she got to the shop and Jonasz was there, she'd just not go through with her plan?"

"You think she did it and killed herself," Hyperion said dully.

"No." I pointed to Strength, a maiden holding open a lion's mouth. "Merry was strong. I don't believe it."

"Which brings us back to Mrs. Henderson." He plucked the High Priestess from the tray—a robed woman on a throne and holding a book. She was a secret keeper, an enigma.

"Which brings us back to Mrs. Henderson," I agreed. "What time did you say that appointment was?"

"Lunch first. Interrogation second. I never interrogate a suspect on an empty stomach."

Chapter Twenty-Seven

UNENTHUSIASTIC, I POKED AT my half-eaten burrito with my fork. It had been a good burrito, and you couldn't beat the atmosphere. Red and green garlands swagged the arched restaurant window beside our table. Outside, mercury ocean and sky melded into one, as grim and gray as my thoughts.

"Maybe you shouldn't have eaten all those cookies," Hyperion said through a mouthful of enchilada.

"I ate half a gingerbread Tarot card," I said, affronted. "And it's Monday. I can eat what I want on my day off. I was just thinking..."

"What?"

I put down the fork and switched to toying with the swizzle stick in my margarita glass. "That there's something Ivette said to us at her office that mattered."

"I'm getting that feeling too, but what was it?"

I scooped up a spill of beans and cheese with a chip. "I was hoping you would know. What does Tony have to say?"

He stared fixedly at me. "Why do you think Tony has to say anything?"

I arched a brow. *Now* who was being defensive?

"Okay." He braced his elbows on the colorfully tiled table. "He might be poking around a bit, but he hasn't been sharing." His face pinched.

"Why not?"

"He's still trying to figure out if he's a cop or something else, I think. He hasn't pulled the trigger yet on getting that PI license."

I frowned. "I thought it was in the works."

"The paperwork's been filled out. He hasn't submitted it yet."

I didn't ask why. For Tony, being a detective had been more than just a job. It had been a calling. There had to be all sorts of emotions and second guessing attached to this decision. But Tony didn't strike me as the kind of guy who'd be happy in limbo.

Hyperion and I were lucky we worked for ourselves. Sure, we could fail, lose our business, but that would be on us. Customers might reject us, but we couldn't be fired.

We finished lunch and walked to the costume shop. "Are you kidding me?" I jabbed a finger at the CLOSED sign in the window. First the missed Saturday lunch and now this? Mrs. Henderson was avoiding us.

Hyperion frowned. "She should be here. We have an appointment." He knocked on the rose-colored door.

After a moment, Mrs. Henderson opened it and peered out. Her eyes were red and her round face blotchy. "Oh. You're right on time." She pulled the door wider and stepped aside.

"Are you all right?" I stepped inside the narrow shop and took back all the rotten things I'd been thinking about her. She looked awful. "Has something happened?"

She sniffed and brushed the top of her red cardigan. Her fingers scraped the Christmas tree embroidered on it. The tiny bell at the top of the tree jingled. "No. I'm sorry. The police were just here, that awful Baranko." She hiccupped a sob.

"What happened?" Hyperion asked solicitously, handing her a community watch sign.

"He wanted to know where I was Thursday afternoon before last. I told him I was here in the shop, but he didn't believe me. I had to give him the number of one of my employees who'd been working with me that day. And then..."

"Then what?" I asked.

"He told me to be careful. I don't know if he meant be careful because he was watching me or to be careful because someone might try to... to come after me too. I hate all this. I didn't want to be Emery's trustee *or* beneficiary. I only agreed because—" She bit her plump bottom lip.

"Because what?" Hyperion asked.

"Because he was so angry at Gino. That's his nephew."

I stiffened. Why would he be—? No. Gino didn't kill anyone. He had his faults, yes. We all did. But the man who'd laughed and argued with me and held me in his arms was no killer.

"It wasn't fair," she was saying. "Gino just was following his own path as a lawyer. And now that Merry's gone, it's such a mess. Everything's a mess. And then Merry accused me of... And then she died... That's why that detective was here."

"It was a confusing time," Hyperion murmured.

"I should never have... Do you know what that detective implied? He actually suggested Emery was after me for my money."

"He what?" I asked, wrenching myself out of my fugue. I'd kind of figured it had gone the other way.

"I know!" She blotted her eyes with a tissue. "Believe me, Emery didn't do me any favors by involving me in his trust. I handed everything over to my lawyer. It's easier to pay him to deal with this mess. The money's going to Merry's estate, minus his fee, of course."

"I've been looking for a good estate attorney," I said. "Who's yours?"

"Gerald McMannis."

I nodded. He was an acquaintance of my grandfather's. If memory served, Gramps thought well of the man. "Did the detective have any idea who might have been responsible for the murders?"

"If he did," she said tartly, "he wouldn't tell me. But I'm very glad you started that watch."

"Do *you* have any new idea who might have done this?" I asked.

She wiped beneath her eyes with the tissue and jammed it in the pocket of her cardigan. "Emery wasn't the most well-loved man. I'm no fool. He did tend to run over people. But he wasn't all bad. He had his moments."

"And Gino?" I asked, throat tight.

"Oh, it was so ridiculous. Gino's father accused Emery of cheating him out of their parents' inheritance. They never forgave each other. Emery regretted it, but he wouldn't climb down. Gino's father was wrong, you see." She shook her head. "I wonder if that's why Gino became an estate attorney—to stop things like that from happening."

"Things like people being cheated?" Hyperion asked.

"No, things like families breaking up over wills. I'm so disappointed Emery didn't get legal help with his own trust. What a mess. But he'd dug in." She cleared her throat and smoothed the front of her cardigan. The bell on the Christmas tree jangled again. "Thank you for the sign. I look forward to the next watch meeting."

"It'll be in January," I mumbled.

Hyperion and I said our goodbyes and left. On the sidewalk, he eyed me. "I'm sure Gino has an alibi."

But Hyperion was wrong. Gino didn't have an alibi, and I knew it.

Chapter Twenty-Eight

I CAME HOME TO Tomas and Gramps repainting the front of my yellow bungalow. You can't let two septugenarians paint your house without chipping in. It's a rule. I spent the rest of Monday helping. It didn't distract me from thoughts of Gino.

As I was putting the paint cans away, Razzzor stopped by to add to the murder board. At least, that's what he'd claimed. His additions weren't that enlightening.

But Gramps and Tomas had fun pinning lines of red string between suspect photos. Then the four of us decorated the new tree Tomas had brought and barbecued on the back deck.

Tomas leaned back in a patio chair. He popped the top off a beer and sent the bottlecap spinning into the deck's redwood fencing. Since Tomas owned the bungalow I rented, I didn't complain about the damage. Solar lights glowed in the garden, and a waxing moon hung low over the bare dogwood tree.

Razzzor patted the front of his band t-shirt. "That was some barbecuing." He raised a beer in Tomas's direction.

Peking quacked somewhere in the darkness of my garden. I hoped he was filling up on bugs.

"The tree looks good." Gramps nodded toward my French doors and the tree glowing behind them. The buttons on his gray, knit vest were in the wrong holes again, rumpling the fabric. My chest squeezed at the sight.

"It's beautiful," I agreed. "Thanks again for bringing it over. I wouldn't have had the time to get one myself."

"Things are busy at Beanblossom's?" Tomas took another pull of his beer, his Giants windbreaker rustling.

"In a good way," I said. "Our first year has been a success, even if—"

A blur of feathers shot across the deck. Peking landed at speed on the table. A plate shot sideways and crashed to the deck.

"Peking," Gramps shouted. The duck ruffled its feathers and quacked, unrepentant.

I laughed. "It's not a party unless something gets broken. And it was a cheap plate. I'll get a broom." I rose and went inside. When I returned, Gramps and Tomas had already collected the bigger fragments.

"Sorry about that," Gramps said. "I don't know what got into him."

"I don't mind." I was just happy to be here with people I loved, and the deck blurred. I blinked rapidly. It was easy to forget they wouldn't be here forever. Every moment with them was special.

Music started up next door, and I winced. Razzzor's brows pinched.

"On a Monday?" Gramps angled his head toward the tall, redwood fence. "Want me to have a word with him?"

"No, it's fine." And I realized it *was* fine. My Christmas gift to Brik would be not to complain about his parties this month. If that was what he needed to get through Decembers, I'd learn to live with the noise. And there were always earplugs.

I'd even forgive him for taking on my decorating role at my grandfather's house. Helping Gramps decorate brought me joy, but opportunities for that were everywhere. All I had to do was take them. Showing kindness, loving others... Maybe those were only a part of the Christmas spirit, but they mattered.

"I heard Mrs. Henderson hired a lawyer to deal with Emery Callum's estate," Tomas said offhandedly.

"Gerald McMannis" I lifted my brows. "Does he happen to be a friend of yours?"

"He might be." Tomas grinned. "Said the trust's a real mess, but it makes it easier that Mrs. Henderson doesn't want a penny of the money. She's handing all the trustee fees to the lawyer. And you didn't hear that from me."

I looked down at the deck, my throat tightening. Mrs. Henderson hadn't been lying about the money. Gino would get it all. Laughter rose and fell next door. A fragment of plate no bigger than my fingernail lay by my tennis shoe. I bent and picked it up.

"How's Gino doing with all this?" Tomas asked. Gramps shook his head warningly.

"I don't know." I set the broken piece of pottery on the table. "We're not seeing each other anymore."

Razzzor's jaw hardened. He took a swig of his beer. The lights of the Christmas tree reflected off his glasses.

Tomas nodded. "Good to figure out sooner rather than later that he's not the right one." He glanced at the fence, covered in jasmine.

"That Jonasz fellow still working for you?" Gramps asked.

"Part-time," I said.

My grandfather nodded. "That explains it. I saw him waiting tables at the Yacht Club the other day."

The Yacht Club *and* the Chinese restaurant? When did he have time to sleep? "You're friends with the owner, Tomas," I said, "aren't you?"

"Sure. You need a table?" The older man laughed.

"No," I said. "I want to confirm Jonasz was working there Thursday afternoon, specifically, from three onward."

"Is that when Merry Callum was killed?" my grandfather asked.

"It looks that way," I said. "She died sometime after leaving Beanblossom's that day. Jonasz left the tearoom not long after she did. Unless you discovered anything more specific?" I asked Razzzor.

The tech entrepreneur shook his head. "The police put her death between four and six-thirty." *Six-thirty*. When Gino had found her.

Tomas pulled his phone from the pocket of his Giants windbreaker. "Let's find out."

My face warmed. I hadn't meant right now. This was supposed to be a relaxing holiday get together. "You don't have to—"

"No time like the present." The older man dialed and pressed the phone to his ear. "Pete, how's it going...? I've got a favor. You've got an employee named Jonasz... Yeah, Jonasz Albrekt sounds about right.... Was he working there Thursday afternoon, between three and seven...? No, no trouble, just trying to clear something up..." He laid his hand over the receiver. "He's checking the timecards."

"Thanks," I said guiltily.

Gramps shook his head. "We don't want a killer in Beanblossom's." The duck hopped into his lap, shook his tail, and sat.

"No." I laughed. "That would be bad. But it's unlikely he is. Jonasz has an alibi for Emery Callum's murder. I just thought... I just thought it made sense to check."

"It does," my grandfather said. "You can't be too careful with something like this." He stroked the mallard's back.

"He applied at ZNS," Razzzor said.

"Did he?" I'd suggested it to Jonasz after talking it over with Razzzor. "I'm glad."

"I just got his background check back from security. It's squeaky clean."

That was a relief. It didn't put Jonasz in the clear for Merry's murder. But since he couldn't have killed her husband, he wasn't much of a suspect. Unless he'd killed Emery before he'd left for the hospital. I studied the plates on the table the duck hadn't sent flying and frowned.

"That's great," Tomas said into the phone. "No, no, everything's fine. Jonasz is fine. Like I said, we just wanted to clear something up, and we did... Merry Christmas to you too." He hung up. "It looks like your part-time employee has an alibi."

"Good news, for once." I liked Jonasz. But I suspected he wouldn't be around Beanblossom's much longer. He needed a full-time job that paid better than a tearoom. "Do you think ZNS will hire him?"

Razzzor shrugged. "Odds are good, but the decision's not entirely mine. The manager he'll be working with gets the final say." He raised his hands in a defensive gesture. "It wouldn't be fair if I jammed my friends onto teams. The managers have to be able to work with them."

"That's all I can ask," I said. "All I ever wanted for him was a shot, not a guarantee. The rest is up to Jonasz."

The doorbell rang, and I stood. "I'll be right back."

I walked inside and opened the door. Brik stood on the steps holding a bottle of wine with a big red bow on it. "Hey," he said. The bottle seemed small in his hands.

"Hey, back." I leaned against the door frame. "That for me?"

"Yeah." He handed me the bottle. "Merry Christmas."

I hesitated. "Gramps and Tomas are here, so's Razzzor. Want to come in?"

Brik wore a dress shirt and jeans, his blond hair pulled into a ponytail. His face was smooth, as if he'd recently shaved. I wondered with a pang if someone special was at the party tonight. Brik deserved someone special.

He nodded. "Sure. Thanks."

Stomach fluttering for no good reason, I held the door wider, and he walked inside.

Chapter Twenty-Nine

BRIK HESITATED BESIDE THE bulletin board, covered in printouts and photos. His brows lifted. "So that's the murder board?"

"The guys just added the yarn," I said, motioning with the wine bottle. Despite the steak I'd just finished, I felt hollow.

"Gotcha." He shifted his weight.

"So what brings you over?" I shut the front door, and the noise from the festivities next door diminished. "Aside from the wine."

Brik dragged his gaze from the board. "An apology. I know I've been throwing a lot of parties lately."

"It's the holidays." I shrugged. "Everyone's having parties." *And I can pretend I don't know your secret. I can pretend everything's fine.* We were friends, after all.

"You're welcome to come over," he said, "if you want."

"Thanks. Like I said, I've got people here now, but maybe some other time. Why don't you come on back?"

He trailed me through the house and past the Christmas tree. We stepped through the French doors and onto the deck.

"Evening Brik." My grandfather grunted and made to rise.

"No, don't bother to get up." Brik shook his hand, then Tomas's.

Razzzor stood, and the two men exchanged grips. "Good to see you again," Razzzor said and adjusted his glasses.

"Nice murder board," Brik said.

"Data is the future of policing," Razzzor's forehead wrinkled. "And, uh, the present."

"Which is why we shouldn't be so quick to give ours away," Tomas said sharply. "People are stupid these days posting so many things online."

"Believe me, you're not wrong," Razzzor said. "It's a dark, dark industry," he muttered. "Really dark. I mean, just—"

I touched his arm and smiled. Dark it may be, but Razzzor was one of the good guys.

Gramps arched a snowy brow. "A party on a Monday night?"

"It was a spur of the moment thing," Brik said. "You're all welcome." He glanced around. "Gino's not here?"

"He couldn't make it," I said quickly and set the bottle on the table.

"If he does," Brik said, "he's welcome too."

"Thanks," I said.

One of those long, awkward silences fell. Razzzor cleared his throat.

"I'd better get back before someone sets the bar on fire," Brik said. "I just wanted to say hello to everyone. Enjoy the wine." He climbed down the porch steps and made his way down the path between my house and our shared fence. The gate rattled shut. The three men stared at me.

"What?" I asked.

"You didn't tell him you and Gino are over," Razzzor said.

I hadn't wanted to disturb our detente. Brik and I were neighbors and maybe friends. I didn't want him to think I was looking for that to change. "It's stale gossip." I shrugged one shoulder. "Why bother?"

"That's why I like you." Tomas winked. "It's no one's business but your own, and you know it." He picked up the near-black bottle and whistled. "This is some fine wine."

"Then let's crack this bad boy open," I said.

I got a corkscrew from the kitchen, and we finished the bottle of wine. There are four glasses to a bottle and there were four of us. So the alcohol didn't disturb my dreams. I had plenty of other reasons for rough sleep, and my sleepy brain kept doing that irritating thing of thinking the same thoughts over and over and over.

I surveyed the morning street through bleary eyes. The light through the tearoom's windows was uncomfortably bright, another beach day. Surfers in wetsuits paraded down Main Street on their way to the beach. I sighed, turned the sign in the window to open, and got to work.

The morning ground on. Though it was a Tuesday, the tables were packed for our first seating. We sold gingerbread houses and Tarot cookies. Jonasz had taken over making the latter. He was a lot neater about lining up the angles and painting the borders than I'd been.

After lunch, I found him at the station we'd set up for the cookies in the kitchen. "How's it going?" I studied the trays lined with frosted gingerbread Tarot cards.

"I'm nearly done with this batch." He frosted the borders of The Empress with a pastry bag.

"They look great," I said.

"Thanks. And thanks for setting up that informational interview with Mr. Razzzor."

I grinned. "I hope you didn't call him that."

He paused, his brown eyes widening with consternation. "I did. Did I insult him?"

"No. But did he manage not to laugh? He's just Razzzor to everyone."

Jonasz smiled weakly. "I'll remember that. I've got another interview tomorrow—a real interview, for a job at one of his companies. But don't worry, the interview won't interfere with my work here."

"I'm not worried. I hope it goes well."

"Their health insurance package..." He swallowed. "We could really use it."

A cold fist gripped my heart. Had his daughter gotten worse? "Has something happened?"

"No." He shook his head. "I mean, something is always happening, but nothing new. After Emery..." He set the pastry bag on the metal counter. "Emery wasn't so bad you know. He got that Cadillac-level health insurance for me. I mean, yes, it was kind of a trap, too. I couldn't leave. But he paid for it. He may have been cheap in other areas, and ill tempered, but he wasn't a bad guy. Not really."

"Which makes what happened to him and Merry even harder to understand. We want our victims and our villains to be dark-hearted through and through." And we could tell ourselves nothing bad would happen to us because *we* weren't villains—at least not most of the time.

"Nothing is easy about this. I don't understand it either." His hand clenched. "I keep going over that phone call. Who would do something like that?"

"Was the voice at all familiar?"

He shook his head. "Maybe. I don't know."

Maricel strode into the kitchen carrying a stack of dirty plates. She set them in a plastic washing rack.

"Were there any other business owners that were particularly upset with Emery?" I asked. "Any other tenants?"

Maricel glanced at me and hurried from the kitchen.

"No." He studied the shiny industrial fridge. "I mean, no one wants their rent raised, especially not by the amount Emery demanded. But I think everyone accepted it. This is California. All the prices are insane and only going up with so many tech companies moving in."

"And now you're interviewing with one."

"I never thought I might work for a tech company. I admit, I complained about them like everyone else. It is their success that drives the prices up. But I need a job with good benefits, and they are the ones who are offering them. I guess reality makes strange bedfellows."

"Yeah," I said, thoughtful. "I guess it does."

"But right now I am just happy to be making Tarot cards out of gingerbread. What a life, eh?"

I laughed uneasily. "I never saw gingerbread Tarot cards in my future either. But they make people happy."

"Yes. I am glad I got to work here for the holidays. I enjoy the festive feel."

"Me too," I said brightly. My Christmas spirit still might be a little spotty, but I was going to fake it until I made it.

The dishwasher made a pained wheeze, shuddered and died. Jonasz froze, pastry bag gripped in one hand.

My heart stopped. "That did *not* just happen."

Water seeped from beneath the dishwasher, and I swore. Clambering on top of it, I reached behind the machine and turned off the water.

Jonasz raced to the walk-in closet and returned with rags and a mop. I slithered to the floor, and we wiped up the mess.

Maricel walked into the kitchen, her arms loaded with dirty dishes. Her face paled. "Oh, no. Tell me you're not cleaning up a dishwasher flood."

I tossed a rag to the linoleum floor in disgust. "It's busted."

She set the dishes on the metal counter. "Should I call Brik?"

"No. He's no plumber." Brik knew his way around appliances, and odds were he *could* fix the washer. But he also had better things to do. And I didn't like our habit of running to my neighbor when things went wrong. Also, I didn't like the way I felt when he was helping me. There was a little *too* much warmth and gratitude, and holiday season or not, we were just friends.

I hung up and managed not to fling my phone against the kitchen wall. I'd finally managed to find a plumber who could get here tonight. But his arrival window was anywhere from two to four hours out.

I should have been grateful he could get here at all. But all I could feel was frustration. I might be here all night.

Hyperion strode into the kitchen. "Ta-dah! I have arrived. Let the rejoicing begin." The wait staff applauded.

I glanced at the wall clock above the kitchen door. It was just after four. Where had he been all day?

He bowed theatrically, then gathered up a handful of Tarot cookies wrapped in clear cellophane. "Excellent. I've got some private readings, and I know I can flog these to my clients. Is this all you've got?"

I slid my hands into the pockets of my Santa Claus apron. "They've been selling well."

"And *you* doubted my genius." He crossed the hall into his office.

I followed him inside. "Jonasz said something that got me thinking."

"Does your head hurt?"

"Hilarious." I watched him arrange the cookies beside the driftwood on his makeshift altar. "I'm serious. It's about the murders. I think I know who did it and how."

"Dazzle me with your brilliance." He collapsed into his high-backed chair and slung one leg over an arm.

I explained. Hyperion's dark brows sloped downward.

"Damn," he said. "You're right. It could have happened that way. In fact, I could easily see it happening that way. Two killers, bonded by mutual hatred and betrayal. But how are we supposed to prove it?"

"I don't know. I hate to say this—"

"Don't say it."

"But I think we should call Baranko."

He clapped his hands to his ears. "I told you not to say it. You know he'll tell us we're delusional. Or worse, he'll arrest us for interfering."

"I don't think he'll arrest us," I said doubtfully. "We had every right to hand out those watch signs personally. It's not like we were doing anything wrong. And we can't prove whodunit. We need the police. They have more resources. They can subpoena phone records and conduct stakeouts—"

He straightened, his foot dropping to the carpet. "We can do a stakeout."

I huffed out a breath. "Only on Mondays, when the tearoom's closed. We can hardly expect the killer to make a mistake on Monday. Besides, who has the time? It's the holidays. I haven't finished my shopping—"

"I thought you got all your shopping done."

"Your gift is a little complicated."

"I have *your* gift," he said with a superior air.

"You said you were waiting for Christmas Eve to shop."

"I had to order yours online."

I jammed my hands into my apron pockets. "Thanks, but—"

"What is it? What did you get me?"

"You'll find out Christmas Eve. And don't you think—?"

There was a gentle knock at the door. Sierra stuck her head inside the dimly lit room. "Your client is here."

"Thanks, Sierra," he said. "Would you mind sending her back?"

"Sure." Sierra vanished.

"Yes, I *do* think Christmas presents are small beer in comparison to murder," Hyperion said. "They're just a much more entertaining mystery to contemplate. I'll call Tony, see what he thinks of our theory. If he thinks it holds water, we'll call Baranko. Fair?"

Since I'd been dreading calling Baranko, it was more than fair. "Deal."

I returned to the kitchen. I'd like to say I was so busy that thoughts of murder were driven like Santa's reindeer from my mind. But they weren't.

There *had* to be a way to prove my theory. Unfortunately, the solution eluded me all through our final seating and cleanup. The latter was running long without a working dishwasher.

Maricel shot me a wistful look, and I laughed. "You can leave," I said. "I'll finish up."

"You sure?" she asked.

"I'm sure. And you've got Christmas shopping to do."

"A party to go to, actually, but thanks." She grabbed her coat and purse and bustled from the kitchen. The rear door clanged shut.

Jonasz checked his watch. "Um, I have to get to my other job. Do you mind...?"

"No," I said. "Go ahead."

"I hate to leave you here alone." His gaze darted toward the wall clock and back to me. "Not after what happened."

"You're not," I said. "Hyperion's with a client in his office, and he's got an online class later. I won't be alone."

"You are sure?" he asked doubtfully.

"I'm sure he's there, and I'm sure you can go. The plumber should get here soon." *Maybe*. "I don't expect you to wait for him."

"Thank you. For everything." He hurried out the back.

I finished cleaning the kitchen, then wandered into the hallway. The door to Hyperion's office was still closed, twinkle lights blinking.

I walked into the dining area, pulled out a chair, and sat. My muscles relaxed in the glow of the holiday lights, and I sighed, rotating my ankles. I glanced at the gingerbread house, then did a double take. Was a chimney missing?

I hurried to the counter and relaxed. The missing chimney had been an optical illusion. Gumdrops were one thing, but only a fiend would steal an entire chimney.

Carefully, I reached around the back for the light cord to switch it off. I hesitated. My grandmother had had an old plastic Christmas village which she'd lit up from inside. Maybe that was why I loved this gingerbread house so much. It reminded me of holidays past.

With a sigh, I switched off the light. The windows in the big house darkened. The past was the past, and I had an electric bill in my future.

The skin on the back of my neck prickled. At the counter, I slowly turned.

Ivette stood behind me. She aimed a gun at my gut.

Chapter Thirty

BRIEFLY, I CLOSED MY eyes. *Jonasz.* I hadn't heard the rear door slam behind him because it hadn't closed properly. It hadn't locked. And I hadn't checked.

When I opened them again, Ivette was still there. The handgun was black and serious looking, and it probably wasn't as big as it seemed, filling my vision. No useless, dainty weaponry for Ivette.

She held it one handed, giving me a good look at her new sapphire ring. And she was all business in her neat suit, not a silvery hair out of place. Lights from the boughs swagging the hall entry twinkled. They glittered off the gold buttons in her red jacket and glinted off the semi-automatic.

"I take it you're not here for a gingerbread house," I said coolly. But my heart thumped in my ears. Ivette had already killed two people. There was no reason for her to hesitate at three.

And I knew Hyperion couldn't hear us, so I hadn't bothered raising my voice. His door was solid enough and soundproof enough to muffle normal tearoom sounds.

"Open your cash register," she said.

I leaned against the quartz counter and wished I'd left a saucer on it to throw at her. But curse my work ethic, everything was spic and span.

"You're here to rob... to make it look like a robbery." I scowled. "Why me?"

"It's not my fault," she said. "I saw you nosing about the alley."

And she hadn't seen Hyperion, because he'd darted ahead, while I'd dawdled to admire the mural. "The alley you used. You left your office through the window while Merry shouted at your empty chair. You killed Emery." I pressed my back against the counter. "You used Merry as an alibi—a willing accomplice—until you killed her."

"Emery pushed us both too far. We had no choice. And she *was* the best person to tamper with his pill box."

"A lot of pills look enough alike that if you're not paying attention, you can take the wrong ones," I agreed. "She made sure he took the pills that made him loopy that morning. The fact that Emery wore glasses made it easier."

"He was always refusing to put them on," Ivette said. "You could say his stubbornness killed him."

I tried to force my muscles to relax, but they didn't want to. They wanted to run. "Merry tampered with his pill box before he left for work that morning," I said. "Then she went to your office to stage a scene."

"It wasn't hard," she said. "She really didn't like me. Not that I did anything to her. My issues were always with Emery. But she couldn't see it. She took everything so personally."

I edged along the counter, moving closer. Keeping her distance, she backed into the hallway. Not that I would have tried to the take the gun from her if I were near enough. I didn't know how.

"Merry kept shouting while you exited out the window into the alley," I said. "You put on a hat and jacket to look like a delivery person. And you called Jonasz from the phonebooth in our parking lot to get rid of him."

"Amazing there are any phonebooth's still around," she said.

"Tourists take photos with it," I said. "They think it's charming. You waited for Jonasz to leave, then you knocked on the delivery door. Emery let you inside, and you struck the blow that killed him. It was easy with him drugged up."

"Open the register."

I walked around the counter. "Then you returned to your office. Merry left. You chewed your receptionist's ear afterward to make extra sure you had an alibi."

She stepped from the hallway and edged closer, keeping the gun trained on me.

I tried to swallow, but my mouth was too dry. "What you didn't count on was that accident on the freeway." I paused behind the gingerbread house. It provided zero actual protection, but it made me feel better. Hey, if denial and self-delusion were all I had, I'd take them.

"Jonasz should have found Emery's body much sooner," I continued. "If he hadn't been caught in that freeway accident, he would have been the prime suspect. The phony call was a sketchy story. He had motive galore. And if he'd found the body, he would have looked guilty as hell."

"Besides which, Emery brought his pill box to work so he could take his lunch meds."

"Jonasz had the opportunity to mess with the pills if he wanted."

"The timing didn't matter," Ivette said. "I still had my alibi." She walked to the counter. Paper snowflakes swayed from the ceiling. The sapphire ring winked on her gun hand. *Her murder trophy.* Would she buy herself a treat after dispatching me?

I dragged my gaze from the gun. "But now Merry didn't have an alibi. The time of death was just wide enough that she could have killed her husband after she left your office. Is that what panicked her? Or was it because Merry learned about your share of the inheritance? Did she decide you didn't make such great partners in crime?"

"I had no idea Emery had forgotten to take me off as a beneficiary," she said. "I had nothing to do with that. It wasn't my fault. But what was I supposed to do? Turn the money down?"

My neck corded, the pounding in my ears growing louder. No, nothing would be her fault, not in her mind. In her mind, she was the victim.

"But Merry didn't believe that," I said. "You realized you couldn't trust her to keep her mouth shut, and you killed her too. Or was that the plan all along?"

She cocked her head. The gun lifted slightly.

"It doesn't matter," I continued. "You slipped her the same pills—how did you get hold of them?"

Ivette raised an elegant brow. "She showed me where Emery kept them when we planned his murder."

"But the police must have taken the extra pills as evidence."

"They did, the ones that I'd left."

Ice spread through my chest. Killing Merry *had* been the plan from the start. "You stole those pills *before* Emery's murder. You always knew you'd use them on Merry."

"It was only prudent," she said. "Now, open the register."

I lifted one hand over the register and hesitated. At this point, I was stalling just to stall. I had no brilliant plan, and little hope one would come to me. All my brain could focus on was the gun. Multitasking in a crisis just wasn't my forte. "Who found out about his affair with Mrs. Henderson?"

"I did. It was the worst kept secret in downtown San Borromeo."

"And you made sure Merry found out. What did you do? Drop hints, make her suspicious? And then when she learned the truth, she came to you. Merry realized Emery might leave her with nothing. Just like he did when he left you for her."

Her hazel eyes narrowed. "That's the problem with stealing another woman's husband. Deep down, you know you're vulnerable to the same trick."

"And sabotaging the Weihnactspyramide?" I asked.

"The what?"

"The big Christmas carousel thing on the beach."

"Oh. That. Honestly, it was too good a chance to pass up. I'd hoped you'd fall off and break something, but no such luck, and here we are. Honestly, I was trying to do you a favor. Do you think I *want* this?"

I opened the register. "Darn. It's empty, because we don't keep cash here. Not after hours."

Her delicate nostrils flared. "Where do you keep the cash? I know you didn't send Jonasz to drop it at the bank."

She *would* know about overnight drops. Emery had probably used the same system. "No, I was going to do it myself. The money bag's in the kitchen."

"I'll get it myself." She raised the gun. My gaze zeroed in on the barrel. Its dark tunnel expanded, filling my vision, blotting out the sapphire ring, blotting out Ivette.

I was going to die. I was going to get blood all over the gingerbread house and God knew what else. And that wasn't the point. *Stop thinking that. Act. Do something. Do—*

"Good heavens," Mrs. Ingram said from the hallway. "Is that a gun?"

Hyperion clamped a hand on the elderly woman's shoulder. He stepped forward, pulling Mrs. Ingram behind him. And though his attempt to protect her was a futile gesture, gratitude spread through me. My partner—quirky, flashy, Hyperion—was a true hero.

"No." Sweat beaded above Ivette's upper lip. "No one hides in the hall. Both of you, out."

"What's happening?" Mrs. Ingram touched the pearls at her throat. Bless her, she'd dressed to the nines for her Tarot reading. "Why do you... Don't tell me *you* killed the Callums?"

"Give it up, Ivette," Hyperion said. "I told the police we suspected you and Merry were in on it together. They know about your office window."

Ivette arched a brow. "Oh, *that's* believable. You're bluffing."

"I *did* call them," Hyperion said in the tone of a child who'd been wronged. "They know we dropped off the watch sign at your office yesterday. No one will believe this was..." He looked around the tearoom.

"A robbery," I supplied.

"A robbery," he said. "And Mrs. Ingram is innocent. You can't shoot her."

"I wouldn't say that," Mrs. Ingram said. "Ivette and I never really liked each other. I always said she was a hard woman."

Ivette's gaze turned flinty. "You old—"

"Sorry I'm late." A burly man in jeans and a thick plaid jacket stepped from the hallway. "Where's the dishwash... Oh, crap." His toolbox clanged to the ground.

BANG.

Several things happened at once. The gingerbread house exploded. Hyperion lunged. Mrs. Ingram shrieked.

The gun clattered to the ground. The plumber tackled Hyperion and Ivette. I swung myself over the counter and grabbed the gun off the laminate floor.

Hyperion, who'd somehow landed at the bottom of the scrum, groaned. The plumber hauled Ivette off him.

"Let go of me," she snarled.

The plumber grunted. "I don't think so, lady."

"Oh, she's no lady." Mrs. Ingram pulled a cellphone from her handbag and dialed. "*I'm* calling the police." She beamed at Hyperion, who was clutching his knee and rolling on the ground. "Your

Tarot reading was spot on. There were all sorts of surprises in my future. I just didn't think they'd happen so *quickly*."

"Thank you, Mrs. Ingram." I dropped the gun in my apron pocket.

Chapter Thirty-One

"Do ya want me to fix that washer or not?" The plumber jammed his hands on his hips. His saggy jeans dipped threateningly.

"No," Detective Baranko said.

"Yes," I said at the same time.

The detective and I glared at each other. Police officers bustled about the tearoom. Their boots ground the remains of the gingerbread house deeper into the laminate flooring.

"This is a crime scene," the detective said.

"My kitchen isn't," I said. "Ivette never went in there."

"And he's a witness." He jabbed a thick finger at the plumber.

"He won't be any less of one if he fixes her dishwasher." Tony ambled up to us and tipped his cowboy hat. "Abigail."

"Hi," I said.

Baranko's scowl deepened, and I tensed. I was surprised Baranko had let Tony inside, even if Hyperion had invited him.

"Fine," Baranko said. "Fix the dishwasher."

"Whatever." The plumber slouched into the hallway.

"Found it!" A gloved policeman pointed to a bullet hole in my shelving, where my teas had once been arranged in neat rows. Now brushed nickel tins lay scattered on the floor behind the counter. A few had opened, scattering dried herbs and tea leaves.

"Now do you see why civilians shouldn't poke around in murder investigations?" Baranko asked.

"I don't know what you're talking about," Hyperion said. "All we did was deliver a watch sign and walk down an alley. It's not our fault if Ivette freaked out and decided we were on to her." His brown eyes widened. "We had absolutely no idea what she'd been up to until she turned up here with a gun."

"I'd call it a successful first outing of your business watch," Tony drawled. "Even if it was dumb luck."

Hyperion's grin turned manic. "Right. Dumb luck."

I took the hint. My partner hadn't had a chance to call Baranko about our brilliant deductions. And I didn't see any need to correct the record. Not when Ivette had confessed in front of so many witnesses.

Mrs. Ingram sat at a table with a policewoman, who nodded and took frantic notes. The old lady's voice floated through a sudden lull in the bustle. "...tearoom is *never* boring."

"Anything else you'd like to add to your statement?" Baranko asked me.

"No. Do I, er, need to go down to the station?"

"Not right now," he said. "Mrs. Callum's denying everything. But her prints are on the gun, and she got a shot off in your tearoom. If things happened like you said they did, she'll have left an evidence trail." He eyed me. "I suppose your little watch is done with now."

"It's not up to us," Hyperion said. "We'll just have to see how many people come to next month's meeting."

And heaven help us, when January rolled around, the watch meeting was packed. I'd like to chalk the crowd up to a love of good scones. But people were there to gossip about Ivette and the

Callum murders. Even Gramps and Tomas had come. So had Brik, who was repairing the bullet hole in my shelf. At least, that was his excuse.

Ivette still hadn't confessed to the cops, according to Tomas's buddy in the prosecutor's office. But the police had found the cap and jacket she'd worn to make herself look like a delivery person.

And she'd left her prints at the phonebooth—not on the phone itself. She'd wiped that. But on the quarters she'd used to make the call. *Heh.*

Hyperion clinked a teaspoon on a teacup, and the crowd subsided.

"Welcome," he said, "to our second business watch meeting, where the dress code is understated and unassuming. After all, good observers don't want to stand out in a crowd. I'd like to welcome back Detective Baranko. I'm sure he'll be happy to answer all your questions about *anything*."

The detective's mouth set. At a table near the door, Tony's grin widened. I bit back a laugh. There was no way Baranko was escaping without telling us the latest in the Callum murders.

"But before we get into that," Hyperion continued. "I'd like to introduce a friend of the community, Razzzor. Some of you may know him from the hit online game, Zombie Nazis in Space, our sponsor in last October's coffin race."

The crowd applauded politely. Razzzor waved from his stool at the bar.

"But what's really important is Razzzor's come up with an app for the watch. It will make it easier for us to report and analyze suspicious activity."

"It's like a murder board," Razzzor said. "But on your phone. And it connects directly to the SBPD online reporting system. You can make your report to the police and let everyone in the watch know as well. It also analyzes data for patterns, and—"

Hyperion cleared his throat.

"I've got a demonstration for later," Razzzor said, reddening.

Gramps raised his hand. "What's an app?"

"It's like a computer program for your phone," Razzzor said.

"Then why not just say it's a computer program for your phone?" Gramps asked.

"Anyway," Hyperion said. "Detective Baranko will be talking a bit about reporting. Also, I've got a new book on Tarot coming out this year and am taking pre-orders now. You can sign up at the counter." He shot me a meaningful look. It had been my gift to him—a professional to turn his Tarot blogs into a book. He'd loved the cover I'd designed using the Eight of Swords card. Or at least he'd said he had.

"Detective?" Hyperion made a sweeping motion and stepped aside.

"Thank you." Baranko shambled to the front of the room. A dozen hands shot into the air. "I'll take questions at the end," he said.

Hands lowered with a disappointed air.

I shook my head and retreated to the kitchen for more scones and sandwiches. From the corner of my eye, I saw a muscular figure slip in after me.

"You don't want to listen to Baranko's lecture?" I asked Brik.

My neighbor leaned against the doorframe and chuckled. "I'm not in your mystery crew. No offense. I wanted to tell you my parties are over."

"I already knew that. You haven't had one since New Year's Eve."

His expression turned wistful. "That was quite a night."

"It sure was." There'd been no sense in turning my nose up at a rocking New Year's Eve party right next door. Even Gramps and Tomas had come.

I jammed my hands in the pocket of my kitschy new apron. Its front was a winter scene with appliqued snowflakes, ruffles, and pale-blue polka dots. Hyperion had got me an apron-of-the-month service for Christmas. I couldn't wait to see what Valentine's Day would bring.

"I saw Gino wasn't there," Brik said casually.

"No. He's a good guy, but we decided we weren't compatible."

Brik grunted. "No hard feelings?"

I glanced at the linoleum floor. Was he talking about hard feelings about Gino or about himself? "No hard feelings." I looked up and smiled.

He hesitated. "I saw Jonasz the other day."

"You did? I didn't know you two knew each other. But of course, you met when you did that repair work for Emery."

"I made some modifications to Jonasz's apartment for his daughter. He said you helped him get a job with one of Razzzor's companies."

"I only connected them," I said quickly. "Jonasz got himself the job."

"And if you and Hyperion hadn't put the pressure on Ivette, he would have been blamed for the murder."

"We didn't put pressure on her. Or at least, we hadn't intended to. It was just bad luck—"

He raised his hands in a quelling gesture. "I know what you told the cops. I'm just saying... You did a good thing. You and Hyperion."

"Oh. Thanks."

"I wish..." His blue eyes darkened. "I wish I'd had someone like you in my corner, back in Eureka."

I lowered my head. I wished that too. I wished I'd known him before his life had fallen apart, before that awfulness had changed him.

He shifted his weight. "And the patch is done on that shelf. It'll need to be painted—"

"I can do that. I've got extra paint in one of the closets."

"Yeah." He grinned, and the kitchen seemed to brighten. "I know you can do pretty much whatever you set your mind to." He studied me, his chest rising and falling sturdily.

The clock above the door ticked. The kitchen smelled of scones and Brik—soap and sawdust. A sudden warmth flooded my heart, leaving me blinking.

"I'll see you around." He turned and vanished into the hallway.

The rear door clanged shut, and I smiled.

Note from Kirsten

Yes, the giant Weihnactspyramide is a thing. I've only seen the life-sized ones in photos and videos, though my parents always had a tabletop-sized Weihnactspyramide when I was growing up. Watching the heat from the candles spin the carousel seemed like magic. It still kind of does.

So what's next for Abigail and Brik? He needs some resolution after what happened to him in Eureka. And Abigail and Hyperion are going to help him get it. So watch for the next Tea and Tarot mystery coming in spring of 2023—*The Sword in the Scone.*

Tea and Tarot. Love and Murder.

A Tarot conference at a holistic resort seems the perfect place for Tea and Tarot partners Hyperion and Abigail to promote their business and enjoy some beachside luxury. But murder cuts their R&R short. And when the evidence points to Abigail's devilishly appealing neighbor, Brik, and an unsolved murder connected to his past, these amateur detectives are on the case.

Years ago, Brik's girlfriend died at the hands of an unknown stalker. He lost everything: his love, his job, his home. Now, he's convinced history is repeating itself. He's tried to keep Abigail in the friend-zone, but he fears another woman he cares about just may be the next victim.

As the investigation heats up, Brik and Abigail are determined to keep each other at arm's length. But as they cross swords with the killer, their feelings become harder to resist. If these two don't learn to trust each other, their chance at love might be cut short. Permanently.

The Sword in the Scone is a fast-paced and funny cozy mystery, packed with oddball characters, Tarot, and murder.

Tearoom recipes in the back of the book!

Can't wait to dig in? Pre-order *The Sword in the Scone* now, and start reading the day it launches on February 14th, 2023!

Sugar Plum Scones

Scone Ingredients:

3 ¾ C bread flour*
¼ C sugar
3 T baking powder
1 tsp cinnamon
½ tsp cardamon
¼ tsp salt
Zest from one large orange
8 T **cold** unsalted butter**
1/2 C chopped pecans
1 C chopped dried Angelino plums
1 ¼ C milk
Coarse sparkling sugar

Directions:

Heat oven to 375 degrees F.

Mix flour, sugar, baking powder, cinnamon, cardamon, and salt in a medium-sized bowl. Add orange zest and mix thoroughly. Cut butter into cubes and mix into the flour mixture with your fingers, crushing the butter, until the mix is coarse and sandy.

Add the milk to the dry mix, and stir until almost combined. Add chopped pecans and chopped dried Angelino plums. You may need to add extra milk, a tablespoon at a time, until the mix is incorporated.

Knead dough in the bowl. Roll out to 1" thick.

Dust with coarse sparkling sugar and lightly press the sugar into the dough.

Cut circles 2 ½ inches in diameter, or cut into triangular wedges 2 ½ inches at the base.

Bake on ungreased cookie sheet until light golden brown. Circles take approximately 15 minutes. Triangles will usually take 20-25 minutes.

* You can use all-purpose flour instead of bread flour, and it will give the scones a denser, more cookie-like texture. Bread flour will "lighten" up the scones, so they're a bit more like biscuits (but not—they're still scones).

**Why cold butter? Cold butter is a big part of the flakiness of scones, because the cold butter expands in the oven. So the colder, the better!

Killer Gingerbread Scones

Scone Ingredients:

3 ¾ C bread flour*

1/2 C light brown sugar, packed

3 T baking powder

2 tsp ground ginger

1 1/2 tsp ground cinnamon

1/4 tsp ground clove

¼ tsp salt

8 T **cold** unsalted butter

2/3 C candied ginger, chopped into 1/8" bits (optional**)

1/2 C molasses

1 C milk

Icing:

1/2 cup confectioners' sugar

2 tsp plant-based milk

1 ½ tsp lemon juice

¼ tsp vanilla extract

Directions:

Heat oven to 375 degrees F.

Mix the sugar, flour, spices and salt (i.e. all the dry ingredients except the candied ginger) in a medium-sized bowl. Cut butter into cubes and mix into the flour mixture with your fingers, crushing the butter, until the mix is coarse and sandy. Add chopped candied ginger and stir to combine.

Add the milk and molasses to the dry mix, and stir until almost combined. You may need to add extra milk, a tablespoon at a time, until the mix is incorporated.

Knead dough in the bowl. Roll out to 1" thick. Cut circles 2 ½ inches in diameter, or cut into triangular wedges 2 ½ inches at the base.

Bake on ungreased cookie sheet until light golden brown. Circles take approximately 15 minutes. Triangles will usually take 20-25 minutes.

Mix icing and drizzle over the scones.

* You can use all-purpose flour instead of bread flour, and it will give the scones a denser, more cookie-like texture. Bread flour will "lighten" up the scones, so they're a bit more like biscuits (but not—they're still scones).

** The candied ginger is what makes these scones "killer." Feel free to take it out. But if you do, they're just gingerbread scones, which isn't a bad thing.

Cherry Lemonade Scones

Scone Ingredients:

3 ¾ C bread flour*
¼ C vanilla sugar
3 T baking powder
¼ tsp salt
8 T cold unsalted butter
Zest of two lemons
2 T lemon juice
1 ¼ C milk
1 tsp. vanilla extract
1 C dried cherries

Directions:

Heat oven to 375 degrees F.

Mix flour, vanilla sugar, baking powder, and salt in a medium-sized bowl. Cut butter into cubes and mix into the flour mixture with your fingers, crushing the butter, until the mix is coarse and sandy. Mix in the dried cherries.

Combine the vanilla extract and lemon juice with the milk and add to the dry mix. Stir until almost combined. You may need to add extra milk, a tablespoon at a time, until the mix is incorporated.

Knead dough in the bowl. Roll out to 1" thick. Cut circles 2 ½ inches in diameter, or cut into triangular wedges 2 ½ inches at the base.

Bake on ungreased cookie sheet until light golden brown. Circles take approximately 15-20 minutes. Triangles will usually take 20-25 minutes.

Serve with lemon curd.

* You can use all-purpose flour instead of bread flour, and it will give the scones a denser, more cookie-like texture. Bread flour will "lighten" up the scones, so they're a bit more like biscuits (but not—they're still scones).

More Kirsten Weiss

The Perfectly Proper Paranormal Museum Mysteries

When highflying Maddie Kosloski is railroaded into managing her small-town's paranormal museum, she tells herself it's only temporary… until a corpse in the museum embroils her in murders past and present.

If you love quirky characters and cats with attitude, you'll love this laugh-out-loud cozy mystery series with a light paranormal twist. It's perfect for fans of Jana DeLeon, Laura Childs, and Juliet Blackwell. Start with book 1, *The Perfectly Proper Paranormal Museum*, and experience these charming wine-country whodunits today.

The Tea & Tarot Cozy Mysteries

Welcome to Beanblossom's Tea and Tarot, where each and every cozy mystery brews up hilarious trouble.

Abigail Beanblossom's dream of owning a tearoom is about to come true. She's got the lease, the start-up funds, and the recipes. But Abigail's out of a tearoom and into hot water when her realtor turns out to be a conman… and then turns up dead.

Take a whimsical journey with Abigail and her partner Hyperion through the seaside town of San Borromeo (patron saint of heartburn sufferers). And be sure to check out the easy tearoom recipes in the back of each book! Start the adventure with book 1, *Steeped in Murder.*

The Wits' End Cozy Mysteries

Cozy mysteries that are out of this world...

Running the best little UFO-themed B&B in the Sierras takes organization, breakfasting chops, and a talent for turning up trouble.

The truth is out there... Way out there in these hilarious whodunits. Start the series and beam up book 1, *At Wits' End*, today!

Pie Town Cozy Mysteries

When Val followed her fiancé to coastal San Nicholas, she had ambitions of starting a new life and a pie shop. One broken engagement later, at least her dream of opening a pie shop has come true.... Until one of her regulars keels over at the counter.

Welcome to Pie Town, where Val and pie-crust specialist Charlene are baking up hilarious trouble. Start this laugh-out-loud cozy mystery series with book 1, *The Quiche and the Dead.*

A Big Murder Mystery Series

Small Town. Big Murder.

The number one secret to my success as a bodyguard? Staying under the radar. But when a wildly public disaster blew up my career and reputation, it turned my perfect, solitary life upside down.

I thought my tiny hometown of Nowhere would be the ideal out-of-the-way refuge to wait out the media storm.

It wasn't.

My little brother had moved into a treehouse. The obscure mountain town had decided to attract tourists with the world's largest collection of big things... Yes, Nowhere now has the world's largest pizza cutter. And lawn flamingo. And ball of yarn...

And then I stumbled over a dead body.

All the evidence points to my brother being the bad guy. I may have been out of his life for a while—okay, five years—but I know he's no killer. Can I clear my brother before he becomes Nowhere's next Big Fatality?

A fast-paced and funny cozy mystery series, start with Big Shot.

The Doyle Witch Mysteries

In a mountain town where magic lies hidden in its foundations and forests, three witchy sisters must master their powers and shatter a curse before it destroys them and the home they love.

This thrilling witch mystery series is perfect for fans of Annabel Chase, Adele Abbot, and Amanda Lee. If you love stories rich with packed with magic, mystery, and murder, you'll love the Witches of Doyle. Follow the magic with the Doyle Witch trilogy, starting with book 1, *Bound*.

The Riga Hayworth Paranormal Mysteries

Her gargoyle's got an attitude.

Her magic's on the blink.

Alchemy might be the cure... if Riga can survive long enough to puzzle out its mysteries.

All Riga wants is to solve her own personal mystery—how to rebuild her magical life. But her new talent for unearthing murder keeps getting in the way...

If you're looking for a magical page-turner with a complicated, 40-something heroine, read the paranormal mystery series that fans of Patricia Briggs and Ilona Andrews call AMAZING! Start your next adventure with book 1, *The Alchemical Detective*.

Sensibility Grey Steampunk Suspense

California Territory, 1848.

Steam-powered technology is still in its infancy.

Gold has been discovered, emptying the village of San Francisco of its male population.

And newly arrived immigrant, Englishwoman Sensibility Grey, is alone.

The territory may hold more dangers than Sensibility can manage. Pursued by government agents and a secret society, Sensibility must decipher her father's clockwork secrets, before time runs out.

If you love over-the-top characters, twisty mysteries, and complicated heroines, you'll love the Sensibility Grey series of steampunk suspense. Start this steampunk adventure with book 1, *Steam and Sensibility.*

Get Kirsten's Mobile App

Keep up with the latest book news, and get free short stories, scone recipes and more by downloading Kirsten's mobile app. Just click HERE to get started or use the QR code below. Or make sure you're on Kirsten's email list to get your free copy of the Tea & Tarot mystery, *Fortune Favors the Grave*. You can do that here: KirstenWeiss.com or use the QR code below:

Connect with Kirsten

You can download my free app here:
https://kirstenweissbooks.beezer.com
Or sign up for my newsletter and get a special digital prize pack for joining, including an exclusive Tea & Tarot novella, *Fortune Favors the Grave.*
https://kirstenweiss.com
Or maybe you'd like to chat with other whimsical mystery fans?
Come join Kirsten's reader page on Facebook:
https://www.facebook.com/kirsten.weiss
Or... sign up for my read and review team on Booksprout:
https://booksprout.co/author/8142/kirsten-weiss

About the Author

I WRITE LAUGH-OUT-LOUD, PAGE-TURNING mysteries for people who want to escape with real, complex, and flawed but likable characters. If there's magic in the story, it must work consistently within the world's rules and be based in history or the reality of current magical practices.

I'm best known for my cozy mystery and witch mystery novels, though I've written some steampunk mystery as well. So if you like funny, action-packed mysteries with complicated heroines, just turn the page...

Learn more, grab my **free app**, or sign up for my **newsletter** for exclusive stories and book updates. I also have a read-and-review tea via **Booksprout** and is looking for honest and thoughtful reviews! If you're interested, download the **Booksprout app**, follow me on Booksprout, and opt-in for email notifications.

Made in United States
North Haven, CT
03 October 2022